LORD OF TEMPTATION

ROGUES TO RICHES #4

ERICA RIDLEY

COPYRIGHT

ALSO BY ERICA RIDLEY

Rogues to Riches:

Lord of Chance

Lord of Pleasure

Lord of Night

Lord of Temptation

Lord of Secrets

Lord of Vice

Dukes of War:

The Viscount's Tempting Minx

The Earl's Defiant Wallflower

The Captain's Bluestocking Mistress

The Major's Faux Fiancée

The Brigadier's Runaway Bride

The Pirate's Tempting Stowaway

The Duke's Accidental Wife

The 12 Dukes of Christmas:

Once Upon a Duke

Kiss of a Duke

Wish Upon a Duke

Never Say Duke

Dukes, Actually

The Duke's Bride

The Duke's Embrace

The Duke's Desire

Dawn With a Duke

One Night With a Duke

Ten Days With a Duke

Forever Your Duke

CHAPTER 1

London, 1817

 *I*n a gambling hell like the Cloven Hoof, most gentlemen were beggared by the cut of the cards or a roll of the dice. For an already beggared lord like Zachary Nash, Marquess of Hawkridge, his best chance for future wealth lay not in games of chance, but with the gamblers themselves. Hawk was not here to spend money, but to *raise* some.

His current prospect, an idle gentleman named Mr. Leviston, motioned over one well-tailored shoulder for a barmaid to refill his glass.

When she arrived with a fresh bottle, Leviston raised his brows in query. "Port, Hawkridge?"

"No, thank you." Hawk allowed the edges of his lips to curve. "As you recall, I'm building my own."

"Touché." Leviston took a healthy swallow of the burgundy wine, then dabbed his upper lip with the edge of a white handkerchief. "When did you say your port would open?"

If Hawk sold the last sticks of furniture and put every penny into the project... He had done these calculations many, many times.

He leaned back. "Twelve months, in the worst of cases."

"One year." Leviston swirled his glass. "And in the best scenario?"

Hawk considered. That depended entirely on funding. On whether Leviston could be convinced to invest. On the size of his contribution compared to outstanding debts.

Outstanding debts. How *tired* Hawk was of spending every waking moment fighting to undo the damage the previous marquess had caused. Ten years ago, when he had first inherited the title, financial recovery had seemed impossible. Now it was finally almost in his grasp.

As long as Hawk's port completed construction, launched on schedule, and became a commercial success.

Which it could do—nay, which it *would* do—if he could secure several thousand pounds of funding.

"Six months," he answered.

Leviston wrinkled his nose. "That will be autumn. Almost winter. Inopportune time to open a port, wouldn't you say?"

"I would not." Hawk leaned forward. "The docks here in London are open year round. The Thames hasn't frozen in three years, and before that, not since 1789. But my property isn't on a river. We're building forty miles south of Dover. The English Channel has never frozen over. Nor will it. And now that the war is over, the coast's proximity to France

2

makes my port's location a strategic advantage for international trade."

Leviston nodded slowly. "How much are you seeking?"

"Ten thousand pounds," Hawk answered without hesitation.

Leviston blinked.

Hawk did not.

Even half that much money would make a significant impact. Finishing construction in the summer months was the key to securing all necessary inspections and permits in order to open before the end of the year.

But offering the exact pounds and shillings required to launch the port on time would be a mistake. Hawk had quickly realized that few individuals had any wish to underwrite the entirety of a project. Too much risk. Even those who did see the potential value were never willing to part with more than a fraction.

"Bit rich for my blood." Leviston swirled his wine. "Best I can offer is five hundred pounds."

Hawk lifted a shoulder. "Five hundred pounds earns five percent interest. One thousand pounds earns ten percent interest and a one percent stake in the venture."

Leviston's jaw worked for a moment.

Hawk waited.

In order to tempt investors, he was forced to give high margins. The terms were in Leviston's favor, and the man knew it.

Hawk's more intangible advantage was that he *wasn't* his profligate father. Not only did Hawk personally pride himself on being the antithesis of that self-serving tyrant, his peers vocally welcomed the diametric change.

Despite his lack of riches and fallen social status, Hawk had brought integrity to his title. He did not spend what he did not have. He worked religiously to pay the debts his father had accrued.

Although he was by far the least eligible bachelor among the aristocracy, the marquessate was much closer to solvent now than when Hawk had first inherited the title.

"One thousand," Leviston said at last. "But not a penny more until the docks actually open."

"My solicitor will send over the contract." Hawk rose to his feet. "Enjoy your wine."

He cut across the crowded room before Leviston could think up any last minute objections or renege on his commitment to invest. Hawk couldn't risk Leviston changing his mind. One thousand pounds was more than Hawk had been able to raise in the past three months.

How he despised the devil's circle of being an impoverished lord. Hawk's new ties to trade had blackballed him from high society venues like Almack's and its ilk. The estate's empty coffers prevented him from retaining memberships in exclusive gentlemen's clubs like White's and Boodles's.

Raising funds was remarkably tricky to accomplish when one had little to no access to wealthy marks.

The Cloven Hoof was one of the few venues at Hawk's disposal. The gaming hell was at the very edge of respectability, both geographically and soci-etally. Exclusive enough to attract the more raffish viscounts and earls. Disreputable enough to allow in those who did not quite belong with the aristocracy.

Hawk eased into the shadows and cast a prac-ticed eye about the crowded interior in search of other potential investors. He did not find any.

The problem with only being able to frequent a notorious establishment like the Cloven Hoof was that one quickly became familiar with the regular clientele.

Every man within these walls had heard Hawk's pitch for investing in his port. The vast majority preferred to risk their money on bouts of Faro and Piquet. The few Hawk had convinced to contribute, however, were the reason the launch date was fi-nally within sight.

A few more investors like Leviston, and Hawk's port might actually open before he and his mother were forced to subsist solely on gruel and broth.

Movement in one of the back corners of the vice salon caught Hawk's eye. With a smile, he made his way to the shadowy recesses of the gaming hell and slid into a small dark table opposite Simon Spauld-ing. London's most celebrated Bow Street Runner... and Hawk's illegitimate half-brother.

Simon moved a small bundle of primroses aside to make room at the table. "Hawkridge."

"Inspector." Hawk nodded at the bouquet of flowers. "Never say you're still unfashionably smitten with your beautiful wife."

Simon grinned back at him. "Incurably so. When are *you* tying the knot?"

"Ask me next year," Hawk said, rather than give a true reply.

The truth was, he didn't know.

He'd been in love once. Might even confess to still being in love, if one were to catch him in the dead of night, jolting awake from the same feverish dream where he relived the best and worst moments of his life with the one woman he could never forget... and never have.

It didn't matter what Hawk wanted. What the title required was a wealthy heiress with a dowry capable of repaying the marquessate's substantial financial debts as well as financing the new port's construction, launch, and ongoing operation.

A difficult task. On rare occasions when he did manage to rub thrice-darned shoulders with those of the elegant set, even the most mercenary of title-hungry debutantes had her sights set far higher than an impoverished lord who could scarce afford to pay his few servants.

"Thirsty?" Simon asked.

Hawk shook his head. "No."

"I'll buy," Simon offered.

"*No*," Hawk repeated, more forcefully than he meant.

Simon had been the one swindled out of his birthright, such as it was. Hawk's childhood had been filled with fireworks and pony rides and expensive boarding schools. Simon's had been spent in a shabby corner of his courtesan mother's townhouse, never knowing what they might have to do to buy bread for their next meal.

Their sire had only been interested in the pleasure he could demand from his lover. Not in being a true father for his unwanted bastard child.

Hawk would never ask Simon to part with so much as a hard-won farthing.

Simon leaned back. "I hoped I might find you here."

"You're a phenomenal investigator," Hawk assured him. "Also I have nowhere else to go."

"Well, I do." Simon gave a crooked smile. "I'm being reassigned across town for the foreseeable future. This is likely to be my last visit to the Cloven Hoof."

And to you, was the unspoken implication.

The two places Hawk was still welcome were his crumbling ancestral home and the smoke-filled gambling rooms of the Cloven Hoof.

Of the two venues, the Cloven Hoof was not only the more semi-respectable, it was also the sole place he could meet with his brother.

Hawk's home was out of the question. Not only did his nonexistent inheritance preclude him from entertaining guests, his dowager mother would rather throw herself from a balcony than allow the bastard child of her husband's mistress beneath the same roof. Hawk would not make her suffer more than she already had.

Yet he didn't wish to lose contact with his brother. Not when they'd just spoken for the first time only a few months earlier and come so far toward establishing a brotherly relationship.

Simon arched a brow. "Have plans for the evening?"

"You know I do not." Hawk couldn't afford plans. Not until the port opened.

"Come to the school." Simon lifted his palms. "Have supper with us tonight."

Hawk's spirits rose. "Dine with you and twenty orphans?"

"Twenty-four," Simon corrected. "And I'm afraid not. The Headmistress Dinner is limited to adults only, although the 'servants' are the students. What, is the occasion not fancy enough for you?"

Hawk laughed. "I haven't received a fancy invitation in years."

"Allow me to change that." Simon lifted his nose and affected an imperious tone. "To the esteemed Lord Hawkridge. The honor of your presence is requested this evening at the St. Giles School for Girls, which you may recognize as the preeminent, most decorated boarding school in the entire rookery." Simon dropped the false hauteur and grinned. "Do come. It's primarily a family dinner. When is the last time you saw your sister-in-law?"

Sister-in-law.

Family.

Zachary still wasn't used to using these words to describe his half-brother. They had resented each other for decades. Simon, because Zachary had been the one to win their father's surname...as well as the marquessate, status, and legitimacy that went with it. Zachary, because despite all that, Simon and his mother were the only ones to occasionally win his father's attention.

It wasn't until after the marquess died—in the arms of his mistress, not his wife—that Zachary and Simon had confronted each other. Although they quickly realized that the enemy was not each other, but rather their late father's irresponsible behavior toward the people who loved him most, the path toward a future resembling true brotherhood required effort on both sides. Trust. Forgiveness. Risk.

"Of course I shall attend," he said immediately. "Consider yourself added to tonight's social calendar. But tell me, what is the occasion? Are congratulations in order?"

Simon paled and coughed into his fist. "We have more than enough children at the moment. You are worse than Lady Grenville."

"You know how we old matrons are," Hawk agreed. "Babies, babies, babies."

Simon laughed, blissfully ignorant of how badly Hawk wished he were in any position to start a family. He had always dreamed of being the sort of husband his father had failed to be.

To Hawk, marriage could be so much more than a cold business arrangement. A wife he loved and doted upon. Someone whose company he enjoyed outside of strained silent meals and requisite nocturnal visits to beget an heir. Likewise, fatherhood meant being there for one's child from the first day. Not only when it suited him, as their father had treated Simon. Nor be present only when one was obligated to, as their father had treated Hawk.

He intended to do it *right*.

"Splendid." Simon straightened the ribbon on his bouquet of primroses. "I'm sure Dahlia will be thrilled to have a guest at the dinner table."

"And if she isn't?" Hawk asked.

Simon grinned wickedly. "If she isn't, then it will be just deserts. I have been the lone male in an abbey full of females for long enough. It is past time to even the odds."

Hawk narrowed his eyes. "That's right, you said 'headmistresses.' Plural. Is one of Dahlia's sisters helping with the school?"

"Camellia is far too busy with the opera, and Bryony..." Simon gave a theatrical shudder. "Can you imagine putting Bryony Grenville in charge of shaping impressionable young minds?"

"Fair point." Hawk inclined his head in agreement. "One incorrigible hoyden is more than enough."

Simon shook his head. "Fortunately, we have Faith."

Hawk's heart skipped. Did Simon just say... No, of course he did not. Hawk's overeager mind had simply misunderstood.

"Faith in the children?" he asked cautiously. "Faith in each other?"

"Oh, I'm sorry." Simon waved a hand. "I meant Faith Digby. The other headmistress."

Faith Digby.

Time in the gambling salon seemed to stall, curlicues of smoke freezing midair, the clink of glasses and the slap of cards drowned out by the sudden rushing in Hawk's ears.

"Faith...Digby?" he repeated hoarsely.

Simon nodded. "She's not only Dahlia's closest friend, but also an exemplary headmistress. If it weren't for Faith's oversight and administration, the school might not be in operation today. She is the star of the show."

She also starred in every one of Hawk's recurring dreams.

The one where he stole their first kiss under a moonlit summer night. The one where he realized he was falling head-over-heels in love. The one where he walked away from the best moments of his life, never to lay eyes on her again.

"Faith *Digby?*" Hawk echoed faintly. "She'll be at your dinner table this very night?"

"Er…" Simon tilted his head in question. "My keen investigative senses are telling me you may have already made this young lady's acquaintance."

"You should get a promotion," Hawk said. "Nothing escapes a Bow Street Runner."

Simon frowned. "My wife thinks the world of Miss Digby. I must admit that I and every one of our students do, too. Have you some reason to dislike her?"

"None at all." Hawk's words flew from him in a rush. "She's an angel. You truly could not have found better. She's everything that I… That is to say… There's a tiny bit of history there you may not be aware of."

Simon crossed his arms. "I'm listening."

"A decade ago, I may have implied our secret courtship was leading to marriage," Hawk admitted. "And then broke off all contact."

"You *what?*" Simon stared at him as if he'd sprouted horns and a tail.

Much like Hawk saw himself in the looking-glass every morning.

"Not my finest moment," he said quickly. "I regretted it immediately. If it makes a difference, I had just turned eighteen—"

"It does not make a difference." Simon reared back in horror. "One does not callously break one's word—or a young lady's heart. What could possibly excuse such unforgivable behavior?"

"I cannot excuse it. No one could. But there is an explanation." Hawk took a deep breath. "Our father."

"Our father died before you turned eighteen," Simon said with a frown.

Hawk nodded. "And spent every penny of the marquessate before he went. Worse than that. He opened lines of credit he could never hope to pay with every vendor and shopkeeper in England, and shamelessly abused their goodwill. The debts he incurred in the pursuits of pleasure are nothing short of astronomical."

Simon grimaced. "I had no idea."

"Neither did I. No one did." Hawk rubbed his face. "Except my guardian. Until I reached my majority, an uncle oversaw the marquessate. And what he saw was that there was a short window of opportunity to squeeze even more credit from unsuspecting vendors before the entire house of cards came crashing down. By the time I gained control of the title, it was already too late."

"And Faith?" Simon narrowed his eyes. "What role had she to play in this?"

"None. She is blameless," Hawk said with feeling. "I wanted nothing more than to wed her. To marry for love. To raise the kind of family children are supposed to have. A home filled with love."

Simon frowned. "Then why didn't you?"

"I could not afford to." Hawk groaned. "Much as it killed me. She was lower class and poor, and I was upper class and completely indigent. Not only was that not at all the sort of life I would ever offer her, our union was financially out of the question. I was forced to begin a hunt for an heiress bride the very next day."

"And you walked away from Faith without a single word of explanation?" Simon asked incredulously.

"Of course not." Hawk winced at the memory. "I wrote her a letter."

"A letter," Simon repeated in disbelief. "No doubt she loved that."

"She sent me to the devil and told me never to darken her door again," Hawk admitted. "You can see how this makes your dinner invitation a wee bit awkward."

"You're an idiot," Simon said baldly. "I have a complete featherbrain for a brother."

"I *was* an idiot," Hawk corrected. "Ten years ago. I was young and foolish and over my head with responsibilities and debts I never knew existed. If I could do it all over again…"

Simon raised his brows. "If you could do it all over again?"

Hawk didn't answer.

He could not have married Faith back then, no matter how much he wanted to. If he could go back in time, the honorable thing would have been never to court her to begin with. He could not provide for her then or now. She had always been better off without him.

And yet the thought of losing a single stolen moment with her twisted a dagger in his heart.

"I never got the chance to give her a proper apology. In person," he added. "With real words. Out loud."

Simon stared at him. "And you think she'll forgive you?"

"No," Hawk said honestly. "I wouldn't, if I were her. But she deserves a heartfelt apology."

"I'll say." Simon shook his head. "Many, many apologies."

Hawk rubbed his face. "I'm just afraid that if I see her, if I speak to her, it will only make things even more complicated."

"*Are* they complicated?" Simon asked dryly. "You were horrible to her a decade ago. You realize this now. You're sorry."

"But there's no way to put it right." That unfortunate reality had tortured Hawk for years. He had never meant to hurt her. And yet, he'd done exactly that. "It's too late. Too much time has passed."

Simon was silent for a long moment.

"Maybe not," he said at last. "Look at us. We didn't speak for nearly thirty years, and now…we're brothers."

Hawk stared back at him, speechless.

For so long, he had yearned to see Faith again. Now that the possibility was at his fingertips, the idea terrified him. Not only might this be his one chance to apologize face-to-face, but also an opportunity to finally move on. To cease carrying a torch for a past they could never relive. He would give the long overdue explanation, and they would go their separate ways.

Someday, he might even stop dreaming about her.

"Am I still invited to supper?" he asked his brother.

Simon let out a deep breath. "As long as you don't upset Faith."

"I won't force her to talk to me." Hawk straightened his shoulders. "And I promise to leave at once if she throws anything at my face."

"I'll hold you to it." Simon glanced at his pocket watch. "Come. We're going to be late."

Hawk tugged his threadbare riding gloves onto his hands. He had no open account to settle. "I'm ready."

Simon scooped up the primroses and rose from the table. "Meet me there?"

"Be right behind you." Hawk pushed to his feet and followed his brother out of the Cloven Hoof.

Simon's horse was tied to a post just outside, which meant he would make it home far faster than Hawk could navigate his old coach through the congested city.

There was no time to go home to freshen up before heading to St. Giles. Besides, not only was Simon's home in one of the poorest neighborhoods in London, Hawk was already wearing the finest outfit he owned.

So be it. Perhaps evening coats and trousers that seemed shabby and unfashionable by Mayfair standards would seem positively glamorous in a rookery.

He shook his head wryly. It had been years since last he was glamorous.

But when his aging horses pulled the old carriage to a stop in front of his brother's boarding school, a niggling doubt blossomed in Hawk's gut.

In a neighborhood like this, leaving one's carriage behind could mean losing it forever. Even with a scrappy young driver inside, Hawk wasn't completely certain the horses would still be attached when he came back out. And he couldn't afford to replace them.

He glanced around and forced his runaway worries to settle. Simon would not have put him in danger. In fact, if Hawk didn't possess entailed properties, a neighborhood like this would perhaps be his home as well. He should not be so quick to judge.

He turned toward the front steps, jaunty hat at a smart angle and walking stick in hand, when a sudden impulse caused him to turn back toward his driver and hand the young man the walking stick. Its hidden sword would be far more useful out here in the street than inside a school.

Empty-handed, Hawk turned his back to his carriage and quickly made his way up the walk to the front steps of the boarding school and banged the knocker.

When the door swung open, Hawk crossed a clean-swept threshold out of the soot-covered rookery and into another world.

The butler was not a portly old fellow with ruddy cheeks and a pompous air, as Hawk was used to, but rather a slip of a girl of no more than twelve years of age, possessed of pointy elbows, crooked teeth, and the brightest smile Hawk had ever seen. He could not help but return her grin.

Despite the crumbling brick comprising the façade of the building, the interior of the school was bright, clean, cheery, and open. Because it had been converted from an old abbey, the architecture boasted flourishes like decorative moldings and beautiful arches.

He shrugged out of his greatcoat. A crackling fire

was just visible through the corridor connecting the next room. The murmur of animated voices and muted laughter bubbled from the other side.

Hawk willingly relinquished his hat and coat to the girl-butler, and then followed eagerly toward the salon containing the voices.

It had been years since he had shared a family meal with anyone but his mother, who often preferred to dine alone in her private quarters. With luck, moments like these with his half-brother and wife would not be a one-time occurrence, but rather the new normal.

He nervously straightened his waistcoat. The only thing better than having a brother would be having a brother he could count as a friend. A cozy dinner with Simon and Dahlia was exactly the step needed to set their awkward little trio off in the perfect direction.

Except tonight, there would be a third party at the table. A third party who belonged even more than Hawk did. A third party who might have forgotten him altogether, although she had never left his heart for a moment. A woman he'd dreamed of for ten long years.

When Hawk rounded the corner, he came face-to-face with his past.

Faith.

A jolt of recognition immediately gave way to a sudden rush of longing. It had been years, but Hawk had never forgotten her face. Or the color of her eyes. Or the scent of her hair. Or the soft feel of her skin as he'd curled against her after lovemaking. Or how *right* she had always felt in his arms.

His heart flipped as years' worth of regret and

yearning surged within him. She was so different, yet the effect was the same. Being near her was the closest to heaven he had ever been.

By the shocked horror in her eyes, she had not forgotten that when his advisors forbade the match, he had not been able to choose love, and instead had walked away from the only happiness he had ever found.

Dahlia leapt protectively between them.

"What the devil is *he* doing here?" she snarled at her husband.

Simon frowned in obvious confusion at the sudden layer of ice blanketing the once-warm room. "Hawkridge? I invited him. He's family."

"He is not my family. And he is certainly nothing to Faith." Dahlia's eyes flashed as she linked arms with the lost love Hawk should never have left ten long years ago.

"His presence means nothing to me," Faith said with bored indifference as she took a seat at the ancient oak table.

The insult of her words indicated his presence very much meant an interminable evening of pain and humiliation for her, and she wished for him to know. He tightened his jaw. The lack of blood in her now pale face would have sent that message even if she had not spoken.

But what was the right path? If Hawk left now, he would certainly never be invited back. But if he stayed... He might tarnish this fragile connection even further.

"Hawkridge is family," Simon announced firmly as he took his seat at the head of the table. "If I can forgive all the wrongs in our past and create a relationship where before there was none, then certainly my wife and my friend can share an hour's meal in polite civility with my brother."

Dahlia sniffed, not bothering to hide her skepticism. "We will discuss this later."

"We certainly will. He's my *brother*." Simon held out an open palm toward an empty seat. "My apologies, Hawkridge. Won't you join us at the table?"

Hawk clenched his jaw. Simon had done nothing wrong. Hawk had created the rift a decade ago.

Faith Digby had every reason to hate him.

Not a day had gone by since then when he hadn't wondered how differently things might've worked out if he had made different choices. He would not be any richer, of course. The marquessate would still be in danger of collapse and ruin. His father would still be dead, his mother would still be disappointed in him, and there wouldn't be a single society invitation on their mantel.

But he would have had Faith. A wife. *Love.*

No. Hawk's stomach churned with regret. Faith deserved better. She had always wanted a family and Hawk still couldn't afford to give her one. He had ruined the moment back then, but at least he had not ruined her life.

She was free to find someone else. Someone better. He had lain with her, yes, but that was a secret only the two of them knew.

Gentlemanly manners dictated that he make an honest woman of her. At the time, there had been nothing Hawk had wanted more. He had confessed his love to her as well as his intention to inform his guardian in the morning. And follow that encounter with a meeting with her father, in which Hawk had fully intended to beg for her hand on bended knee if need be.

But Hawk's guardian was his self-serving, vainglorious uncle, who had more than forbidden the unequal match. He castigated Hawk for his duty to his family, to the title, to the marquessate, to their name.

His uncle had called him stupid to consider even for a moment marriage to a chit as common as Faith. His mother had agreed, tearfully pointing out that Faith had been spawned from a family to whom a connection would make the Hawkridges a laughingstock. His advisors confessed that the point was moot—Hawk could not *afford* to marry for love. Not with the estate's ballooning debts beggaring them all. They'd be lucky not to be chased out of England.

Each word had been a painful reminder of where his duties lay. He was now Lord Hawkridge. His wife must be his equal in society. Good blood, good family, even better connections. And above all, wealthy. The fate of the marquessate depended on Hawk making a brilliant match. The breaking of his heart—or hers—was inconsequential.

Love was for common people. Duty was for noblemen.

So here they were.

"Thank you," Hawk said, hoping his voice did not relay the turmoil within.

He took a seat because this might be the last time he saw his half-brother and his sister-in-law. And would undoubtedly be the last time he saw Faith.

Even though she clearly hated him, his love for her came rushing back a thousand-fold with every stolen glance in her direction. He'd never forgotten her. Not for a single night. Perhaps this was a sign that he could finally give her the apology she'd been owed for ten long years.

His chest grew tight. As the years had gone by, the apology had become harder and harder to make. A dragon that could never be slain. A confrontation best avoided.

Until now.

CHAPTER 2

Faith Digby's fingers trembled far too violently to risk lifting her teacup and saucer for a calming sip of chamomile. With this many butterflies in her stomach, she doubted she'd ever feel tranquil again. The last person she had ever expected to see sat three feet away from her on the other side of the dinner table.

Zachary Nash, Lord Hawkridge.

Her skin had prickled before he'd even walked into the room, as if her body had sensed his presence like a flower senses the sun.

The years had been both cruel and kind. His jaw was stronger, his muscles more defined, his shoulders wider… But the jacket that contained them was faded from repeated use and worn at the seams. The cravat was close to threadbare, though brilliantly white and folded into effusive perfection.

His cheekbones and jaw were impeccably free from whiskers, leaving nothing to distract the eye from that full, sensual mouth Faith remembered so well. His hair was the same dark brown and perfectly coiffed, his eyes the same long-lashed hazel, brilliant and captivating. But she would not let herself be captivated. Not again. Not by one such as him.

The package might be as tempting as ever, but the man inside was not.

Her presence at dinner tonight was partly because she was as much a fixture of the school as the chandelier overhead—and just as tarnished—but also because she was looking forward to speaking with Dahlia and Simon about the exciting new plans for the next fundraising show they'd been working on for so many weeks.

The words were no longer on the tip of her tongue. She didn't wish to speak of her charity work in front of Hawkridge. She didn't want him to know about her life at all.

Her lips tightened. Why should she? He had already turned down the chance to share it.

But she would not give him the pleasure of seeing her inner turmoil. She never gave anyone that satisfaction. She would remain as stoic today as she had been the day he'd left her behind so many years before. She would present her façade of ice. No. Not of ice; ice could melt, and she was done melting for him. Her façade was now porcelain. It could crack, it could break, but for now it would remain as emotionless and unreadable as that of a doll.

It was her only defense. She could not let him see how he affected her so long after he'd broken her heart. He need not know the way her heart thundered in her chest, the way her breath caught in her throat, the way her lips parted every time she glanced his way.

Not that she meant to glance his way. She could

not possibly let him back into her life. He'd broken her heart once. Now, he was even more dangerous. He could never know.

"We splurged for meat today," Dahlia whispered to her under her breath. "Which means there are knives at the table. Just let me know if you'd like me to slide mine between his ribs."

Faith dared not attempt even a weak smile, lest her carefully crafted mask begin to crack.

Dahlia had been her first friend and, for a long time, her only friend. Now they were like sisters. Their bond was unshakable. But Dahlia's temper was as fierce as her loyalty, and Faith could not allow her best friend to destroy her marriage by stabbing her brother-in-law at the dinner table.

"Not required at present," Faith whispered back. "If I change my mind, I will give you a sign."

Dahlia's husband, for his part, appeared uncharacteristically mystified. As the most decorated inspector of the Bow Street runners, Simon was used to knowing all the facts of any given situation he had been assigned to investigate. Being caught unawares was an uncommon circumstance.

Out of loyalty to her best friend, Dahlia had clearly kept Faith's secret, just as Dahlia had sworn to do for her when they were both young. However, now that Simon knew there was a mystery afoot, he would not rest until he had uncovered every rancid speck of past history.

Faith froze. She could not allow Simon to poke about in her life any more than she could allow Hawkridge to upend it. She would have to act as though there was no mystery here. Just a little misunderstanding. Water under the bridge. Why, she'd forgotten about that old drama. It never crossed her mind anymore. Nothing to investigate. Everything perfectly normal.

She straightened her spine. This was her chance to sell him on that fiction by acting the part.

"How was your day today, Simon?" she asked pleasantly as one of the student "footmen" presented the table with a large tray bearing spiced vegetables.

The skeptical look in the investigator's eyes indicated he was far from forgetting the ripple of shock Lord Hawkridge had caused with his exalted presence, but Simon was an absolute love, and would not purposely make anyone feel awkward. That trait might be her saving grace.

"It was my last day in the old neighborhood," Simon answered after a moment. He glanced at Hawkridge. "I am glad you joined us. You are family, after all."

Guilt picked at the scarred edges of Faith's heart. While she personally would have been thrilled never to see Hawkridge again, he *was* Simon's estranged half-brother.

Because Hawkridge was a lord and Simon a lowly bastard, the inspector would not be welcome at the marquessate. It was very likely that the two would only be able to see each other going forward by planned meetings such as this, well out of the public eye.

Faith's heart ached in sympathy. Her parents were not of his class, but she could see her family whenever she pleased.

She would simply have to make it through dinner before falling apart.

Faith did her best to focus on her boiled vegetables and not on her one-time lover. She was determined to think of him not as Hawk, as he had become in their youth, but as untouchable Lord Hawkridge, who he was now. A marquess and a stranger. Nothing more, nothing less.

"How was your day?" Hawkridge asked, meeting Faith's eyes for the most fleeting of moments before focusing pointedly on Dahlia. "Er, ladies?"

Dahlia glared back at him without responding until Faith kicked her ankle beneath the table. Her fingers shook with embarrassment.

She would not make a scene. Not out of any desire to spare Hawkridge, but because she had moved on. She'd had to. They had both done unforgivable things in the past. Faith had decided long ago not to compound those errors with additional reckless choices. She was no longer a foolhardy, lovesick girl. She was the administrator of a boarding school. A model teacher. An adult.

It was time to act like one.

Faith glanced over at the student footmen keeping dutifully to the shadows and gave them a proud smile. "My day has been wonderful, because our students make it so. Thank you, ladies. You've outdone yourselves with this meal."

All three of the uniformed girls blushed in unison.

Once a week, the students put on a special meal for their headmasters. The girls loved the ritual and the chance to show off their culinary talents. Normally, Faith loved their shared evenings, too. Tonight, however, she would rather be anywhere else.

No matter how hard she tried, she couldn't escape Hawkridge. Not in her mind, not in her dreams, and now not even at her boarding school.

If she could make it through this dinner with the least interaction possible, she would dedicate herself to figuring out how to never let such an occurrence happen again.

"Is this the first time your students have served a meal?" he asked.

"Not at all," Simon replied with obvious pride. "They take turns performing all the duties required to run a school of this size, in order to be better prepared to work in various capacities, should they choose to stay on."

Hawkridge's brows lifted as though he were impressed despite himself. "That's an ingenious idea."

"Not mine, I'm afraid." Simon gave a crooked smile. "One of Faith and Dahlia's many strokes of brilliance. Tonight is a 'Headmistress Supper.' A special occasion, where a limited number of the most outstanding students are selected to perform each role. The girls must vie for jealously guarded slots."

"This meal is leagues better than anything conjured from my kitchen," Hawkridge said with a self-deprecating smile.

Neither Faith nor Dahlia smiled back.

"We hold Headmistress Suppers fortnightly." Simon's eyes brightened. "You're more than welcome to join us at any time."

"I wouldn't want to intrude," Hawkridge demurred.

Faith did not wish for him to intrude either. Her stomach clenched. She hoped this didn't mean her former paramour would be hanging around the school more often, but suspected she was out of luck.

Panic slid beneath her skin at the thought of having to sit across from him again and again. She hid her trembling fingers beneath the serviette on her lap. God help her. Faith didn't know which was more in jeopardy: her self-respect or her self-control.

Hawkridge was as impossible to resist as a whirlpool at sea, breaking her defenses, dragging her under, drowning her with his power. When he'd promised to marry her and never returned, she'd sworn never to allow herself to be hurt again. But just seeing him tonight hurt. Hearing the familiar timbre of his voice hurt. Smelling the familiar scent of his soap. Sharing the same space.

She tried to keep her eyes focused on Dahlia and Simon, but it was impossible not to stare at Hawkridge's soft brown hair, his soulful hazel eyes, the curve of his smile. She tried to listen to Simon discuss his new assignment, but all she could hear was the old memories rushing back. The afternoon at the lake, the evening under the stars.

Desperate, she tried to focus on the unusual treat of a succulent lamb shank being served at the school, but all of her favorite foods tasted like nothing in her mouth. Not with her tongue remembering the taste of his kisses, the scent of his skin, the feel of his mouth against hers.

Her breaths tangled. The wooden chair was too hard, her linen bodice too tight, her heart pounding far too loud.

She'd survived the past ten years by reminding herself that she would never, ever see him again.

That even if their paths should someday cross, her broken heart was now cold as stone. Impenetrable. Unable to be hurt anew. Certainly not foolish enough for all the old feelings to come rushing back.

The wanting. The hurt. The anger.

She could not possibly make small talk with him over the dinner table as if none of it had ever happened.

"Faith has been an instrumental help to Dahlia," Simon was saying to Hawkridge.

"A help?" Dahlia's chin jerked up indignantly. "Faith is a godsend. She enriches the lives of everyone she touches. She makes me a better person and she does no less for the four-and-twenty students in our care."

Hawkridge's eyes widened with surprise and interest. "Faith—that is to say, Miss Digby—teaches at this school?"

"She owns it," Dahlia shot back before Faith could respond. "We are co-administrators, but there is no doubt Faith is the backbone. When I started this school, I could scarce raise enough money for three meals a day. Faith turned everything around with insight and efficiency. Thanks to her five-year plan, our venture is well on its way to being self-sufficient."

Hawkridge's expression could only be described as stunned. Then, impressed.

Faith resented him for it. And herself for caring. 'Twas bad enough to be forced to have dinner with the "gentleman" who had taken her virginity and left her behind. The last thing she needed was for him to be *proud* of her for making something of herself despite him.

Very well, perhaps not the last thing. The one hundred percent very extremely last thing she needed was the way he had been looking at her every other moment. The way he was looking at her right now. As if his soul had been waiting for her all his life.

It wasn't new, she reminded herself sternly. That was how he had always looked at her. When she was young and foolish, she'd believed she was special. Now she knew it was how he looked at everything. He might even have loved her once...

But she had never been special. Not to a man who loved everything. Hawkridge had forgotten her just as easily as any of the myriad other pleasures that came and went from his charmed life.

Her spine caved. What hurt most wasn't that he hadn't cared about her. It was that he *had*, yet he'd nonetheless walked away without a second thought. She had been foolish to think she would somehow be an exception.

That was not a mistake she would ever make again.

"Faith." Hawkridge's voice was low, his eyes intent. "May we talk?"

"No." Her voice was so hoarse, even Faith herself was uncertain she had spoken the word aloud.

She glanced at her friends. Simon and Dahlia were too deep in a conversation about his current Bow Street investigation to realize Faith and Hawkridge had spoken.

He followed her gaze, and shook his head. "Not here, of course. Privately. This is between the two of us."

Privately? Vertigo assailed her. She could not

possibly entrust herself alone with him. That was exactly how this disaster had begun.

"There is no 'us,'" she bit out in anger. "There hasn't been in years. You made your position quite clear in your *letter*."

"I am sorry." Hawkridge lowered his voice, his eyes pleading. "You've always deserved better. All I want is the chance to—"

"You already had your chance," Faith interrupted. Of course he was not serious. He had never once been serious about her. She was done with his lies. "Once you got what you wanted, you walked away. I've no doubt you intend to do so again. You will have to find someone else."

She tore her gaze from his before she could glimpse his expression. She didn't want to know how he felt. She didn't want to know anything else about him at all.

A trio of student footmen with pinafores and plaited hair skipped up to the silent table to present their coup de grace: blackberry tarts for dessert.

God save her. Faith lifted her fork with trembling fingers. The blackberry tart looked wonderful. There was no way she could eat it.

Stomach churning, she wondered if Hawkridge remembered the last time they had eaten blackberries together. He had told her he loved her. That the moment he assumed control of the marquessate, his first act would be to make her his wife.

None of it had been true. Overnight, he had disappeared completely from her life.

She would not forgive him.

CHAPTER 3

*S*till reeling from the unexpected guest at the Headmasters' Supper, Faith slipped into the most calming room in her parents' home: the sumptuous Digby library.

Although her parents would not approve of giving their hard-won books away to indigent students, Faith could see no harm in borrowing a few from time to time as a special treat for the girls.

As she knelt to browse a colorful collection of illustrated volumes about England's flora and fauna, the door to the library flew open and a four-foot-tall bundle of pure energy burst into the room with a squeal of delight.

"Aunt Faith!" Christina sprinted across the room and launched herself into Faith's arms, causing Faith to tumble backwards and Christina to dissolve into hiccupy laughter.

"Grandmother and Grandfather took me out on a boat! There was water, and fuzzy ducklings, and men selling pies... The only piece missing was you!" Christina hugged Faith as if they hadn't seen each other in years rather than since this morning at breakfast time. After a long moment, she leaned back and clapped her hands. "The ducklings were ever so cute. I counted them. First there were seven, then there were twelve, and all of them left and followed the mama."

Faith's heart soared as she cradled the child in her lap and listened to her recount her adventures. Faith tried to imagine sweet Christina with a stranger's eyes. She could not. Thick brown hair, sparkling hazel eyes, infectious smile. The spit and image of Christina's father.

Faith shook her head. She would not think about Hawkridge right now. Or ever again, if she could help it. He had disrupted her life more than enough. She would not allow thoughts of him to ruin her favorite bedtime ritual with Christina.

"Are you ready to pick out a book?" she asked as she hauled herself and the excited ten-year-old to their feet.

"One book?" Christina wheedled, dramatically puffing her lower lip. "You mean two books?"

Faith grinned at the familiar ritual. Of course she meant two books. There were always two books, sometimes three books. Part of the game was to pretend there could be only one. And every night, Christina would stick out her lower lip and beg for just one more book... Or two... Or three. Faith had never once said no.

Christina loved their time together just as much as Faith did. Remembering such moments were limited only made them all the sweeter.

They were inseparable. The best of friends. No matter how many meals they shared, books they read, games they played, stars they counted, puddles they splashed in, hills they rolled down, it was never enough. Faith missed her desperately whenever they were apart. She would read shelves of books until half midnight if that was what Christina wanted.

Christina held up a volume on horses. "How about this one, Aunt Faith?"

"Of course." Faith smiled indulgently to hide her wince of pain. Every time Christina called her Aunt Faith, it was a dagger to her heart. Even after all these years. But pretending Christina to be an orphaned niece had been the only way to save both of their futures.

"One more," Christina announced, and dashed off amongst the tall stacks of books.

Faith leaned back against one of the many shelves bulging with leather-bound volumes. There was such a stark difference between the Digby library and the boarding school library. Her parents' collection was as new as the books it contained, many of which had been acquired specifically for Christina. The school's "library" was a ramshackle collection of castaway tomes, many of their battered pages not meant for children at all.

It seemed like such a waste not to share the wealth. But all this opulence was purchased with her parents' money, not Faith's. They were unwilling to donate much to the school. Mother and Father considered doing so "spending Christina's inheritance" and could not understand why Faith would want them to divide their interests.

Faith sighed. She wanted the best for Christina and the girls at the school. Her parents wanted the best for her and for Christina. Their horns remained locked for now.

"These!" Christina flew around the corner with a book held high in each hand, skidding on the lush imported carpet.

Faith's heart twisted. She could not imagine a life without Christina in it. She would give up every other comfort in the world as long as this little girl with a big smile and the sweet-smelling ringlets was always at her side.

But life had a way of dropping marquesses at the dinner table.

She pressed her lips together. Damn her traitorous heart for skipping a beat when he'd asked to speak with her alone. She shouldn't be anywhere near a man like that. She definitely shouldn't be wondering how he had been, what he was doing now, if she would ever see him again.

He was poison. An addiction. But she was through. No matter how pretty his words, he had shown his true colors long ago. She would not fall for the magic of his embrace anew. There was too much at stake.

She straightened her shoulders, determined to spare Christina pain at any cost. One could not undo the past, but Faith had dedicated the last ten years to making the best she could of their present.

Faith wanted Christina to have what she had not. To grow up and fall in love with a man who cherished and appreciated her. To be free to marry without any hint of scandal that would stop her from living the best life possible.

"After such a busy day, I believe you deserve a treat," Faith said as she accepted the two slim volumes. "How about a third book tonight?"

Christina's only reply was a high-pitched squeal

before she disappeared between the stacks in a whirl of ribbons and ringlets and lace.

Faith hugged the two children's books to her chest and smiled affectionately. She considered herself a logical person, possessed of a practical mind, not a creative one. Yet she was a dreamer after all. She could not help but hope for new opportunities for the girls at her school, for the daughter she protected at all costs, and sometimes, even for herself.

The library door swung back open and her ruddy-cheeked parents barreled into the room.

"There she is!" Mother pointed at Christina dashing between two tall stacks of books, then turned to Faith. "Did she tell you about the little ducklings?"

"Of course she did," Faith said with a grin.

Christina loved her grandparents as much as they loved their grandchild. They doted on her like she was the princess in a fairy story, and in turn Christina believed her grandparents to be the equal of any king and queen.

Faith supposed that was the power of money. Her parents hadn't been able to shower her with toys and attention when she'd been Christina's age. She had not lived a sheltered childhood, because her parents had not been wealthy enough to shelter her. She had been elbowed, shoved aside, trod upon. Sometimes because she was invisible to the others. Sometimes because she was not invisible enough.

Her fingers tightened about the books clutched against her chest. She would never let her daughter's wrist be bruised by a stranger's careless yank. A shiver slid down Faith's spine from all the old memories. That was then. She was no longer invisible. Christina would never be.

She turned to her parents. "Have you given thought to the list of schools I researched?"

"Oh, darling." Mother exchanged a telling glance with Father. "We simply haven't had time."

They had time. They had nothing but time. Time and money. What they didn't have was any desire to let Christina out of their sight, even in the name of education.

As much as Faith understood their reluctance, sometimes letting go was the best way to give more. Christina deserved a good school, to have good friends. Real friends. She deserved to have the kind of life that little girls like Faith had always dreamed of.

She intended to ensure it happened. Her only goal was to keep Christina healthy and happy now and in the future. She leaned forward. "If Chris's schooling is not a priority at this moment," Faith said smoothly, "perhaps now is the perfect time to invest a small sum into my boarding school."

The amount of money her mother spent on a single gown would transform the girls' pitiful library into a haven for the rest of their school years. Her parents' pocketbooks wouldn't even register the donation. But the lives of her students would be forever enriched.

"I think it's time you reenter society," Mother began, ignoring Faith's request.

"I was never *in* society," Faith reminded her. "You tried your hardest, but I was never worthy in their eyes. I shall stay right where I am, thank you."

"That was back then," her father put in. "Our factories were new, our money was new, our situation was new. It's a different world than it was ten years ago."

"Is it?" Faith hoped so, for Christina's sake.

Nonetheless, she had taken care when crafting the fictional circumstances of Christina's birth. Chris had not been born to a family of social-climbing trade-mongers with bad manners and good intentions, but to a mysterious wealthy cousin twice or thrice removed whose family had never worked a day in their lives. The untimely demise of Christina's very genteel birthparents was a dreadful tragedy, but since the distant Digby relatives had been visiting nearby, of course they had done their Christian duty and agreed to raise the orphaned newborn as their own.

A story like that was hard to disprove. Tragic enough not to invite nosy questions. Faith simply wished for Christina to be accepted for who she was: a kind, wonderful, curious, bighearted little girl.

"I've increased your dowry," Father said, tensing as if he expected this news to incite a war.

Faith would not disappoint him. "I told you to invest that money in my school. I will not be needing it."

"And I told you," Mother put in, "that instead of going to work in a rookery, you should be outfitting yourself with the very best modistes in the whole of London. The Season is underway. You did make one friend amongst the *ton*. If you attend the Grenville routs in the right gown, you might even catch the eye of a duke or an earl."

"I decline." Faith crossed her arms. That was how

she had ended up ruined and alone ten years ago. She would not be making that mistake again.

"Doesn't Chris deserve an...uncle?" Mother insisted. "Lord knows you deserve a husband."

"A good one," Father put in quickly. "A man with a title, full coffers, and the bollocks to do what's right."

Faith forced a brittle smile to hide her clenched teeth. Not because her parents were wrong. But because they were right.

Yet finding a good man with the stones to do what was right was not that easy. Faith was no more likely to scoop up an errant duke today than she was ten or twelve years ago. Less likely, even. For one, she was far too old. For two, well, the only eligible bachelor she had come across in all that time was... The same one who had ruined her the first time.

Her resolve hardened. Hawkridge hadn't been part of her life for over a decade. She would not change that now. Especially not to benefit *him*.

She knew what he wanted in a wife. Everybody knew. Back then he had been looking for an evening's distraction. Now he was looking for money.

Well, he could keep looking. Her family's money was for *family*, not selfish blackguards. She didn't need him. She didn't need any man. Spinsterhood was far preferable to how she'd suffered in her failed attempts to fit in with the fashionable set. She wasn't one of them. She didn't need to be. 'Twas better the devil one knew, and what Faith knew was being a good mother.

Er, *aunt*.

Once was more than enough.

She gazed at her daughter, whose pert little nose had already disappeared into a book.

Faith was neither proud nor embarrassed of her place in society. Or lack thereof. She loved her friends, her family, her career. She didn't want to lose any of it. She was finally happy. How could anyone be anything less with a wonderful child such as Christina in her life?

"Let's go upstairs to read!" Christina latched onto Faith's elbow and dragged her from the library toward the nursery.

"Only if you help," Faith replied as she did every night.

What had begun as marathon sessions of Faith reading bedtime stories to her child had transformed into blissful evenings of Christina snuggled tight to her chest, reading aloud at a level quite advanced for her young age.

Faith was so proud of her daughter. Christina deserved the best education they could find. Loving friends, a happy childhood, every possible advantage.

Which could only happen if things continued exactly as they currently stood. Under no circumstances could she allow any hint of gossip that Christina was a by-blow.

Faith knew firsthand how cruel society could be. The fashionable set wouldn't accept Faith because her family was in trade. Their "betters" would positively rip apart an innocent bastard child.

Her child.

CHAPTER 4

*B*ond Street. The fashionable heart of London. Hawk stood at the edge of the bustling district and stepped forward into its midst.

Early spring sunlight glistened off of store windows. Street sweepers cleared the way for bright-cheeked ladies in sumptuous gowns. Metal wheels and the smart clop of hooves met on wet cobblestone. Fancy carriages, elegant clothes, French perfumes...

If he allowed himself to dream, Hawk could almost let himself believe he was still a part of this world.

Now, only his title belonged.

He straightened his worn gloves and shoved them out of sight behind his back. He walked with his head held high, as if he hadn't a care in the world. As if he were here to actually shop, rather than slowly pay off a long overdue account created by his father.

Not that Hawk was completely innocent of all such expenditures. One must clothe oneself, although a new jacket or a fresh pair of trousers every few years wasn't the sort of purchase that would impress anyone strolling on Bond Street.

He kept his eyes forward, trained on no one in particular. He needed to let the tailor know the account was late but not forgotten. Hawk would pay as much as he could as soon as he could—sooner, if he could talk a few more investors into hurrying the port's development along.

He exchanged smiles and polite words with everyone who tossed him a greeting. Most were too intent on their own shopping expeditions to notice Lord Hawkridge's hands were as empty as his pockets.

That suited him perfectly. Hawk tortured himself over his financial difficulties enough quite on his own, thank you very much. He dreaded becoming town gossip. Another empty title among the relentlessly mocked *ton* caricatures.

At least it had not yet come to that.

Just as he reached the door to the tailor, it swung open from the inside and a familiar, well-dressed gentleman strolled out.

Hawk straightened involuntarily, although the last person on this earth he was likely to bamboozle was Mr. Grenville. He would know at a glance that Hawk wasn't on Bond Street for an idle bout of shopping.

Yet he didn't hide his face. Normally, London's most enigmatic secret-keeper *would* be the last person Hawk wish to run into, but today it just so happened that he possessed a few secrets Hawk would do anything to unlock.

Mr. Grenville was Dahlia's brother. Dahlia was Hawk's sister-in-law... and the bosom friend and business partner of Hawk's former paramour Miss Faith Digby.

Grenville would know everything there was to know.

If Hawk wished to learn more about Faith, he could not ask for a richer source. Grenville's fame came not just from the wealth of his knowledge but his legendary discretion. Far more important men than Hawk paid handsomely to keep their secrets well out of the public eye.

Not that Mr. Grenville was anything so common as a blackmailer. Men of power sought him out, confided their worst indiscretions, so that he could make all potential problems disappear. Hawk had no idea how Grenville had stumbled into such a profession, if indeed it could be considered as such, but he was a nonpareil.

If anyone in all of England could tell Hawk how Faith was doing, what she was doing, how much happier she was without the penniless Lord Hawkridge in her life, Mr. Grenville would be that man. There is not a single secret all of London that Mr. Grenville was not privy to. The trick would be getting him to reveal even a tiny morsel.

"Grenville," Hawk exclaimed with a bright smile he instantly regretted.

His exclamation was too exclaim-y, his ingratiating smile a bit too desperate. Grenville would guess in an instant why Hawk was so delighted to see him.

"Hawkridge," Mr. Grenville said smoothly, his quick, intelligent gaze displaying neither suspiciousness nor curiosity. He did not inquire whether

Hawk was in the fashionable quarter to outfit himself in the latest mode, or to pay a bill.

Why would he? They both knew what Hawk was about. And now the conversational ball was back in his hands.

"I dined with your sister yesterday," Hawk said, as casually as he could manage.

Mr. Grenville was no doubt far more acquainted with the details of the encounter than Hawk. Gossip had it, the very walls confided to Grenville.

A faint smile curved his lips. "I trust Dahlia was well."

"She appears to be thriving at her boarding school," Hawk replied, thrilled at how quickly the conversation had given him the perfect foothold. "Miss Faith Digby was also there. They seem to be getting on well with their school."

"Mmm," Mr. Grenville murmured, his tone non-committal.

The moment stretched on awkwardly.

Did Grenville know about Hawk's past involvement with Faith? Did he suspect Hawk had stolen something far more valuable than a kiss? But if he knew about Faith and Hawkridge, why would Grenville never have mentioned it?

"Is she well?" Hawk blurted, not bothering to specify to which lady he referred.

Mr. Grenville lifted dark eyebrows. "You said you saw her. Did she appear unwell?"

The skin at the back of Hawk's neck prickled. Perhaps he did know. Grenville knew everything, after all.

Hawk relinquished all pretense of artifice. "I had

not seen her in far too long. I shan't beg for details. Just tell me she's been well."

Mr. Grenville tilted his head and considered him in silence.

"Please. Faith is a mystery. Her name has never graced the scandal sheets, nor has it been called with any of the banns." Hawk set his jaw in frustration. "I know nothing. It is torture. Surely there must be something you can tell me."

A sympathetic smile curved the corners of Grenville's lips. "I can tell you are very much interested in personal details. You mention scandal, wedding banns, whether she has found happiness. I am sorry that finding yourself so distant from her life tortures you. Yet it is not my place to amend that gap, but yours. I cannot help."

"You could," Hawk muttered under his breath. Very well. He did not deserve Faith then or now, which meant he likewise did not deserve to be privy to her life. No matter how he wished otherwise.

"Are *you* happy?" Mr. Grenville asked, surprising Hawk with the question.

Happy? The weight of his many responsibilities had weighed on Hawk's shoulders for over one third of his life.

No, he was not happy. When he was younger, he had often wished he could be a headmaster or street sweeper or pie maker. Anything at all where his life and his fortune was under his control.

But he could not and he was not. He was a marquess with a title he could not be rid of by any means other than death. The same for his debts, and the lands entitled to him by law, unable to be sold or bartered or used as leverage to gain investments that might actually lift them out of the pit his father had dug for their family.

"It isn't my duty to be happy," Hawk said wryly, rather than give a direct answer.

"The curse of the aristocracy." Mr. Grenville inclined his head in commiseration. "And yet without such rules, I would have no clients."

True. Scandal was his specialty. Whether plots were being devised above board or below, Mr. Grenville was always in the thick of it. Protecting those who could afford his protection. Unmasking those who deserved to be unmasked.

"Am I keeping you from a job right now?" Hawk asked.

"This is the job." Mr. Grenville swept his hand in the direction of the endless store windows. "You don't happen to know the identity of the penny caricaturist poking such dreadful fun at the upper classes, do you?"

"If I could draw, it would probably *be* me," Hawk said with a sardonic grin.

His mother would not appreciate the jest. Nor would the many peers whose faces had graced the anonymous sketches sweeping London by storm.

Caricatures had long been a part of town entertainment. Mocking the Prince Regent, pointing out genteel hypocrisy, providing commentary on the recent war with Napoleon Bonaparte. But of course Hawk knew to which caricatures Mr. Grenville referred.

A new artist had risen up out of nowhere, an illegible signature scrawled amongst the inked lines.

This artist provided more than idle commentary. He outed peccadilloes, mocked his betters, submitted illustrated scandals to gleeful gossip columns. The Cloven Hoof still boasted copies of the *Lord of Pleasure* sequence, which had recently upended the life of one of their friends.

Indeed, Hawk's mother's greatest fear was her face appearing in one of Betelgeuse's caricatures. Or Hawk's.

Of course a man like Mr. Grenville would want the name of the villain behind so much havoc. The only surprise to Hawk was that the secret-keeper did not already have it.

"I'm afraid I don't get out enough to be privy to any scandals," Hawk admitted. "The only reason my dancing slippers are in serviceable condition is because I haven't used them in years."

"Mmm, I see." Mr. Grenville raised his brows. "You are lovesick, and you are bored. A precarious combination."

"What?" Hawk stammered. "No, I—"

"There may be a solution," Mr. Grenville continued, his eyes alight with mischief. "As it happens, I occasionally serve as substitute dancing-master at my sister's boarding school when the usual dancing-master cannot be present. I am expected tonight, in fact."

Hawk frowned. "What have your dancing lessons to do with me?"

"I cannot imagine. All I know is that it would be dreadful if I were to not keep the appointment. There would be no one to take my place. And I feel the ague coming on." Mr. Grenville gave a laughably delicate cough into a pristine riding glove. "But I suppose beggars cannot be choosers when it comes to volunteer dance instructors. If some other gentleman were to be present at around six o'clock this evening, Dahlia—and, perhaps, her business partner —might find such a circumstance serendipitous. You did say your dancing slippers were in serviceable condition, did you not?"

Hawk's breath caught. A second chance with Faith in as many days.

Which could only mean Grenville did not know about their sordid past. Right? Of course he would not. Why would Faith confess ruination to anyone, when she could simply find someone better than Hawk and carry on without him?

Faith's pool of potential suitors was not limited to peers of the realm. Perhaps the reason Mr. Grenville had not wished to speak of her was because she'd done exactly that. Found a beau that was not Hawk. Someone who would not disappoint her.

Someone who could marry her.

Hawk's shoulders tightened. Even if the best he could hope for was another stolen hour in her company, he could think of no better way he'd rather spend an evening.

He felt as though he had been bestowed a benediction. "Thank you."

"For what?" Mr. Grenville gave another false, mincing cough. "I find myself so out of sorts that I fear I have already forgotten our entire conversation. I must bid you good day."

Hawk nodded quickly, his heart soaring. His friend had given him a far better opening than he deserved, but it was still up to Hawk not to bollocks the opportunity.

He fumbled in his waistcoat pocket for his battered timepiece. It was three o'clock in the afternoon.

Barely enough time to go home and draw a bath, dress in the handsomest clothes he could find, and casually happen to be in the neighborhood of the St. Giles School for Girls at a quarter to six.

And just happen to have his dancing slippers in his carriage.

CHAPTER 5

*J*ust as the sun was beginning to sink behind the jagged, soot-covered horizon of the St. Giles rookery, Hawk alighted from his coach with more hope in his heart than he'd dared allow himself to feel in years. He tossed his driver one of the few remaining coins in his purse and squared his shoulders.

He strode across the street with an air of relaxed confidence that was pure fiction.

This would likely be his only opportunity to see Faith one more time. He was powerless to resist the pull. They had never belonged to the same circles. Back then, Faith had been too poor for his. Now he was too poor for his own circles, too. Ironic that they should cross paths again in a rookery.

He rolled back his shoulders and made his way up the strikingly clean walkway. Why would she have sought employment here, of all places?

Her father had been dabbling in some sort of textile manufacturing venture years ago. If it hadn't worked out, perhaps that could explain why Faith would be working as a headmistress in one of London's poorest districts.

No matter what the others said, Hawk had never minded any of that. Faith didn't require priceless jewels or a royal lineage to outshine every other debutante he had ever met. Their souls had been like two halves of a whole. She completed him in ways he hadn't even known he was lacking. He'd been empty ever since he'd walked away from her.

He raised his hand to the warm brass knocker and hesitated. For years, he had specifically not asked around about Faith because he'd already burnt that bridge and there was nothing he could do to mend things. To change things.

Knowing little details about her just twisted the knife deeper. And yet here he was.

Hawk straightened. Of course a professional secret-keeper had been the wrong man to beg from whom to beg scraps of intelligence. If he wished to know about Faith's life, Hawk would have to talk to her himself.

And it was past time he did so.

Whether she would be willing to grant him a private audience, if only for a moment, was outside of his control. Yet he owed it to her to try. To both of them. He might be unworthy of forgiveness, but Faith very much deserved a more honest explanation than the letter he'd been forced to write all those years ago.

Resolved, he banged the brass knocker once, twice, thrice.

The door swung open and a pinafored butler of no more than twelve years peered up at him suspiciously. "You are not Mr. Grenville."

51

"I am not," Hawk agreed. "I am Lord Hawkridge and I was hoping to speak with your headmistress."

"They're both in the ballroom and dreadful busy. We are awaiting this evening's dancing-master."

"If they're both standing around waiting for a guest to arrive, then perhaps they are not *dreadfully* busy," Hawk suggested with a smile.

The freckled butler did not smile back. She crossed skinny arms over her chest and glared back at him with an air of cool self-confidence.

Hawk tried a different tack. He had very few calling cards remaining—he hadn't been in a position to pay calls or accept an invitation in so long that the expense of printing more could not be justified—but this gatekeeper would not be swayed with mere words.

"Would you please do me the honor of informing Headmistress Digby of my presence on your front stoop?" He handed the girl his second-to-last card.

Its embossed coat of arms failed to impress her.

"Stay here." She turned without another word, allowing the door to close in his face as she presumably presented his card to her headmistress.

Hawk fought the urge to straighten his cravat. The starched linen was almost transparent from repeated washings, and he did not wish to risk jabbing a hole into its painstakingly creased folds.

Moments later, the door swung back open. Hawk's heart leapt until he recognized the angry eyes glaring out at him.

He sent the pigtailed butler a reproachful glance. "I asked you to deliver my card to Miss Digby."

"And Molly will be given an extra biscuit for being wise enough not to take orders from the likes of you," Dahlia snapped. She crossed her arms, mirroring her student's stance. Or perhaps the other way around. "What do you want?"

"To talk to Faith," he said honestly. "It's past time, don't you think?"

"It's over and done," Dahlia said flatly. "There's nothing left to say."

He lifted his brows. "I think that is up to Faith and me, is it not?"

"It is not." Dahlia pointed across the road, where his battered and rusty carriage practically sparkled, so out of place was it in a rookery. "Shouldn't you be somewhere else?"

"Five minutes," he said quickly. "Two, if that's all she will give me. Even if you don't think I deserve the opportunity to apologize, she deserves to receive one."

Dahlia did not waver. "What good would it do now?"

Perhaps none. Perhaps she was right. But after finally glimpsing the opportunity for a second chance, Hawk was not willing to give up so easily.

He was here not just in the hopes of seeing Faith, but to take Grenville's place for the evening. Even if Hawk was not invited to join the dancing, he possessed strong muscles quite capable of helping in any other capacity the school might require.

"An apology may not change anyone's life," he admitted. "But perhaps my hands might. I can wield a hammer, a broom, a fire iron. I am more than willing to trade an hour's labor for the briefest moment of her time."

Dahlia's eyes narrowed. "You don't care about my school."

53

Hawk did not respond.

"Which can only mean you truly do care about..." Dahlia's antagonistic stance softened briefly before her gaze shuttered once more. "My girls are self-sufficient and do not require your pity."

A handful of little girls ranging from perhaps eight years old to fifteen bounded into the room behind her like a pack of puppies.

"Is Mr. Grenville here yet?"

"It's late! I'm bored!"

"When will the dancing start?"

Some of the hardness melted off Dahlia's edges. She sighed. "I suppose you can acquit yourself somewhat respectably on the dance floor?"

A sudden rush of hope infused Hawk with warmth. "I am your servant."

"Just until my brother gets here," Dahlia said quickly. "We shan't need you for more than a few moments."

"But Mr. Grenville never has time to dance anymore," piped up one of the eavesdropping schoolgirls. "And Mr. Spaulding's new schedule means he can't anymore either. What if there *is* no one to teach us to dance?"

Dahlia glared at Hawk as if the situation were his fault. "Very well. While I *am* desperate enough to allow even one such as you to perform dancing-master duties when no one else is available, do not mistake this concession as a blanket welcome into our home."

Hawk nodded. "I understand."

"Do you?" Dahlia glared down her nose at him. "This is not an opportunity for you to cozy up to Faith again. In fact, I shall ensure she has the option to stay completely out of your sight whilst you're under our roof. Although I cannot turn away an offer of free help, your continued presence is contingent on our combined goodwill."

Her words were more than clear. They were fair. Perhaps more so than he deserved.

This was his opportunity to prove to her and Faith both that he was not the lad they remembered, but a man they could trust. And if even that was too much, then hopefully one day Hawk would at least be able to apologize as Faith deserved.

"Understood," he repeated firmly. "I am at your disposal for as long as you need me."

"Dancing lessons are every Saturday at six o'clock," one of the girls piped up. "Right, Headmistress?"

Dahlia pressed her lips together. After a long silence, she gave a tight nod. "Saturdays at six. But only until we find a more appropriate replacement."

He inclined his head. "Until you find someone more suitable."

Dahlia's eyes narrowed into slits. "If you hurt her again, I will kill you. They will never find your body."

Hawk's throat thickened at the strength of her loyalty. She and Faith were practically sisters. He expected nothing less from her. His only hope was that someday they would expect more from him.

"Then we understand each other." Dahlia spun on her heel and strode through the gaggle of children toward an archway farther down the corridor.

Hawk hurried forward, lest the door once again slam in his face.

Light and laughter spilled out of the converted

ballroom at the rear of the abbey. Two dozen gleeful schoolgirls danced a chaotic minuet as the sweet, soaring notes of a violin filled the candlelit air with music.

Dahlia's sister Bryony was the source of the rousing tune, and stood on a raised dais on the other end of the ballroom. She was a gifted musician, world-class by some standards, genius by others, but Hawk only had eyes for the green-eyed headmistress at her side.

Faith turned as if she had felt him enter the room the same way he felt her presence from across the well-trod carpet.

Dahlia leapt up on the dais to whisper into Faith's ear.

He flinched when her smile immediately fell.

Faith turned to Dahlia in obvious anger and whispered back words Hawk could only imagine.

Dahlia lifted up her palms in supplication and gestured at the two dozen bright-eyed schoolgirls waiting expectantly for their turn to dance.

Faith rubbed a hand over her face as if hoping the entire situation would disappear. Or at least Hawk.

He did not.

His muscles tightened. This was torture. If Faith had rejected him, asked him never to return, he would have to respect her wishes.

Dahlia's face softened. She touched her fingertips to Faith's arm and gestured toward the stairs.

Faith shook her head and squared her shoulders as if preparing for battle.

She was going to stay.

She was going to stay.

Hope rushed within him. He ached to speak with her, dance with her, hold her once again. But he'd settle for making an apology, if she would only let him.

Perhaps tonight would be too soon to apologize, but at least she hadn't run away. That in itself felt like a second chance. Not like forgiveness, of course —even when he could make his overdue apology, he had no expectation of being forgiven—but at least it meant another hour in the same room as Faith.

After a far too insightful glance between the two of them, Dahlia clapped her hands for attention to silence the crowd. "Mr. Grenville unfortunately appears to be delayed, but Lord Hawkridge has graciously agreed to be our substitute dancing master in the interim."

The violin stopped. Every pair of eyes swung in Hawk's direction.

"Well, then." Dahlia motioned for him to take center stage in the middle of the scuffed wooden floor. "Who will be the first to dance with Lord Hawkridge?"

Hawk smiled at the wide-eyed orphans surrounding him.

None of them smiled back.

Even the girls who had helped coax their headmistress into accepting him as a temporary substitute were suddenly far more interested in plucking invisible lint from their pinafores than being the first to dance with Hawk.

The moment stretched on to infinity.

"*Fine*," Dahlia said in exasperation at the same time Faith said softly, "I'll do it."

Hawk's heart stopped.

"What?" Dahlia stared at Faith. "Did you say—"

"You go ahead," Faith stammered in haste. "I think you said it first. I don't need to dance. I'll just—"

"You were totally first." Dahlia stepped away from the dais. "In fact, I think I smell smoke in my office. It's my duty to investigate. Bryony, some music?"

Faith opened her mouth, but was drowned out by the suddenly deafening melody sailing from Bryony's violin.

Hawk glanced over his shoulder to help, but Dahlia was already disappearing upstairs.

Very well, then. Time to dance.

He made his way from the center of the salon to the dais where Faith stood rooted with bright pink cheeks. Heart racing, he lifted an outstretched hand and held his breath.

Faith's indecision was palpable. So were the thumping feet of the rowdy students, the fairylike sparkles of the mirrored candles, the intoxicating sweetness of the violin's melody.

It was not going to work. She was not going to take his hand. Hawk was being given the cut direct in front of two dozen indigent orphans and he had never felt a keener blow.

Just as he started to lower his hand, she lifted hers.

His breath caught. Faith's eyes were not full of forgiveness but resignation. Yet it was more than he had hoped for. More than he deserved. It was a start.

He helped her down from the dais and placed his other hand about her waist.

The last time he had touched her, she'd had thin,

coltish limbs in debutante pastels. Now, she was nothing but soft, womanly curves. Even more perfect than last he'd seen her. Even more perfect than last they touched.

Faith's gait was stiff, her muscles tense, but she allowed him to guide her into a waltz.

He tried his best to look lordly and not like a mooning ninny. He wasn't even certain how he'd been lucky enough to win this dance.

"For the children's sake. This is their favorite moment in the week." She answered his unspoken question with surprising prescience. "I will throttle Dahlia the moment this 'lesson' is through."

In that case, he was glad for the children. He hoped they never quit this room. He would live in this moment, in this waltz, in this embrace for the rest of his life, if only Faith would let him.

"I am so sorry," he said without preamble. "For everything."

It was not how he meant to start, or the way he meant to say it, but it was true. It had always been true.

"Don't apologize," she said, surprising him with her lack of rancor.

He blinked. "You deserve it, and more. I've so much to apologize for."

She shrugged. "Don't bother."

The hopefulness he'd felt earlier evaporated. Perhaps Faith had ceased caring about him to the point that nothing he said mattered to her at all. Hawk swallowed his hurt. Her disinterest was far worse than the righteous anger he'd expected. The anger he deserved.

Anger would mean she still cared in some way. This...*emptiness* meant there was no hope at all.

"I'm not looking for forgiveness," he said quickly, lest she had misjudged the reason why he was here. "I'm not trying to ferret my way back into your life. I just want to apologize for my actions before. To explain why—"

"I don't care why." She sighed. "Apologizing to each other can only lead to new hurts. It is best we leave the past in the past where it belongs. You may have this waltz, but we do not have a future."

"Apologize...to each other?" Hawk frowned in confusion. What had she to apologize for? "Surely, you don't think you owe me anything. It is I who treated you unforgivably. The last thing I ever wished to do was hurt you—"

"Then why did you?" she interrupted, a glassy sheen to her eyes. "Why did it have to be this way?"

His cheeks burned. But he would not back down from the truth.

"Because I was weak. Because I was young. Because I thought I had more freedom than I actually possessed. None of those reasons excuse my actions, but perhaps I can explain why it happened. You were not at fault. You were all that I wanted—"

"You had me," she said bitterly. "And the next morning, discarded me."

"I don't deny it," he said softly, hating that his apology was hurting her. "That is the truth, but it is not the whole truth. The marquessate was out of money. My guardian forbade the match—"

"You had already despoiled me," she hissed angrily. "You ruined me without a second thought."

"It didn't feel like 'ruining' at the time," he said

quietly. "It felt like lovemaking. It felt like I'd finally found the other half of my soul."

She laughed in derision. "The half that wasn't good enough to keep?"

"You have always been good enough," he said, his voice firm.

She did not bother to hide her skepticism. "Clearly."

"You were never the problem. When my life started falling down around me, I let them talk me out of pursuing the best thing that had ever happened to me. My mother, my guardian, my advisors. They said the only way to save the marquessate was by marrying an heiress."

"Where's your heiress?" she asked dryly. "Did you walk away from her, too?"

"I didn't want an heiress. I wanted *you*. But I couldn't have you until I could undo the damage my father had done to the estate. To our finances. I had a title but nothing else. I couldn't *afford* to marry you."

"So you said in your charming letter." Her eyes flashed. "Which you sent in lieu of speaking to my father. In lieu of giving me the dignity of calling off in person. Not that you were concerned about my dignity. Or anything else I might have once had. You'd already taken what you wanted."

"I am sorry," he whispered. "I should not have done that. I should not have done any of it. I knew it from the moment I left you. I've hated myself every day for not telling them all to go rot and follow my heart instead. I never meant to hurt you."

"And yet here you are. I told you to stay away from me. Were my words unclear?"

"Your words were ten years ago," he burst out. "Just like mine. I've respected those wishes all this time. But when I saw you at dinner, I realized it wasn't enough. It wasn't *right*. I cannot rest until I've apologized for every foolish—"

"Because you're so noble?" She arched a brow. "Or because doing so unburdens your conscience, without a single care about what I might want?"

"All I care about is your happiness, Faith. I swear on my soul, I thought you would marry someone else!"

"Once upon a time, perhaps I could have." Her lip trembled. "I suppose now we shall never know. I wasted too much time believing in *you*."

He winced. While he deeply regretted hurting her, he couldn't provide for her back then, and he still couldn't now. "I am so sorry, Faith. If there had been issue, I would have defied my family and offered for you despite the consequences. But you were so smart and sweet and beautiful. I knew you'd find someone better. Someone who could give you the life you deserved."

"You would have lowered yourself to wed me only under the direst of circumstances?" Her laugh was hollow. "What girl does not dream of such romance?"

"I wish I could have married you," he said urgently. "I have thought about it every day of the rest of my life. It wasn't that your dowry was not enough for me, but that *I* could not provide for *you*. I was too young to realize I wasn't the right man for you until it was too late."

"Because you became a lord?" Her eyes were dead. "If my presence in your life tarnished your precious title to such a degree, why play with my heart at all?"

"I was never playing." His eyes bore into hers as he tried to make her see the truth. He had known tempting himself with her in his arms for even a moment was a terrible idea. He had never stopped loving her. But he still couldn't have her.

"Poor little marquess." Her lip curled in contempt. "It must be so dreadful being a titled member of the aristocracy. You couldn't wed the gauche spawn of a textiles mogul, and I couldn't wed anyone at all."

"I shouldn't have ruined you," he said firmly. "I don't deny it. You deserve better. I should never have taken what should not have been mine. I should never have made promises I was unable to keep."

She raised her brows. "Are you any different now?"

"I'm trying to be." He lowered his voice. "I've spent the past several years building a large commercial port on one of my entailed properties. As soon as it opens, the marquessate—"

"The precious marquessate?" She burst out laughing. "You couldn't marry me because I was merchant class, and now you're saying you're about to be a merchant yourself. Your advisors are brilliant."

"They dislike the port," he admitted. But it was the only way to save the estate. Another year or two, and he could be solvent. Be able to make his own decisions again. "But I didn't come here to talk about me. I came here to apologize to you. To let you know how truly sorry I am for everything I've done to hurt you."

"Your words were as empty then as they are now." Her tone was scathing. "It's been *ten years* since last I saw you. If you called off our affair in order to wed an heiress, you'd have done so by now. You never cared about me. These excuses mean nothing."

Hawk flinched. The only reason he hadn't married an heiress was because he hadn't found a wealthy debutante willing to marry *him*. Not with so many far more eligible bachelors haunting the Marriage Mart at Almack's.

But although that was the truth, saying so would not make Faith feel any better. It would only prove what she no doubt already suspected.

If some heiress appeared on his doorstep tomorrow with enough money to pay off all the debts, restore the estate, secure the tenants, support his dowager mother, and replenish both the title's coffers and its former glory...

He and Faith both knew that when he had to walk away again, he would.

CHAPTER 6

*E*very muscle in Faith's body was poised to flee, but she could not save herself.

As happened every week at this time, four-and-twenty pairs of curious, engaged eyes scrutinized her every move across the dance floor. As they paired up with each other, every student attempted to copy her exactly.

Faith tried to hide a grimace. She didn't even wish to copy herself. Against all odds, she was in the one place she had sworn to never again find herself:

Lord Hawkridge's arms.

It was heaven. It was hell. It was home and memories and broken promises. Dancing with him was like nothing she'd ever dreamed and everything she'd ever feared. He was the same temptation he'd always been. The same poison. The same mirage. She shook her head to clear it.

How ironic was it that, so many years after they had found and lost each other, she and Hawkridge should share their first public dance?

Back when she had been young and hopeful and desperately trying to fit in with a crowd like his, she would've done anything to have a name on her dance card. Hawkridge's name. For a few short months, she had even hoped it would be possible.

But she was not one of his exalted set, then or now. And he was not of hers. The difference was, she now accepted her place. She had carved out a life of her own. People of her own. A family of her own.

Here, in the boarding school she managed with her best friend, was the one place where a woman as unremarkable as Faith held any power over a lord as well-connected as him.

The moment Heath Grenville arrived to take over as dancing master, Faith could show Lord Hawkridge out the front door and insist he never ever return.

That knowledge was the one thing keeping her mechanical limbs in motion. That, and the sense of rightness she'd always felt in his arms. Even though she knew it was wrong. That as soon as the music stopped, reality would come rushing back. Cold and unyielding. The tear in her heart, reopened.

This was just a waltz. It wasn't forever. It wouldn't even happen again.

She just had to survive a few minutes more in the arms of a man whose every aspect reminded her of the girlish dreams she'd once believed would someday come true.

From this position, she could not keep an eye on the front corridor in the hopes of espying the late arrival of Dahlia's brother. Instead, all Faith could see was the angle of Lord Hawkridge's jaw, the slant of his cheekbones, the dark curve of his eyelashes as his hazel eyes gazed soulfully into hers.

It was all so familiar. Every dream, every memory, an echo of moments just like this. Moments she'd feared would never happen again. Moments she had prayed would not. He was her biggest mistake and her greatest weakness. She should not thrill at his touch. At being the object of his focus, if only for one dance.

No matter how loudly Bryony played her Stradivarius, Faith knew from experience that the asynchronous stomping of two dozen little girls was more than capable of drowning out music, no matter how beautifully it was played.

Yet tonight she could hear nothing at all over the pounding of her own heart.

He smelled the same. Like man and musk and promises. He smelled like a lord. Like a daydream. Like a nightmare. He smelled so painfully familiar it was like discovering a part of herself that had been lost and finding the pieces no longer fit back together.

If her fingers trembled in his, Faith could not tell. He gripped her hands so firmly she could not possibly run away... Or slap him, if that was what he feared.

He need not. She had no moral high ground from which to exact vengeance.

At first, perhaps. At first, absolutely. He had ruined her. There was no excuse possible for not doing the right thing.

She had been *so* young back then. So naïve. So hopeful.

And then she'd received the letter.

Despite tossing it into the fire where it belonged, Faith still recalled every word of that precise, no-

nonsense script. When he had inquired as to whether their ill-advised encounter had incurred a permanent consequence, she hadn't completely understood the question.

Possibly because it had arrived on impersonal sheet of parchment rather than direct from his lips.

When she realized he was saying that the only possible circumstances in which a lordling like him would even consider leg shackling himself to a peasant like her, was if an unwanted child forced his hand in the matter, she had been furious.

What woman wanted a man who didn't want her? A life of inferiority and resentment with the man she'd foolishly believed loved her would have been consigning herself to a hell worse than anything she could imagine.

Perhaps, unwanted pregnancy or not, he still wouldn't have married her. That was not what men of his station did. Most likely, the cold dispassion of his letter was Lord Hawkridge's discreet way of enquiring as to whether the stupid country girl required hackney fare to someplace where their "indiscretion" could disappear.

She had expected so much *more* from him. From herself. From love.

Of course a child could not come from a single union that lasted scarcely more than an hour. She would not embarrass herself chasing after a rogue who had no wish to be captured.

With all the scraps of pride and dignity she could muster, she had grabbed her quill with shaking fingers and informed him in no uncertain terms that he was under no obligation to so much as lay eyes on her ever again. That if what they'd shared was such a mistake, she had no intention of making another.

Somehow, she managed to force her steps to keep time with the music.

Being in his arms felt so wrong. So right. So infuriating. How dare he show up after all this time? Of course he could whisk her about the dance floor with the grace of a prince. He'd had years of practice. Scores of other dances. Other women. Her hand in his wasn't special to him at all. It was perfunctory.

She wished she could feel the same. Or better yet, feel nothing at all.

Her family was no longer poor. She was no longer hopeless. But he was still a lord, capable of doing anything he wished in or out of the law with virtually no repercussions.

If he would not wed her back when their nights were full of stolen kisses, he certainly would not do so now. Who knew how he might react? He had the power to take Christina away. Perhaps even take Faith to court for fraud or child-stealing and any other charges *ton* barristers could bring against her.

And he might. He would be furious.

She could never let him know.

Her heart stuttered as she forced herself to keep dancing. To ignore the feel of his palm against the small of her back. To waltz as if she hadn't a care in the world.

Only recently, after Dahlia had wed Hawkridge's half-brother, did Faith discover how deeply his father's infidelity had scarred him. Hawkridge hated his father as much as he loved him. Vowed to be nothing like him. Promised his half-brother Simon that he would never make the same mistakes. Swore to be an exemplary father. When Hawkridge sired children, he would raise them under his roof as their father had been too selfish to do.

He would rather die than sire a bastard.

Except that was precisely what he'd done. And he had no idea. Because Faith hadn't told him in time.

Not that it would stop him from taking Christina from her now. Hawkridge would believe raising his daughter himself was the right choice. The *only* choice.

And to punish Faith for her deception, he would ruin her even worse than before.

Her feet tripped. She gulped and tried to tamp down her rising panic.

Whether she found herself in prison or simply alone in a big empty house that had once contained her daughter, the moment Hawkridge learned the truth she would never see either one of them again.

"Bryony is a prodigy at the violin, is she not?" he asked, as if Faith's entire fate did not rest in the palm of his hand.

She forced herself to nod. It was true. Almost all of the Grenville siblings were musical prodigies. "Yes. She is remarkable."

His eyes focused on hers. "Do you play?"

Faith shook her head. "I enjoy music, although it is not something I myself can produce."

What was she babbling about? God help her. She was trying so hard to hide her fears and act normal that it was hard to follow the conversation.

This waltz was longer than any musical score Faith had ever endured in her life.

Bryony, the blasted traitor, must be dragging out

the moment on purpose to give them time to talk. That witch would be next in line for a throttling. If the bloody music would ever end.

Lord Hawkridge's gaze searched hers. "You seemed so lost in thought. What were you thinking about?"

Faith bit back a hysterical laugh before it could escape her throat. What if he could see in her eyes that she was hiding something from him?

She tried to calm her breaths. He wasn't going to take Christina from her. All she had to do was act natural a few minutes longer.

And definitely not look into his eyes.

"Dare I hope you'll quit London as soon as the Season is through?" So what if the question was rude. He expected it. And probably wouldn't notice the trembling in her hands. She hoped.

Besides, men loved to talk about themselves, did they not? Especially if they were rich, titled, or powerful. "Hawkridge" was bound to be Lord Hawkridge's favorite subject.

To her surprise, he winced rather than began to boast.

"Honestly?" He hesitated. "The Season I shared with you was the happiest I've ever been. Everything I do, I do for the estate, for the title, for my tenants, my mother. It is exhausting. And it is never enough."

Faith clenched her teeth, angry that his unexpected confession engendered the same instant empathy she had always felt toward him. He did not deserve it. Hawkridge had behaved dishonorably to Faith, but *he* was the one who had suffered?

She pursed her lips. Fortune had smiled upon her despite him. She loved her life, her family, her daughter, her friends, her career. Her loved ones adored her right back. Believed her to be strong and capable and worthy of respect.

Lord Hawkridge's intense gaze suddenly swung her way again. "Your school is marvelous. I am impressed, even more so than I expected to be."

"I can't take all the credit," Faith said quickly. "Or even most of it. Everything you see was Dahlia's idea. Her dream, her sweat, her tears. I came on board when she realized she could no longer do it alone. Thank the stars. I wouldn't change this for the world. The students are wonderful."

Hawkridge beamed at her as if he hadn't heard a word about Dahlia. "With your love of children and your love of books, it's no wonder they love you. You must be a brilliant headmistress." His eyes softened. "One of my favorite memories is my head in your lap as you read aloud to me during a picnic along the Serpentine. The expressiveness of your voice has always had a way of transporting me to another world."

Her throat caught at the unexpected compliment and she glanced away.

Faith wished she could transport into another world right now. One where she wasn't sharing the air with the one man capable of stealing her breath. A world where her heart, life, and daughter were not at risk. A world where she didn't find herself in the unenviable position of wishing to undo the past.

If only he hadn't sent that terrible letter. If only she had not responded so hotly before discovering herself with child. If only she had been born to his class, or him to hers.

If only, if only, if only.

This was the world they lived in. The decisions they were forced to live *with*. The past could neither be altered nor undone, no matter how good he smelled or how easily he twisted up her insides until all she could think about was him.

Faith jerked her head up as the interminable waltz finally drew to a close.

So as not to find herself in his arms for so much as another moment, she immediately declared herself a "male" partner for the girls and swept the closest student into Bryony's next minuet.

Although it killed her to do so, she forced herself not to look at him again until the hour was through, but she could not trust herself to personally escort him to the door.

Instead, Faith thanked the school's unexpected guest and dismissed her students all in one breath and raced up the stone staircase to murder her best friend.

Dahlia barely glanced up from the paperwork on her desk when her door banged against the wall as Faith stormed into the room.

"What the devil were you thinking?" Faith demanded, her cheeks flushed with heat and her limbs still shaking. "Promise me, swear to me, you will never allow Hawkridge to darken our door again."

"Difficult, as he is our new dancing master," Dahlia said. She pulled a pile of decorative scarves into her lap that she had been embroidering for the next school fundraiser. "I'm sorry."

"I can't do it." Faith gripped the back of a chair. "*We* can't do it."

"What choice did I have?" Dahlia eyes were

pleading. "I'm so sorry, Faith. You don't have to come to lessons anymore."

Of course she did. Dance lessons were the girls' favorite part of the week, and up until now, one of Faith's favorites, too. She wouldn't let her feelings for Hawkridge ruin that. Even if it meant her choices were to bow out completely...or to find herself back in his arms.

Dahlia bit her lip. "Simon's new schedule precludes him from continuing on and my brother rarely has the time to substitute once the Season begins. When Hawkridge offered—"

"He *offered?*" Faith couldn't believe her ears. "How would he even know we were teaching the girls to dance?"

"He didn't. He offered to wield a hammer or a broom or a mop." Dahlia shrugged. "I cannot recall his exact words, but the essence was him volunteering to help in any capacity needed." She looked up from her embroidery with sympathetic eyes. "You know how much help we need. Should I truly have turned him away?"

Faith rubbed a hand over her face. Of course they could not turn him away. No matter how long she'd been angry at him.

Or how badly a small, secret part of her heart already longed to see him again.

CHAPTER 7

$\mathcal{T}$he following afternoon, Hawk was en route to pore over his ledgers in search of a miracle, as he had done every day for the past several years. In his distracted state, he nearly walked directly into one of their few remaining servants.

The young girl held a heavy silver tray in her arms and bore dark circles under her eyes, but she somehow managed to smile and bob at her master as if she couldn't be more delighted to deliver her heavy load.

Perhaps she was. After all, she had survived the latest round of heart-wrenching sackings when Hawk realized even their pared down staff was more extravagant than they could afford to keep on.

"Let me take that," he said impulsively.

There could be no doubt the laden tray was headed to his mother. The dowager refused to rise from her bed each day until she consumed a pot of fresh-brewed tea and broke her fast. It had been a ritual for as long as Hawk could remember.

"'Tis no bother at all," protested the maid, but she gratefully allowed him to relieve her of her burden.

"Thank you. I shall return to the kitchen to work on supper."

Hawk's jaw tightened as he realized this maid also pulled shifts as cook and housekeeper.

He nodded to dismiss her and headed toward his mother's chambers. Only when he glimpsed the golden glow of particles sparkling between the slender cracks in the curtains did he realize how late the hour had become. Mother had never been one to rise before noon at the earliest, but surely four in the afternoon bordered on excessive, given the Hawkridge family no longer attended evening soirées.

His mother lay in repose amongst a heap of silk-covered feather pillows in the center of her bed. Her eyes were closed as if she had not heard him enter the room or set the tray on the sideboard within arm's reach of the mattress.

Birds chirped outside the shuttered windows, but the air inside the room seemed oddly suffocating. Dust. Stale perfume. Mother's once brown hair was now mostly gray, her papery skin like dry powder.

She looked *old*, he realized suddenly. A sinking feeling twisted in his gut.

His mother had been the only family he had left for so many years that the thought of losing her had never crossed his mind. He pulled a chair next to the bed and lifted her frail hand in his. Hawk was glad he had not gone straight to the ledgers. A man must not forget to take advantage of the time he had been granted with his remaining parent.

"I don't suppose you resolved that silly issue with

my credit at the modistes," she said without opening her eyes.

How quickly tender moments could turn bittersweet.

Hawk patted her hand and refused to feel bitter. "Not yet, Mother. I shall let you know the moment you can once again spend indiscriminately."

"I should not have had to stop," she said petulantly. She opened her eyes. "Where's my tea?"

"I'll pour." He rose to his feet.

Her too-bright eyes scanned the room. "Where's the maid? You should sack her if she's too busy to serve a dowager marchioness her morning tea. *You* should not be performing manual labor. I'm certain I taught you better values than that."

"The maid is following my orders," he said calmly as he filled an antique cup with steaming tea. "And it is not morning but late afternoon. Why are you still abed?"

Her chin lifted. "Should I not be? Am I not in charge of my own schedule?"

"Of course," Hawk demurred.

What neither he nor his mother mentioned aloud was that being in charge of her own schedule was a fairly new occurrence in her life.

Hawk's father had held very firm ideas on how his marchioness should look, behave, be treated. When the accident claimed him, the new guardian had been even worse. Neither of them had escaped tyranny until Hawk had finally become old enough to take control of the title.

Yet those dark shadows persisted. Everything Hawk had thought he was inheriting was either in shockingly poor condition or nonexistent. But the thing he hadn't seen coming, the saving grace bestowed upon him despite all the strife, was the freedom not only to be his own man at long last but also to grant that same freedom to his mother.

With him, her tone was always sharp, but Hawk was determined to allow her to speak her mind. They both knew he held the title and thus could do as he pleased. But Hawk had no interest in becoming a tyrant.

Instead, he handed his mother her tea and retook his seat at her side. Their financial straits weren't her fault. They had his father and his uncle to thank for that. As soon as he'd secured enough investors to open his port, he would finally be able to spoil his mother as a dowager marchioness deserved.

Until then, he would do what he could to keep her safe and happy.

"Did you stay up late reading again?" he asked.

"I tossed and turned worrying about my son's utter lack of heirs." She cupped both pale hands about the warm teacup. "You should have everything a man with your title deserves. A wife. Heirs. And servants," she added pointedly. "If you tried a little harder I'm sure you could find an heiress with more fortune than we could spend in our lifetimes."

Hawk gritted his teeth. He had *tried*. For years, every night had been spent hunting an heiress. Now, every moment of every day was spent trying to build the new port on a waterfront section of desolate entailed land.

When the port's obvious ties to trade barred him from Almack's assembly rooms, Hawk had lost more than easy access to the Marriage Mart's famous balls. He'd finally realized he wasn't *going* to find an heiress.

Perhaps once his port was profitable, he could sell it for a small fortune and once again be an attractive catch to the daughter of a peer. Combine the right bloodlines, beget "an heir and a spare" for the title. Everything a lord was duty-bound to do. No matter where his true interest lay.

But all that was someday in the future. Until then, financing the estate was up to Hawk.

"Have you given more thought to the dowager cottage in the country?" he asked.

Mother still hadn't forgiven him for letting out the primary country estate, and thus far had refused to consider the idea of doing the same with the unused cottage designated for her use.

Yet until his port was in operation, rents from entailed properties were the only income keeping them afloat.

"It is beneath us," Mother snapped, her eyes wild. "I refuse to be talked about worse than we already are. If my countenance appears in a caricature, I'll lock myself in that dowager cottage and never leave."

Hawk leaned back in his chair.

This was not the first time she had threatened such a thing. Mother was still furious at him for moving them to an even smaller London townhouse. There was barely room for the two of them, and he wouldn't even have spared the coin for that much, were he not obliged to attend the House of Lords during the Parliamentary sessions.

And of course, he could not forbid his mother from being in town for the Season, when all her friends were out spending their fortunes and attending exciting events. Even if not being able to join them was its own special hell. While her friends were out shopping and dancing, the dowager marchioness could only afford activities that did not require ball gowns or jewels. More often, jealousy kept her from leaving the house at all.

But it was temporary.

It had to be.

As soon as the Season was over, however, Hawk would cease paying this rent. He would move his mother to the country and live in a shabby, unrentable property he could neither repair nor sell until the port turned a tidy enough profit to finally give them their lives back. Which it could do in less than a year, if he could just lock in a few more investors before quitting Town.

The prospect of living so far from London was less enticing than ever. He yearned to find room for himself in the lives of the two people he had thought lost forever: Faith Digby and Simon Spaulding.

"I took dinner with my brother the other day," Hawk said without thinking.

"He's no son of mine and no brother of yours," Mother snapped, slamming her teacup back into its saucer with enough force to crack the porcelain. His mother struggled to sit up straight amidst her sea of silk-covered pillows. "You owe no allegiance to a *bastard*. We are Hawkridges. Never forget what that means."

Hawk winced. For a moment, he had forgotten that his relationship with his brother was a part of himself that he could not share with his mother. The thought of having to keep separate versions of himself, to never be able to truly and completely share his life, was as sad now as it had always been.

But he would not upset his mother with his contrarian ideals. Not when he was just starting to realize how old she was becoming. How little time they might have left. Very soon, Simon could well be Hawk's only remaining family. He would not waste what time remained with his mother.

"It's a beautiful day, Mother." He leapt up from his chair to throw back a curtain to let her see. "We could take a stroll along the—"

A wracking cough from the center of the bed interrupted his train of thought. Hawk turned in shock to see his mother convulsing with each violent round of choking coughs.

He ran to her side and leaned her into his arm in order to lightly pound her back to open her airways.

She felt like nothing in his arms. The bones of a bird, and not much more weight than one. The light from the open curtain illuminated the gauntness of her cheekbones. Her skin was no longer porcelain, but ghostly. Her body was no stronger than that of a child.

"What is happening?" he demanded as soon as her coughing fit ceased. "Are you ill? Shall I fetch a doctor?"

"I'm fine," she snapped, jerking her frail shoulders from his loose grip. "If we don't have enough money to pay for my modiste then we certainly don't need to waste a coin on some quack surgeon."

"It was just a cough. Haven't you ever coughed? And I don't feel like taking a walk. I feel like being alone." She waved a thin hand in the direction of her chamber door. "Go about your business,

Hawkridge. I order you to leave. I am perfectly fine."

Hawk rose to his feet out of respect for his mother, but with the disheartening suspicion her sudden attack was not as meaningless as she would like for him to believe.

CHAPTER 8

*H*awk charged into the Cloven Hoof, his blood racing as rapidly as it had when the long-awaited summons first arrived. His investment payout was finally here.

When Maxwell Gideon had first come to Hawk with the idea of investing in a fledgling gambling salon meant to somehow rival exclusive gentlemen's clubs like White's and Boodles's someday, despite allowing less savory clientele through its doors, Hawk had been unconvinced of the Cloven Hoof's potential appeal to the high-in-the-instep upper crust.

Hawk, however, had been desperate. He'd come up with the idea of creating a thriving port but, as yet, had been unable to secure enough financing to begin. Only he could see future fortune amidst the jungle of weeds covering the rocky coast.

That was to say, only Hawk and Maxwell Gideon.

So they'd struck a devil's bargain. Hawk would invest in the gaming hell for a guaranteed two hundred percent profit, and when the money came due,

Gideon would match the payout as an investment into developing Hawk's port.

Today, the money was due.

He elbowed through the crowd of drunkards and gamblers, excusing his brusqueness by promising to stop and chat as soon as his meeting with Gideon was through. To Hawk's delight, the Cloven Hoof appeared busier than ever.

His step lightened. If business was good for Gideon, that should mean the return on investment should be good for Hawk. Perhaps his return would be even greater than double the initial sum. If so, he would be able to move the development schedule up by months. Open the port well ahead of schedule. Finally put an end to years of wading against the riptide of crushing debt.

But no matter how much or little his investment in the Cloven Hoof had earned, his primary goal was to send a doctor to check on his mother's health whether she admitted her symptoms or not.

Although days had gone by since the last of his mother's coughing attacks—at least as far as he knew—Hawk still wanted to ensure a medical professional looked her over and assure him nothing was wrong.

The tall oak door to the Cloven Hoof's back office was ajar by a few inches. Hawk rapped his knuckles on the thick doorjamb.

"What is it?" snarled a deep voice from within the depths of the office.

Hawk pushed open the door and stepped inside.

To call a man like Maxwell Gideon intractable or formidable was akin to claiming the sea to be somewhat damp. The Cloven Hoof and its infamous owner were both of deservedly questionable repute. Gideon was as impossible to predict as the turn of his cards, and just as likely to change the outlook of one's fortunes overnight.

Or, in Hawk's case, over an investment of five long years.

Gideon glanced up from a few small stacks of obsessively neat piles of paper and motioned for him to enter. "Lord Hawkridge. Do come in."

Hawk closed the door behind him and blinked as a total and eerie stillness descended upon the shuttered office.

Gideon preferred to work in complete silence. To conduct business from within the eye of the storm.

Hawk would never get used to the drastic change. Or the irony of a vice merchant cloistering himself inside walls designed to combat the din of his own gamblers.

There was neither a decanting port nor a glass of chilled ale on Gideon's desk, but rather a simple mug of black coffee. The walls of the office were bare of adornments. Every surface sparkled. Hawk imagined Gideon hired a team of employees to ensure every file was perfectly square, every seal perfectly centered. Everything within sight was relentlessly managed and in its place, just like Gideon ran his entire business, and likely, his life.

He seated himself on the other side of the wide desk.

"There is a new opportunity I believe could interest you," Gideon began without preamble.

"I am not interested in a new opportunity." Hawk leaned forward and said slowly and firmly, "I'm here to reap the rewards of the last opportunity…and to collect your portion as well."

"Don't be hasty," Gideon said, his legendary calm in place. "Everything in its time. I would like to ask your opinion about—"

"You are not listening. I am truly out of time." Hawk's voice was hard. "Is the money here or not?"

Gideon leaned back in his chair and touched the tips of his fingers together, unperturbed by the frank coldness of Hawk's question. One could be forgiven for almost believing him a completely different man than the laughing, dark-eyed rogue who had discussed the new Dulwich Picture Gallery over drinks with Zachary not a fortnight earlier.

But that was friendship. This was business. And Maxwell Gideon did not blur lines.

Neither did Hawk.

"I repeat," he said quietly. "Do you have the money?"

Gideon's cool gaze and hard features did not so much as twitch. Vauxhall Gardens boasted carved statues with greater range of emotion than the blackguard currently displayed.

Hawk stared back at him without backing down.

These walls had seen more secret deals brokered than he could even imagine. Gideon had his thumb in all of the pies. His office might be closed off to the noise of his clients, but Maxwell Gideon was well-informed about everything that happened under his roof. He spread the word about opportunities to the right ears, gathered speculative funds from the right investors, took an impressive percentage from every deal.

And now it was Hawk's turn to benefit from the arrangement.

Gideon gazed back at him without blinking. "Yes, I have the money."

"Good." Even if all Hawk had earned was a measly shilling, he wasn't walking out of this office without it. "Double, as promised?"

"Double," Gideon agreed. "For now."

Hawk frowned. "What is that supposed to mean?"

"It means," Gideon said as he leaned back in his chair. "That I have another opportunity. *You* have an opportunity, that is. What I have is a counter offer."

"I am not interested. Prepare the bank draft at once."

Gideon shook his head. "Hear me out."

"I don't have time," Hawk said simply. "My mother is ill. The port is nearly a year away from opening. And my father's overdue accounts are still—"

"You'll earn back six times your investment," Gideon interrupted. "Six times the amount as it *currently* stands."

Hawk's teeth clacked shut.

Five years ago, he had invested one thousand pounds in the Cloven Hoof. It had been risky. Some might even say foolish. But it had been worth it. To-day, those one thousand pounds were now worth *two* thousand pounds.

And Gideon was saying he could turn it into six times *that* amount?

Hawk only needed half that sum to finally wrangle the port into operational condition. The rest could be spent on a fleet of doctors. Servant salaries, overdue accounts, estate repairs. A bouquet for Faith. His throat went dry.

"When would the investment pay out?"

"Two years." Gideon leaned forward, his dark eyes glittering. "Twelve thousand pounds. Think about what you'd do with the money."

Hawk had already thought about it. In the split second since Gideon had made the offer, Hawk's mind had already spent every penny. The port would be functional. Hawk's *life* would be back on track. His bank account would be healthy, his estate would be healthy, his mother would be healthy.

But only if he had the money today.

"Two years is too long." He pointed toward a pen in the standish on the desk. "Request the bank transfer."

"One year," Gideon said quickly. "Twelve months from today. Six hundred percent. You can't beat this offer."

"Why are you even making it?"

"To buy out my silent partner." Gideon's lip curled. "The jackanapes currently owns fifty percent of the Cloven Hoof and refuses to sell unless I can buy back every share. This club is mine. I want to prove it."

"You don't need me for that." Hawk gestured toward the door. "Not when you have an entire gaming salon full of fools eager to toss their fortunes into the wind."

"They're happy to hand over money," Gideon agreed. "In exchange for shares in the Cloven Hoof. Exactly the situation I wish to be rid of. You're different. All you want is money. I'm willing to lose some in the deal as long as it gives me full ownership of the business I built with my own sweat and blood. You and I both come out ahead."

Hawk's pulse pounded at his temples.

Gideon was right. Hawk needed short-term funding far more than he needed ownership shares in a semi-reputable gambling den. This deal would be perfect for both of them...if he had the money today. Even a single year was too long to wait.

On the other hand, it was his best hope to secure the rest of the funding for his port. He could not afford to turn it down without careful consideration.

Hawk crossed his arms over his chest and narrowed his eyes at Gideon. "How long do I have to think it over?"

Gideon lifted a perfectly tailored shoulder. "You have twenty-four hours. I cannot wait a single minute more."

Hawk nodded tightly.

The twenty-four hours were already dwindling. And there was no time to waste.

He had to get out of this club, out of this environment of risk and gambling in excess, and focus on what mattered most. His mother. His brother. Faith's happiness. He had to get home and find somewhere quiet to think. For better or for worse, this decision might well affect the outcome of the rest of Hawk's life.

"You will have your answer by tomorrow." He rose stiffly and let himself out Gideon's office lest he be persuaded to make a rash decision.

He knew what was at stake if he didn't take the deal. And he knew what was at stake if he did. The question was which was the wiser choice, if indeed he had any wise choices left to him.

He glanced at his pocket watch. Five thirty. He could be home in less than an hour. Review the port's ledgers, have supper with his mother. Return to trying to squeeze a penny out of a rock.

Chaos assailed him the moment he stepped outside Gideon's office and into the corridor. Milling bodies covered every square inch of the Cloven Hoof. The din was overwhelming. He gripped the back of the closest chair and tried to block it all out. The clink of glasses, the slap playing cards, the rattle of dice, the crows of the scattered winners, the devastated groans of the many losers.

Hawk forced his way through the crowded salon toward the door, but escape was impossible. The more he tried to flee, the more familiar faces threw themselves in his path.

"Hawkridge!"

"What do you think of this hand?"

"When are you going to get rid of those horses and acquire a matched pair?"

"Should I hold or roll one more time?"

"What do *you* think of my cravat? Is there truly such a thing as too many folds?"

Normally, Hawk loved wasting a few minutes in inane conversation with his friends. Moments like these made him feel like the carefree young man he once was. No greater concern than the color of his horses or the starch in his cravat. But he was no longer that man and this was not one of those moments.

"Excuse me," he said for what felt like the hundredth time. "I must get through."

The warring smells in the gambling salon were as heady as its sea of colors and textures. Expensive port and cheap gin, perfume and desperation. Hawk did not belong here. He had to get out. He tried to wade toward the door.

Some of these men had long been lost to the allure of drink and easy fortune. Playing cards. Dice. Hawk no longer believed that anything came easy, but he did believe it possible to be in control of one's own life. He intended to prove it.

It was more than wanting to be unlike his father, or wanting to be his own man. Hawk needed to be the kind of father he'd always dreamed of being, the kind of husband he'd always dreamed of being. It had to be possible. He could not let himself believe differently.

He was the master of his own ship, yet he could not help but feel badly in need of a compass.

"Hawkridge," came a delighted voice. Hawk's old friend Anthony Fairfax emerged from the shifting crowd. "How are you, old chap? Has it ever been an age."

"You know what the bachelor life is like," Hawk answered without saying anything at all. Talking about himself would only depress them both. "How is married life?"

Fairfax's eyes shone. "I have never been happier. Life has turned out better than I had ever imagined. We're even expecting our first child."

"Congratulations," Hawk forced from his lips. He was thrilled for his friend. So why did Fairfax's news make Hawk feel as though he had taken a punch to the gut?

Shame prickled his skin. He hated how jealous he was that other men could marry for love, could start a family, could say unequivocally that they were happier now than they had ever imagined being.

But it was more than what they possessed and Hawk lacked. He envied how much easier their lives were in comparison. No unsurmountable debts, no weighty obligations, no heavy question marks pressing on their chests. His throat went dry with envy.

Men like Fairfax knew where they would be five, ten, twenty years from now—arm in arm with the woman he loved.

Hawk didn't even know what answer he would be giving to Maxwell Gideon twenty-four hours from now. But he would have to figure it out soon.

"Have you seen these?" Fairfax pointed at a few faded caricatures nailed to one of the walls.

The errant drawings were remnants from a few months ago, when Gideon had all but wallpapered the gambling salon with drawings mocking the "Lord of Pleasure," one of Gideon's closest friends and a frequent visitor to the Cloven Hoof... Until he'd fallen in love, that was.

Now the earl was just another happily married man. Likely working on an heir or two of his own this very minute.

Hawk shoved down his envy and quickly finished his conversation with his friend.

The room was too loud, the drunken gamblers too rowdy. More than that, the sight of errant caricatures had brought to mind his mother's recent admonition. Her concern about how she and her son were viewed by Society was more than valid. Hawk narrowed his eyes. He refused to allow her to become a laughingstock.

Which meant what? He pushed upstream toward the exit, determined to escape. Should he take Gideon's investment opportunity or not? And what about the rest of his life? What could he do about Faith? Where did he really stand, and was there anything he could do to improve it? He had no answers.

But now that she was back in his life, he could not bear to let her slip away again.

Guilt tightened his throat. He was not proud of how he had treated Faith in the past. But he was a different person now. They both were. He would like nothing more than to start anew.

When his port launched, perhaps, he could finally court Faith the way he'd always longed to.

He reached the front door just as it opened from the outside and a prissy gentleman with a sour expression pranced into the salon. Hawk's stomach sank at the sight.

Phineas Mapleton, London's worst gossip.

Just his luck.

"Hawkridge, my friend!" Mapleton called out in a voice designed to carry. "I didn't think you had enough ready blunt left to show your face in an establishment even as poor as this."

"And I didn't think you lacked the self-awareness to realize we are not friends," Hawk responded with a disarming smile.

Mapleton blinked in confusion then slapped him on the shoulder. "What on earth are you doing here? If you're looking for an heiress to marry, you won't find any skirts within these walls."

Hawk clenched his teeth. His mother was right. People were already talking. "Who I marry is none of your business."

Mapleton chortled. "But your choices are so amusing! The only chit you truly seemed half sweet on was the daughter of that disgusting textiles fellow. I heard you visited that ridiculous boarding school. I suppose you went nosing back around her as soon as you realized her family now has more money than yours ever did."

Hawk blinked. Her father's ill-advised textile investments had borne fruit? The Digbys were richer now than the Hawkridge title had ever been? Then why on earth would Faith be working in a boarding school?

She *wouldn't*. Mapleton was inventing gossip whole cloth.

Hawk returned a cold stare. "As usual, you have no idea what you're talking about."

"I know everything," Mapleton corrected smugly. "I know you haven't a ha'penny for day-old pies, and that the Digbys still think their filthy factory money can buy them entrée into the aristocracy." He gave an exaggerated roll of his eyes. "Why are commoners so deluded?"

Blood rushed in Hawk's ears. Was it true? *Could* it be true?

He pushed past Mapleton and out into the relatively fresh air of the alleyway.

Mapleton was a loudmouth and a terrible person, but he had no reason to lie. He drew too much pleasure from wreaking havoc with the truth. He was right about Hawk, which meant he was probably right about Faith's family, too.

Hawk leaned back against the rough brick of the façade and tried to quell his rising panic. This was wonderful news. And terrible news.

The last thing he wanted was for Faith to think that after all these years, he was only lowering himself to speak with her again because she now had money.

Whatever gossip she'd heard about him was probably true. He did need money. And he did want to marry. He had always wanted it to be her, but was a long way from making that happen—if he even could.

In the meantime, Hawk didn't want to lose her. But that was precisely what would happen if she thought his interest was in her family coffers, rather than herself. How could he convince her of his sincerity?

He pushed away from the wall and strode toward his aging carriage. It was six o'clock. She wouldn't be expecting him at the school until tomorrow, but perhaps that was for the best. She would know he came to call for her, not out of obligation.

His heart lightened. There was no time like the present to tell her she was still in his heart.

When he raced up the front steps of the boarding school to bang the brass knocker, Faith was just leaving. Hope fluttered within him.

She looked beautiful. Bonnet tied tight about flyaway golden-brown curls, woolen scarf looped twice about the high neck of a smart blue pelisse that complemented the green in her eyes.

If she was pleased to see him, she did not show it.

"What are you doing here?" Her tone was just short of long-suffering, as if the universe had conspired to throw him into her path as often as possible despite her best efforts to avoid him.

He deserved her disinterest. He'd lost any claim

on her time when he'd failed to offer for her after strongly implying church bells would be in their very near future. Marrying Faith would have been the cruelest thing he could do. That selfish act would simply have ensured that they both starve.

And now look at them. She in the first stare of fashion, wealthy enough to afford to volunteer her time without hope of recouping her investment, and he almost as indigent as the orphaned girls in her school.

Not that he hadn't tried. He had wrought miracles. The dwindling Hawkridge coffers had eked out not one year, but ten. Against all odds, he had paid off over half of the estate's debts. He was still a far cry from being the catch of the Season, but at this rate... he'd be in a position to beg for Faith's hand in no more than another decade or two.

Never had the dichotomy seemed so bleak.

"I wanted to see you," he began. His heart beat so quickly he could barely think.

Faith did not bother to hide her displeasure. "I'm busy."

"Ten minutes." He would feel no shame at the plea in his voice. This was too important. *She* was too important. "If I cannot keep your interest for longer, then I deserve to watch you go."

Her eyes narrowed and she crossed her arms. "Five minutes. I'm running late."

"Five minutes." He nodded stupidly. Now that a ticking clock had been granted to him, all his carefully constructed conversation points vanished from his mind. He straightened his shoulders. At least they weren't being spied upon by a gaggle of little girls. "I admire your loyalty and dedication to the school."

Her brows arched. "You drove to a rookery after nightfall to compliment my work ethic?"

"No. I came to say…" Frustration pounded at his temples. This was impossible. He didn't know how to say the things he came to say. Their roles had completely reversed. He was the one holding on to something he couldn't have, and she was the one trying to walk away. "I'm sorry, Faith."

"You already told me."

"I mean it." He took a deep breath. "I would apologize from now until eternity if it could change the past, and I'm willing to do so even though it can't."

"I don't want your apologies."

"You have them anyway." His *let's try again* speech was not going well. If he proposed a courtship of any kind, she would laugh in his face. "If you would rather leave the past behind us, I am happy to accommodate your wishes. I would rather talk about our future."

Her eyes shuttered. "We don't have one."

"We could," he insisted. "Not right away, of course. There is too much unresolved between us and I'm not yet in a position to offer—"

"Miss Digby?" came a small voice from inside the foyer.

Still blocking him from entering the doorway, Faith bent eye-level to greet one of the children. "What is it, Beatrice?"

The little girl held out a crumpled scrap of paper in a grubby hand. "I drawed a doggy for Chris."

"Thank you, Beatrice," Faith said solemnly. "I'll see that it gets delivered."

Hawk melted inside. His heart went out to little Beatrice and all other schoolchildren rescued from unspeakable lives on the streets. He truly did admire Faith and Dahlia both for the lives they were changing with their school for girls. They were miracle workers.

Because his own half-brother had been born a bastard, Hawk was painfully aware of the societal roadblocks and self-loathing and lifelong inequality that comes from being born on the wrong side of the blanket. He would never inflict such pain on an innocent child.

Faith kissed Beatrice on the crown and turned back to Hawk. "Three minutes."

He glanced down at the indecipherable ink squiggles clutched in her hand. "That was kind of Beatrice."

She slipped the parchment into her reticule. "They're kind girls."

"Who is 'Chris?'" he blurted. His cheeks immediately heated. It wasn't until the question had left his mouth that he realized it was borne of jealousy.

"Chris" could very well be the name of a suitor, and none of Hawk's business at all. Any man in his right mind would be blessed to win Faith's hand. There was no reason to think her heart wasn't already promised elsewhere.

Faith's lips tightened as if she had no intention of answering the impertinent question. Just when he could no longer hold his breath, she sighed and said simply, "My ward."

Hawk was relieved beyond all reason. Having a ward did not preclude the possibility that Faith was also in possession of a fiancé, but at least he could pretend he still had a chance.

And then reality set in.

"You have a ward," he repeated.

He was not surprised. Faith was goodhearted to a fault and had always loved children. If this boarding school was not proof enough, he would not be shocked to learn she spent her parents' textiles fortune on an entire house full of wards.

"One minute," she said. "Now you understand why I must get home."

He nodded. Of course he could understand putting a dependent first. He had to do the same. Guilt assailed him as his mother's frail countenance flashed in his mind.

Faith was the one woman he had always hoped to marry. If she truly was an heiress, life had finally given them the only circumstance in which Hawk's responsibilities to his title and the desires of his heart both pointed in the same direction.

But it was far from easy. Or straightforward. Heiress or not, Faith's blood was not of the proper pedigree a peer was meant to mix with. Even though Hawk had never given two figs about Faith's lack of ties to the aristocracy, right now he was forced to consider any dowry with cold practicality.

As much as he hated the thought of squandering any woman's fortune on his predecessor's past mistakes, being noble had long since ceased to be an option.

CHAPTER 9

Faith's heart was beating so quickly she feared her ribs would crack. She did not wish to speak of Christina with Hawkridge. She did not wish to speak to Hawkridge at all.

And yet she could not simply push past him and go. For touching him was out of the question. Just being in his presence was enough to weaken her knees and empty her head of all the reasons why she should not let him tempt her. Sliding her fingers over his leanly muscled forearms would be her undoing.

Even anchored in the open doorway with the wind in her hair and the cold sooty air bracing against her cheeks, his familiar scent and the warmth of his presence transported her from the dirty rookery to the brilliant starlit night they had shared so long ago. Back then, a chill in the air was simply a fine excuse to nestle deeper into his embrace.

Not so today, despite what her treacherous body might wish.

Her pulse skipped. Preparing herself emotionally

for their hour-long weekly dance lessons was difficult enough without also having to worry about him dropping by the school unannounced at all hours of the day or night. Especially with that way he had of completely focusing on her to the point where it was easy to believe she was the only thing that mattered in his world.

It wasn't true. It had never been true. Yet believing the lie was so, so tempting.

"Time's up," she said. "Good night, Hawkridge."

Faith wasn't fleeing. She had to get home to her daughter. If she tarried any later, her parents would have carried Christina to bed and Faith would have missed their nightly storytime ritual.

"Let me take you home." The intensity of his gaze did not waver.

She shook her head. "I have plenty of hack fare."

"I have a carriage waiting not ten feet away." He lifted his palm toward the street.

"Even more reason to say no." She did not know whether her cheeks had turned pale or pink at the thought of sitting next to him in a carriage. "We should not be alone together."

"I know," he admitted. His hazel eyes seemed so sincere. "I just want to do the right thing. Please allow me to be gallant. Just this once."

"Gallant without strings?" she asked archly before she remembered that with him, there were never any strings. No ties between them at all. That was why he had been able to walk away. Her voice went flat. "Am I to receive a curt, emotionless missive on the morrow?"

Anguish flashed across his gaze. "Can we not try to be friends?"

"How?" she asked hoarsely, wanting it so badly she could taste it. If only they could have what they once shared. If only they could have *more*. "Why?"

"I don't know," he answered honestly. "But I would very much like the opportunity to try."

She closed her eyes and forced herself to listen to the truth of where she was rather than the dream of where she wished to be. This was real life. The thunder of footsteps in the dormitories overhead. The nightbirds hawking their wares on the streets outside. The emptiness in her heart that she dared not refill with more empty promises.

As co-owner of a boarding school, her first obligation was to whatever most benefited the girls in the institution. Even if it meant occasionally allowing her former paramour through the doors. Even if it meant dancing with him.

However, she was not obliged to open herself up to being rejected anew.

He claimed to wish to be friends, but were his motives pure? Dare she trust him again, even a tiny bit? She licked her suddenly dry lips.

Perhaps their encounters would be easier to survive if she just accepted that she had missed him. Being near him was torture because she was forced to admit part of her *wanted* to be near him. But it didn't mean she'd forgiven him or that she was inviting him back into her life.

Although Faith wished with her entire being that things had gone differently between them, no amount of apologizing would change the past.

"I'm scared," she said suddenly, unable to stanch the words. She was too vulnerable. He was asking too much. "I want to believe you. But last time, trusting you was a foolish mistake."

"I am not the same man I was before," he said, his tone firm and his gaze intense. "Are you the same woman?"

She swallowed her guilt. "You may not wish to be friends with who I am now."

"Can I not decide for myself?" He lifted her hands in his as if he were about to clutch them to his chest, then abruptly let go as if the mere act of touching her wounded him more than he could bear. He stepped aside, allowing her free passage to come or go as she pleased. "As you wish, Miss Digby. You may call a hack, or you can allow me to escort you. Friendship cannot be forced. Your choices are yours alone."

She nodded. Very well. There could be only one decision. Had Hawkridge resorted to manipulation, she would've sent him to the devil. But politeness and respect had managed to melt the edges of a heart even as cold and scarred as hers.

He had made her choice by allowing her to choose for herself.

"It's not the same house as before." She latched the front door of the school behind her and joined him on the stoop but did not take his arm. "Little more than a fifteen-minute drive if the streets are clear."

He stared at her as if she were speaking in tongues. Then his face lit with surprise and joy, and he nodded so quickly she feared he would unravel his cravat.

"Fifteen minutes is a trifle. I am honored to escort you." His cheeks flushed with pink. "You may now have a new residence, but I fear my conveyance is the same as before. With perhaps a few new creaks to augment the dull edges."

"I was going to take a hack," she reminded him gently. "I will not be offended by a marquess's coach, no matter its age."

His driver opened the side door before they had even crossed the street, and Hawkridge helped her up into his antique carriage as if she were more precious than any jewel.

He took the seat beside her at a respectable distance. Neither hugging the window on the other side nor arranging himself alarmingly close. To an outside observer, they might even look as though they were exactly what he wanted: friends. His gaze shone with unconcealed hope.

Faith tamped down the butterflies in her stomach. Perhaps he *had* changed. Perhaps this time, his interest was sincere.

Hawkridge looked at her expectantly and she realized she had missed the driver inquiring as to her destination.

She directed him to her parents' elegant new home in the heart of stylish Mayfair and tried to collect herself before risking another glance at Hawkridge.

He was too close.

He was not close enough.

She longed to reach for him. Did he miss her touch as much as she missed his? When he looked her in the eyes, did his gaze drop to her lips and remember how they felt against his, as she did every time she looked his way?

"If you like," he said hesitantly, "I should be pleased to escort you home after dancing lessons."

"I'm not sure that's wise." Her voice was throaty, so full of desire and skittishness and longing that Faith could scarcely recognize herself.

He lifted his hand and reached toward her so slowly, so tenderly, so hesitantly, that she had plenty of time to stop him long before his warm familiar fingers curved against the side of her face.

Yet she did not.

"I missed you." His voice was gravelly, his gaze anguished. "I still miss you."

Faith did not trust herself to respond. She doubted she needed to. Allowing him to cradle her face in the palm of his hand was as much a confession as torture.

Now he would know.

She yearned for him. Had never stopped yearning. Her body could not be trusted to accomplish self-preservation. Nor could her heart. It was cracking open even as she gazed up at him in wordless need.

He might've kissed her then, had the driver not abruptly reached their destination. She might even have let him.

Oh, who was she fooling? Of course she would have let him. Her face was still nestled in his hand. He could kiss her now, right in front of her parents' home, and she would not pull away.

And then she realized what was missing: Surprise. Surprise was missing.

Hawkridge had not blinked when she'd given her direction to a neighborhood five times as elegant as the one her parents had been able to afford when they were younger. He was not surprised she now resided in one of the largest homes on the most expensive street.

He *knew*.

She jerked her face from his touch, the old hurt roiling inside her like bile.

Of course his offer to "do the right thing" was just as insincere now as it had been back then. A man like him would always want something from her. No matter how much she longed to believe otherwise.

He lowered his hand and frowned. "What's wrong?"

"I'm home. Let me out," she said rather than answer directly.

There was no sense in starting an argument.

That explained the sudden renewal to his attraction. Lord Hawkridge was after her pocketbook, not her heart. Rekindling a pointless "romance" with him was as foolish as ever.

She all but elbowed past him as she scrambled out of the carriage and onto the front walk of her parents' home. If his sudden interest was due to her dowry, then she had no interest in him at all.

Besides, Christina was waiting inside, which made this street the last place to be airing old wounds. Her stomach constricted as she gazed up at the flickering candle in her daughter's bedroom window. This was far too risky.

Faith didn't know what would be worse—for Hawkridge to disbelieve her if she were foolish enough to confess the truth, or the brunt of his vengeance if he did.

He stood beside the carriage, clearly bewildered

by the abrupt way she had closed herself off from him. "Faith?"

"Miss Digby," she corrected, forcing herself to resume a professional mien that fit the headmistress of a boarding school.

"I should not have touched you." He stepped forward, his gaze full of self-recrimination. "I only—"

"I can't." The words exploded out of her as if her hungry heart had clawed from her chest. "Good night, Lord Hawkridge. Thank you very much for your generous assistance. I will not impose upon you again."

Faith turned and hurried into the house as if the devil himself were behind her, but she suspected the greatest danger lay within her own heart.

The moment she was safely inside, she closed the door against the night and her own desires and collapsed against it to catch her breath.

Alarmed, the butler offered to fetch her a brandy, or smelling salts.

Faith waved the idea away. The situation required a far more drastic solution than smelling salts. Or expensive brandy.

She had been so close to giving Hawkridge a foothold back into her life. Back into her heart. Back into her *arms*.

How could she be so foolish? Had life taught her nothing?

She pushed away from the door leading back to temptation and hurried instead to the library at the rear of the house.

It was empty.

However many books Christina had chosen tonight, Faith had not been there to read them.

A flash of anger coursed through her. Not at Hawkridge. She had given up long ago on staying angry with him. Rather, her ire was directed at herself for letting him distract her from the only thing that mattered.

She tossed her bonnet on a side table and raced up the stairs to the sleeping quarters. As soon as she reached the landing, she slowed her steps so as not to startle Christina awake.

The door to her daughter's bedchamber was ajar, and Faith's parents stood just out of sight in the corridor. They held twin fingers up to their lips in a gesture for silence.

Faith sighed. She had indeed missed the bedtime ritual. She nodded at her parents and tiptoed to the crack in the door to peer in at her peacefully sleeping daughter.

Christina was beautiful, awake or asleep. Her golden-brown curls framed her cherubic face like a halo. Soft breaths and the occasional crackle in the grate were the only sounds.

A sense of peace enveloped Faith. Seeing her daughter, knowing she was safe and happy, filled Faith with a richness far more valuable than money. She was more fortunate than she had ever dreamed.

For now.

Darkness gripped her heart as she considered all the ways allowing Hawkridge back into her life could have catastrophic consequences. She would allow nothing to bring her daughter pain.

Her parents motioned her away from the open doorway toward the rear of the corridor where they would not wake Christina.

"Have you tired of that school for indigents yet?" her father asked jovially.

Perhaps it was a jest. Perhaps it was not.

"I recall quite clearly what it was like to have very little," Faith replied without rancor. "I shall never tire of giving children a reason to hope."

Her mother's eyebrows lifted. "Then why do you look like you've just come from battle?"

Faith winced. "Because I have. Lord Hawkridge escorted me home."

This time, it was her father whose eyes narrowed suspiciously. "Why?"

"His proposition was far different than any one of us could have imagined." Faith's self-deprecating smile was wan. "He wants to be friends. He wants us to forget the past and start anew, as if such a thing were possible."

"But that's wonderful!" her mother said in delight. "I've always said you were meant for better things. This is your chance to turn your life around even more dramatically than your father and I did."

Faith cast her mother a flat look. "No."

"Is a potential courtship with a marquess not worth the risk? Even if it's *that* marquess?" her mother insisted stubbornly. "*Especially* if it's that marquess?"

"No," Faith repeated softly, gazing through the parted doorway at her sleeping daughter. "It is not."

As far as anyone knew, Christina was a perfectly ordinary ten-year-old. Branding her a bastard would invalidate her status in society, but worst of all, it would make her think *herself* less valid.

Faith didn't wish to give anyone a reason to slight her daughter. To mock her. To reject her. To make her feel worthless and meaningless and unwanted. More importantly, Christina must never doubt she was important and loved.

If Hawkridge became involved, everyone would know Christina had been born out of wedlock. Being the by-blow of the marquess would give her no advantage. Dahlia's husband Simon knew that better than anyone. Hawkridge's father had abandoned Simon and his mother in order to wed a *suitable* bride. For a peer of the realm, class differences were a chasm too wide to cross.

Faith had learned that the hard way. Although she had been born on the right side of the blanket, she still hadn't been good enough to make a desirable match. Or a match at all. Faith pressed her lips together. The last thing she would do was make life even harder for her daughter.

"Any money that goes to Hawkridge's failing estate will not be able to go to Christina," Faith reminded her mother. "If you don't want two dozen innocent little girls to benefit from my dowry, do you really want that money to disappear into the bottomless pit of Lord Hawkridge's debts?"

Mother's eyes widened and she vigorously shook her head. "Absolutely correct, daughter. I don't know what I was thinking. Never get into his carriage again."

"For any reason," her father added darkly.

Faith gave a tight nod. She deserved that rebuke.

No peer would lower himself to wedding Faith unless he were in desperate circumstances. Hawkridge wasn't interested in her. He needed her dowry. Well, too bad. Faith was not in the marquess charity business. In fact, she had no business with Hawkridge at all.

Across the corridor, Christina sighed in her sleep and rolled on her side to curl deeper against her pillow.

It would destroy her to know the truth, Faith realized bleakly. Would Christina still love her "Aunt Faith" if it turned out she was the mother who had lied to her for her entire life?

Sick fear turned in Faith's guts. It would be hard for a ten-year-old to understand that the secret Faith kept was meant not to protect herself, but her child. This necessary fiction was the only way Faith could ensure Christina even had a chance.

From time to time Faith couldn't help but wonder what would have happened if she had confessed the truth back then, back before it became a tempest too wild to call back.

But those sorts of thoughts inevitably invited the return of reality. Hawkridge hadn't wanted her. She hadn't been good enough for him or his title or his family.

Even if he believed her, even if he'd gone against everyone's wishes and made an honest woman of her, she still wouldn't have been wanted, still wouldn't have been good enough, still would have been living in a far greater hell than the happy life she had now.

Christina would not be reading from a plethora of child-focused books, or have access to an in-home library. She would not have the best tutors money could buy, or perhaps any tutors at all. She would not be clothed in dresses that fit, with fine warm fabric, and shoes that didn't pinch.

Instead of possessing bright eyes and rosy cheeks, she might be pale and gaunt. And bored. And lonely. And miserable.

Whether Faith had made the right decision for herself or for Hawkridge was no longer the question. She had made *a* decision. It had resulted advantageous for Christina. A mother could wish for nothing more.

So why was a traitorous part of her so tempted to tumble right back into the arms of the one man she could never have?

She closed her eyes against the familiar pain. No matter how much she might wish there was a way, she could not rekindle any sort of relationship with a shameless fortune-hunter like Lord Hawkridge. Even if she were still stupidly, hopelessly, in love with the man.

Especially because she was still stupidly, hopelessly in love.

CHAPTER 10

*H*awk grabbed the last vacant seats in the bustling tea shop and motioned above the crowd for his brother to join him.

Simon abandoned his own search and began to make his way through the sea of fashionable ladies and gentlemen queuing up for sponge cakes and fresh-made ices. Although spring had finally arrived, it was not a warm enough day to sit outside. Which meant half of London was between these walls.

Hawk sent his brother a hesitant glance out of the corner of his eye. He hoped Simon would not regret accepting the invitation.

Enjoying Gunter's flavored ices was a perfectly normal activity brothers might do… If they were twelve years of age. But just because neither man had lived the childhood he dreamed of didn't mean it was too late to do it right.

Before, they had been silent enemies. Although they had not spoken until this past year, they had known about each other since birth. Now they were family.

"Splendid job," Simon said as he slid into the empty seat across from him.

"As soon as they realized I was a marquess, they couldn't get away fast enough," Hawk joked.

When Simon's jaw tightened, Hawk regretted his words immediately.

Of course his brother would not find humor in such a jest. As the bastard child of a courtesan, worse indignities would have befallen him daily. Although Hawk would never abuse the power of his title, Simon was still getting to know him. Tasteless jests were not the best way to strengthen his relationship with his brother.

"Did you decide on violet or jasmine?" Hawk asked quickly, as if his previous words had not been spoken.

Flower flavors were all the crack this season. Surely that was a safer topic.

"Violet." Simon glanced over his shoulder at the incredible crush of people. "I considered ordering both, but I am not convinced this establishment has enough ice to last the afternoon."

"It's worse in the summer," Hawk said with a laugh. "The queue stretches all the way outside where those wishing to be seen await their ices in a long line of open carriages wrapping about the square."

He wondered if that had been the wrong thing to say as well.

Simon had mentioned that he never before tasted Gunter's famous wares, but that did not mean he had not watched the fashionable set indulge themselves from afar.

He likely did not need Hawk to tell him about

the quarter-mile of colorful bonnets encircling Berkeley Square, the gentlemen in perfectly tailored riding outfits leaning beneath the trees, the harried waiters dodging the constant flow of horses and carriages to deliver freshly scooped frozen cream before it could melt.

His brother had probably been one of the many on the outside looking in.

Hawk grimaced. Perhaps meeting here had not been the wisest idea.

But then a waiter appeared with two delicate bowls and Hawk was transported back to his childhood. This had long been one of his favorite places. There was no one he'd rather be sharing it with.

"*Bon apetit.*" Simon lifted a spoon in salute.

Hawk grinned and did the same. "Likewise."

He closed his eyes for the briefest of moments to allow the sensation of orange blossom and sweet cream to fill his mouth and his heart. Delicious. He opened his eyes and grinned to see his bemused brother lifting a hand to the back of his head.

Simon winced and gave a lopsided smile. "You warned me."

"It's cold," Hawk agreed with an answering grin. "Go slow and enjoy it."

A wave of happiness flowed through him. He loved moments like these. A favorite treat, good company. Simple pleasures had always brought him joy.

"How I wish the right gentleman would look at me the way you look at orange blossom ices," cooed a cloying voice to Hawk's right. A cloud of perfume enveloped the table. "Capturing the full attention of a man who knows how to savor a treat is every woman's fantasy."

He glanced up to see Mrs. Epworth, a young widow who had joined the fast crowd the moment she was done mourning a husband three times her age. The old roué had left his young bride with both money and unprecedented freedom. She now enjoyed pushing the boundaries of scandal at every opportunity.

"The confections here are masterpieces," he replied placidly, ignoring the shameless flirtation. He was not interested in becoming one of Mrs. Epworth's many conquests amongst the *ton*.

"Always so polite." She batted her eyelashes at him and sighed in mock resignation. "More's the pity."

Hawk did not watch the deliberate swing of her hips as she sashayed away from his table. All her parrying had done was reinforce Hawk's unceasing yearning for Faith.

He should have brought her here, back when she still loved him. Back when he still could. He rubbed a hand over his face in regret. Their courtship should have been public, not relegated to shadows and stolen moments. Suddenly his flavored ice did not taste as sweet.

Faith probably wondered if the only reason he'd paid her any attention was in the hope of seducing her. She would never believe he had truly intended to wait until he had at least secured permission for her hand before indulging in anything more than heated kisses.

In the end, he had let the moment be ruled by emotion rather than propriety. No doubt he had proved her worst fears true when he failed to appear the following morning with a request to visit with her father.

And now what must she think? Even though he couldn't have her, he had never stopped wanting her. But she would have no reason to believe such a claim. Especially given that it had been years since last they spoke, and now that her family had money, here he was again.

No doubt that was why Faith had all but leaped from his carriage last night.

"Orange blossom not to your liking?" Simon's tone was light but his gaze perceptive. "There's still time to order the violet. Or chase after that woman."

Hawk shuddered. "No thank you. My interest lies elsewhere."

But he would not elaborate. He didn't want to talk about his relationship with Faith with anyone but the woman herself.

Nor did Hawk wish for Simon to think the reason for the date in Berkeley Square was not an earnest brotherly outing but rather a shameless ruse to weasel his way back into the life of a woman Simon counted as a friend.

"How is your new assignment coming?" he asked instead.

Simon's eyes brightened.

Hawk was sincere in his desire to make up for lost time. His brother was the sort of man he would love to call a friend, regardless of familial connection. Brilliant, successful, kindhearted. Dahlia had married a man anyone could be proud of.

"The hours are less convenient, but the increase in pay is a boon for the school." Simon's voice softened. "How are *you* faring, brother? If you are in need of a little help—"

Speechless, Hawk shook his head in horrified denial.

The last thing he wanted was to accept anyone's charity. Especially not from his brother.

Even if Hawk were finally desperate enough to beg for spare coin, Simon was in no position to offer any. The man had sold his house to provide for his family. To purchase the abbey that now housed two dozen little girls. Hawk could never take food from children's mouths.

"Well, I'm here," Simon said, likely not realizing his presence in Hawk's life was a balm in its own right. "I should be even better advantaged this time next year if I'm awarded the promotion I've heard whispers about." His eyes lit with excitement. "We will finally be able to make repairs to the school that we've been holding off."

"I am an expert at repairs," Hawk said. Circumstance had made it so. "If all you need is labor, I am your man."

"I accept," Simon said quickly. He set down his empty bowl, eyes twinkling. "Too late to take it back. I and my entire extended family preemptively thank you for your generous offer of unpaid servitude."

Hawk bowed his head, battling an irrational flash of jealousy at the idea of possessing an extended family. How delightful that must be. For the past ten years, all he'd had was his mother. Including Simon in his life had already doubled Hawk's fortune. Sawing wood and pounding nails could allow him to show his brother that Simon's needs were as important as his own.

"Are there many repairs?" he asked.

"More than I'd like," Simon admitted. "My new assignment provides even less leisure time than before, and of course we haven't the means to purchase much in the way of materials. Faith has been trying to get her parents to donate her dowry to the cause, but I can certainly understand why someone might be reluctant to part with ten thousand pounds. We'll find a way. We always do."

Ten… thousand… pounds.

Hawk's throat went dry. No wonder Faith had distrusted his overtures for friendship. Such a sum would erase the lion's share of the marquessate's debt.

He groaned. There was no chance of her believing that she herself was the primary attraction.

Still dazed, Hawk set down his bowl and lifted his eyebrows toward the throngs still awaiting their ices. "Shall we relinquish our seats to the masses?"

"Unfortunately," Simon agreed. He rose to his feet. "Much as I'd prefer to get back in line and sample every flavor."

"Next time," Hawk promised as he led the way back to his carriage. But it was likely to be his last visit to a tea shop for quite a while. He could not afford to repeat even an extravagance as small as this very often. If he reinvested his recent earnings with Gideon, there wouldn't be any spare coins left at all.

When his aging horses pulled the carriage alongside the school for girls, Hawk expected his brother to leap down, bid his leave, and hurry inside to his wife. Instead, Simon took him by surprise.

His dark brows lifted expectantly. "You will come inside, won't you?"

Hawk blinked. This was Simon's first free afternoon in a fortnight. Surely he wished to spend it with his family. "I don't want to intrude—"

"Poppycock." Simon laughed. "Family cannot intrude. You're welcome under our roof any time."

Warmth infused Hawk at his words. "Just long enough to pay my respects to your wife, then."

Simon grinned and led the way.

Dahlia was bent over the desk in her study when they reached the second floor.

Simon kissed her forehead. "Give me just a moment, if you don't mind. I'll check to ensure the hearths are lit for the evening."

The moment her husband quit the room, Dahlia leapt up from her chair and jabbed a finger into Hawk's chest. "Worthless rogue! I don't know what you said last night to upset her so, but if you hurt her again I will find the closest sharp instrument and *gut* you."

Hawk held his palms up in peace. "I swear I will not harm her."

Dahlia glared for a moment longer, then dropped her hand. Her gaze was sharp and considering. "You cannot speak to her for another quarter hour. Story time is sacrosanct."

Hawk stared back blankly. "It is?"

Dahlia sat back down at her desk and turned away as if she had already allotted him all the time he deserved. "Third door on the left. You can peek in from the corridor so that you do not distract the children."

Hawk hurried to the corridor. He found the room with little trouble. It was full of Faith's voice and hushed energy as she read aloud from within a circle of two dozen rapt faces.

How he wished he were among them at her feet. He had missed the sound of her voice, the pleasure of reading a book aloud. Her students were more than fortunate to have her. He smiled to himself at their enthralled expressions.

Most of the girls wore identical outfits of plain dresses and simple pinafores. One of the children, however, was dressed fine enough to match the crowd he had just seen in Gunter's.

Hawk frowned. He could not imagine someone donating such expensive fabric and precision hand-work to a boarding school for indigents, but Dahlia's skill with exacting charity from the *beau monde* was unparalleled.

Faith was also dressed as finely as any lady of the *ton*. Her elegant day dress was just practical enough to fit her environment. The added soft blue hue brought out the peaches and cream of her com-plexion and contrasted beautifully with the soft shimmering brown of her hair.

Hawk would never tire of gazing at her. Faith would be a vision no matter what she wore. But watching her from the shadows felt like the same endless torture of reaching for her in his dreams only to jerk awake empty-handed. He could not have her in fantasy or reality. But nothing could stop him from longing for her.

Her smooth, animated voice stuttered to a shocked halt when her eyes flicked toward the cracked doorway and she glimpsed him watching.

Embarrassed heat crept up Hawk's neck at her

obvious horror. He had meant to stay and talk to her, but that was clearly not something she desired.

He stepped back into the corridor and out of her line of sight. If she wished to speak with him, she knew when and where she could find him. He would not shoehorn himself into anyone's life.

No matter how much he yearned for her.

CHAPTER 11

*F*aith clutched a pristine edition of *The Mysteries of Udolpho* in her lap and thanked her stars for Bryony Grenville.

Were it not for Dahlia's younger sister, Faith never would have received an invitation to one of the fashionable set's exclusive book clubs.

Strictly speaking, she still had not received an invitation. She was here as Bryony's guest. Seated in the drawing room with a dozen women of far more varied backgrounds than Faith would've dreamed the *beau monde* could tolerate.

The Fairfax parlor was simple, but clean and elegant. The plain silver tray on the table in the center of the room laden with fresh tea and lemon cakes.

But the best part, the thing that Faith loved the most, was the heated argument raging over whether Udolpho was truly Radcliffe's greatest Gothic romance, or if the novel were no more substantial than the exaggerated imagination of its heroine.

The ladies talked over each other to make their points.

Disappointment that scarcely a third of the novel

took place in a Gothic castle, raptures at the sequence in Italy, which everyone agreed was one of the most romantic of countries, rolling eyes at the heroine's unprovoked fainting spells which occurred so frequently as to be laughable.

It was heaven. Faith had always dreamed of finding a group such as this. Of finding herself amongst a fellowship of women who valued each other's minds more than their titles. Now that she was here, she hoped to return again and again.

But her presence today was not due to her own recognizance. Faith struggled to think of what she could do to ensure a return invitation of her own.

Thus far she had yet to express any of her views aloud. More correctly, she had yet to speak at all. Faith was not shy with her family, not shy with the Grenvilles, not shy when she spoke for hours in front of a group of two dozen schoolchildren.

But this was something else. A dream so close to her grasp it was in danger of popping.

She gripped her book tighter in her lap. If she spoke out of turn, she and her unfashionable opinions would be roundly rejected. There would be no more book clubs.

However, if she remained quiet, she would be completely forgettable. An opinionless mouse would not receive a second glance, much less an invitation to return.

The question was achieving just the right balance to join the conversation.

"I think there should have been more kissing," announced Bryony with her characteristically scandalous flair.

"Kissing!" exclaimed Lady Roundtree. "In a *romance* novel?"

"That wouldn't be gothic, but scandalous!"

"But perchance a better ending, no?"

"Imagine if she kissed him instead of fainting..."

"Then he would never have preferred gambling!"

"What say you, Miss Digby?" Bryony twisted toward Faith, her eyes laughing at the lively discord she had sown. "To what lengths should our dear Emily have gone to ensure Valancourt be more attracted to her than to the gaming tables?"

"None," Faith said, far more vehemently than she had intended. "If he is not sufficiently charmed with who and what she is, he does not deserve to take more from her than she is ready to give."

"Well said!" Mrs. Fairfax clapped her hands together. "If only the rakes of London were half as wise as Miss Digby."

Faith sagged in relief that her outspoken opinion had been accepted.

"I've a splendid idea!" Bryony banged her spoon against her saucer for attention. "We should have Miss Digby select the next title. Her library is even larger than Prinney's, and she has read every single book in it."

"Oh, is it true? If so, I am vexingly jealous," Mrs. Fairfax said in delight. "Do say you will invite each of us over to browse your wonderful collection."

"I... That is... If you like, you are more than welcome," Faith stuttered. "Although I am not certain any library can be half as wonderful as Miss Grenville would have you believe."

"Not true," Bryony countered with sparkling

eyes. She held up her palm to the blond woman on Faith's other side. "Just ask Mrs. Turner."

Mrs. Turner blushed. "I knew my husband was The One when I discovered he had built a library just for me."

Faith smiled shyly. "It sounds like you chose very wisely."

"Do you spend every afternoon enjoying the fruits of his labor?" Mrs. Fairfax asked.

"I used to," Mrs. Turner replied, seeming chagrined. "But now that the children are older, I find myself dedicating an extraordinary amount of time to determining whether increased tutorage or finishing school would afford them the greater benefit."

"Dreadful to decide, is it not?" Faith blurted before she could stop herself. "Both are splendid choices with strikingly different advantages. The hiring of governesses and tutors allows one to select each instructor with great care and provide the child with one-on-one attention, whereas finishing school grants them a plethora of group activities, the chance to make friends, the ability to learn and grow with others."

Appalled, Lady Roundtree's teacup rattled against her saucer. "Are you a *mother*, Miss Digby?"

"I have a ward," Faith said hurriedly as she realized her mistake. "I do not pretend to know what motherhood is like, but it is my duty to give my niece the greatest advantages I can."

"You phrased it so well." Mrs. Turner smiled at her in kinship. "That is exactly what it is like. And if you are interested, there remain a few openings in what most of us agree to be the finest finishing school in the area."

Lady Roundtree cast her gaze heavenward. "Never say you refer to the Fitz-Dwyer Academy."

Bryony rolled her eyes toward Faith. "Since the review process isn't quite as stringent as Almack's"—the other ladies tittered—"those with vouchers may find affiliation beneath them."

Faith didn't give a fig what the patronesses of Almack's believed beneath them. All she wanted was the best possible education for her daughter. An opportunity for Christina to grow and blossom with richer resources and better advantages than Faith or her boarding school could provide.

"You must know that the *best* families educate their children in the home." Lady Roundtree sniffed. "No one of truly fine breeding would want their daughters anywhere they might be influenced by those who are unworthy. A governess is the *only* answer."

Mrs. Turner ignored the comments and turned to Faith. "I can pass your name along, if you like."

Faith's breath caught at the unexpected offer.

The Fitz-Dwyer Academy was legendary among families who could not boast ducal connections the likes of Lady Roundtree's. It would be perfect for Christina. The best environment, the best tutors, the best chance for an unparalleled education and a truly happy childhood.

"I would like that," Faith said softly.

Her fingers shook as much in terror as excitement at the idea. She had such mixed feelings about sending Christina out of sight, even if it was nearby.

This particular institution was not dreadfully far from London. With Mrs. Turner's gracious offer of an introduction, Chris had even more of a chance of acceptance. If Faith were willing to relinquish her.

Perhaps the best thing for Christina would be not to have her "Aunt Faith" hovering over her shoulder.

She sagged in gratitude. "Thank you."

"Consider it done." Mrs. Turner reached for another lemon cake. "I shall send a personal letter the moment I return home. On one condition."

Faith's stomach bottomed with dread. "On what condition?"

"That you join our club and host next month's meeting in this famous library of yours," Mrs. Turner said with a wide smile.

"Splendid idea," Mrs. Fairfax agreed. "We're still working out the schedule. Will you be in town all year or just for the Season?"

"All year," Faith stammered, unable to believe what she was hearing. Her mind was dizzy with disbelief and pleasure.

For the first time in her life, fashionable women actually seemed to like and respect her.

Of course she wished to be part of their book club. She would let them borrow every book in the family library if it kept her in their good graces.

Which, she realized with a sinking feeling, would not last long if the truth about Christina were to come out. Were Faith's history as a fallen woman ever to become common knowledge, she would be nothing but an outcast forevermore.

And so would her daughter.

CHAPTER 12

*I*t was the middle of the morning when Dahlia swept into Faith's study later that week and collapsed onto the spare chaise longue with a pile of documents and a frustrated sigh.

Faith put down her quill. "What is it?"

Dahlia lifted the papers from one corner as if their contents were toxic to the touch. "Have you seen the state of our accounts?"

Faith motioned towards the open ledgers on her desk. Of course she had seen the accounts. It was her job to balance the unbalanceable.

"I'm still in a dreadful row with my parents." Faith turned her chair to face her best friend. "If they would just donate my dowry money, all of this would disappear. We could buy new clothes for the girls, new materials for the schoolroom, attend more activities…"

"May luck be with you." Dahlia fell back against the armrest and gazed up at the ceiling. "I tried my damnedest to gain control of my dowry for the same purpose, and my mother would have nothing to do with the idea."

"Ah, but your parents believed your work here to be beneath you and their title as baron and baroness." Faith closed the ledgers. "My parents know perfectly well where we come from. They have no complaint against aid for the poor. They just fear giving away so much money that they risk returning to poverty themselves." She rubbed her temples. "Or ruining my chances of attracting a prince."

"Just do that," Dahlia suggested with a grin. "Gaining a prince's money might be easier than gaining your dowry."

"Probably true." Faith's shoulders sagged. "My parents now have more money than they are ever likely to spend. But anyone who has ever been un-sure that there would be supper on the morrow never becomes completely confident, no matter how secure their station might seem."

Dahlia propped herself up on one elbow. "How did your father come to own that first factory, by the way? When we met as children, he already man-aged a sizable chunk of the industry, and it never occurred to me wonder how he got started."

"That, or your gentle breeding prevented you from broaching a topic as vulgar as textile factories," Faith teased her best friend. She lifted a shoulder. "He worked in a factory. My mother's father owned it. Grandfather bequeathed it to Father when he died, and Father set about turning a warehouse full of whirring looms into an empire."

"He made it happen," Dahlia said, impressed. "Just like that."

"Just like twenty years of frustration and famine, risk and reward, setbacks and growth, riches and rejection." Faith was proud of her parents. Their path had not been easy. "When I met you, my family was wealthier than we had ever been, but of course that was nothing compared to the boom in the textile industry this past decade." She drummed her fingers with frustration. "There is plenty left over for charity. They aren't heartless. I just need to find the right argument."

The banging of a hammer sounded somewhere in the abbey and Faith winced. "Story time is in thirty minutes. Should I reschedule?"

Dahlia frowned. "Perhaps. It must be Simon. He won't rest until our school shines like a palace. Even if we can't afford it."

"There *is* another option," Faith said slowly.

"Don't start," Dahlia interrupted. Her nostrils flared angrily in warning.

Faith kept talking. "If we opened the school to paying students, not the *beau monde*, just ordinary paying students—our revenue stream would stabilize considerably."

"Who would come?" Dahlia asked as if the question had no answer. "Our girls are happy with their lot for the first time in their lives. The last thing they need is an influx of better-than-thou snobs to make them feel unworthy all over again. You of all people know how damaging that can be."

"Not the *beau monde*," Faith repeated. "Listen to yourself. The parents of that kind of student would not allow them anywhere near our school in the first place. I'm talking about girls like me. Children in the position I was. With enough money to do something better but lacking the prestige to be accepted. *We* could accept them. This is exactly the sort of place where their presence as well as their pocketbooks could do a world of good."

"Do those students exist?" Dahlia asked, her expression skeptical. "Your family managed to send you to a boarding school. What makes you think parents like yours would send their children to a place like this?"

"How many friends did I make at that school besides you?" Faith asked, rather than reply.

"Bryony," Dahlia said quickly. "Camellia."

"Your sisters," Faith repeated dryly. "In other words, no one else. That's exactly why parents might choose to send their students here. With enough money, we could rival comparable boarding schools while providing what none of the others can: the chance for such children to make friends."

Dahlia pushed herself into a sitting position. "Your parents would never have sent you here. The St. Giles School for Girls is not an environment for those seeking to increase their status."

Faith laughed in surprise. "That's exactly what it is. You rescued these children from the streets, from brothels, from workhouses. It is an *absolutely* status-increasing environment. Perhaps children with parents like mine are doomed to societal purgatory, but there are plenty of families whose desire for their children's happiness would make them consider another option."

Dahlia's expression was skeptical at best.

"My parents believed expanding their factory stronghold would raise enough money to make me a contender for a title. As if the factories were a magic wishing stone that would grant me the life of a princess. But I am not my parents." Faith tightened her fists. "I don't care if Christina ever lays eyes on a duke. I want her to be safe and smart and happy. We must believe there are many other parents whose outlooks mirror mine."

Dahlia shook her head. "A pretty speech, but even you will be sending Chris to a finishing school fancier than this one, are you not?"

"Only if she gets in," Faith answered with bald honesty. "Despite my parents' money, despite a letter of recommendation from a member of the *ton*, for people like us there are still no guarantees. But there *could* be. The St. Giles School for Girls could be exactly the sort of certain bet someone of medium affluence and marginal influence might choose for their child."

Several long beats of silence stretched out between them.

"Think about it," Faith insisted. "For all the little girls who cannot gain acceptance into schools like the Fitz-Dwyer Academy, why not make our boarding school the next best choice? We have the experience and the expertise. We just need the resources. Accepting paying students would make an enormous difference for all of our students."

"Two beds," Dahlia said in defeat. "That's all I'm willing to grant."

Faith clenched her jaw. "Two beds aren't enough money to make a—"

"Two beds may be more than enough *children* to change the dynamic amongst our current students," Dahlia said firmly. "We start with two, and if all goes well I shall concede the point and open as many beds as we have room for. Income from paying students should make us able to provide even more lodging for those who cannot pay."

"That's exactly the idea," Faith agreed in relief. She was still certain her parents would come around, but it might take them months or years to do so, and their school did not have that kind of time. She glanced at the clock on the mantel. "I'll tell the girls we'll have story time later this afternoon."

Dahlia nodded and threw herself back on to the chaise. "They're doing art projects right now. That will keep them busy through suppertime if you let them."

Faith grinned. The watercolor sets had been a donation by her parents, proving they were far more softhearted than they would like Faith to believe.

At least, when it came to their granddaughter's requests.

She shook her head in amusement. Perhaps she was going about this all wrong, and all she needed was for Christina to ask her grandparents to donate the money.

She rose to her feet. She would unveil a new collection of books during story time on the morrow. With the new watercolors as today's entertainment, Dahlia was probably right that not a single girl would notice a delay to story time.

Faith still thought it wise to check on them.

As she made her way down the corridor toward the schoolroom, the hammering grew louder. What in the world was going on?

She pushed open the door to the schoolroom and came to an abrupt halt.

Hawkridge stood at the rear of the room nailing brand new shelving to the far walls.

"Almost done," Simon called from the other side of the schoolroom. "We've already reinforced the windows and these are the last of the new shelves."

"What are you doing?" Faith stammered as if Simon had not just explained precisely what was happening.

She wasn't looking at Simon. She couldn't tear her gaze from Hawkridge.

With his jacket unbuttoned and his cravat askew and a damp strand of golden brown hair clinging to his forehead, he should have appeared a fright.

Instead the schoolroom had turned into a mirage.

He appeared almost ethereal bathed in the morning light, with his muscles flexing and his aura of concentration. Hawkridge had always been the most handsome lord Faith had ever seen, but here he was more than that. He was a *man*. Strong. Sure. Larger than life.

He met her eyes and gave a little crooked smile that melted her heart with its bashfulness. Hawkridge had not intended for her to see him like this. Was likely embarrassed to have been caught in a state of anything less than perfection. But he could not possibly have designed a manner in which he could appear more appealing.

"Thank you for helping," she said in a desperate attempt to hide the depth of her attraction.

"As our fortune ebbs, I have become increasingly adept at mending and home repair. I am lately far handier with a hammer than I am with a fencing sword." There was that bashful grin again. "I am indebted to my brother for this opportunity to show off my growing expertise."

"What's he talking about?" asked one of the girls in a loud whisper.

"He's a lord," returned one of the older students.

The younger girl's eyes widened. "Lord of what?"

"Lord of nothing much, I'm afraid." Hawkridge pulled silly faces to make them laugh. "Lord of the Handsaw? Lord of the Hammer?"

No. *Lord of Temptation.*

Faith fled back out into the corridor lest she betray her emotions.

Out of sight, she leaned against the wainscoting and let out a deep breath to calm her nerves. She took stock of this new perspective on Hawkridge.

So he was hopeful. And altruistic. And kind to children. It changed nothing at all between them.

But she had not fled quite far enough. She was still standing there alone in the corridor when a slender shadow fell out from the open schoolroom. Hawkridge stepped into sight.

Also alone.

Alone with her.

Her pulse fluttered as he slowly and inexorably strode her way.

An abbey like this had innumerable nooks and crannies she could have fled to. Places to catch her breath. To hide her flushed cheeks. To try to regain control of her runaway heart.

Staying anywhere within reach of him for even a moment was a terrible idea. They'd never once succeeded in being alone without touching each other. And if he touched her now…

Faith licked her lips. She should run.

But she stayed.

CHAPTER 13

*H*awk put one foot in front of the other, walking as slowly and deliberately as he could to give Faith plenty of opportunity to flee rather than join him in conversation.

She was beautiful. A few dark tendrils had escaped from her unbonneted hair and a pair of spectacles he hadn't even known she owned perched forgotten on the edge of her nose. She might as well have been draped in nothing but pearls, such was the desire he had for her.

It was the same magnetism they had always shared. Fighting a losing battle against a pull more powerful than their will to resist. From the moment she stepped into the schoolroom, every beat of his heart had belonged to her, every breath from his lungs a whisper of her name.

He had meant to ignore the attraction. Had tried valiantly to pretend it was all in his head. That there was nothing between them. That she didn't care. That neither did he.

But here she was. Gazing up at him with huge

green eyes as a telltale pulse fluttered at her throat. Close enough to kiss.

Now was not the time for conversation after all. Words were the enemy that kept cropping up between them. Every time he attempted to tell her how he felt he only succeeded in pushing her away.

He was done talking. He would show her. There would be no chance of misunderstanding.

Hawk lowered his mouth to hers, fully expecting her to push him away before their lips could touch.

Instead of a battle, he got a firestorm. Her fingers curled in his hair, tangling possessively even as he crushed his mouth to hers.

He wrapped one arm about her waist and hauled her flush against him. Rather than protest, her lips parted to allow him further plunder. He cradled the back of her head in his hand. No matter how hard he tried to take what was offered, he was giving even more. Complete surrender.

Her taste was simultaneously familiar and new, an intoxicating conundrum that only made him thirst for more. Every kiss was his soul unburdening itself to her, every lick of his tongue a confession of a love felt too deeply for one man to bear. This was the sort of kiss he had dreamed of once again sharing. A kiss that laid waste to reality and lifted them up into the clouds until nothing existed except the heat between them.

Her fingers were demanding, her lips sweet. She did not *want* to want him, but just like him, she could no more break this kiss than halt a hurricane.

Hawk didn't want to stop. He never had. If he got his way, he never would.

The magic of her kiss could be the sustenance

that gave him life for the rest of his days, if only she would allow it. He was hers. That he could not keep her, in no way prevented his helpless heart from belonging to her completely.

The thought made his blood pulse faster. Damn him. If marriage was not in their future, he almost certainly should not be kissing her.

Yet he could not bring himself to pull away. Not when she fit so perfectly in his arms. Her body flush with his was a brew as heady as any potion, making him feel as though they were not opposing forces but rather two jagged halves that had finally become whole.

He could fall into her forever. She was the sun and the stars and the ocean, an entire landscape of taste and sensation waiting to be explored. She was no gentle breeze, no wilting rose, but a goddess capable of destroying all hope or granting eternal life.

With each breathless kiss, he was finally born anew.

"Hawkridge?" Simon's jarring voice came from just inside the school room, his footfalls ever closer. "Where did you go?"

Hawk and Faith leapt backwards from each other as if the shock of the outside world had physically jolted them apart.

In frustration, Hawk glanced over his shoulder. "I'll be right there!"

But when he turned back to Faith, she was already gone, the distant click of a door latch the only clue as to where she had disappeared.

He ran his fingers through his tousled hair and turned back toward the schoolroom in a daze. After a kiss like that, his brain could think of nothing except sweeping her back into his arms. Hawk shook his head to try to clear it of the magic of her embrace.

With a shaky breath, he squared his shoulders and marched back into the schoolroom. "Here I am."

"Splendid." His brother dropped a heavy box of assorted tools into Hawk's arms and bent down to scoop up a large leather satchel. "We're off to the kitchens next to patch up the pantry."

Hawk nodded absently. His feet might follow Simon's, but Hawk's head would remain in the clouds where he shared an endless kiss with Faith.

"Never have twenty-four children," Simon joked as he raced Hawk down the stairs.

Hawk laughed and forced himself to focus on the moment. "Luckily, they're not your children, or you really would be in trouble. Can you imagine if you had raised all twenty-four little girls since birth?"

"Not in the slightest," Simon said cheerfully as they reached the first landing. "But not siring them doesn't make them feel any less like my children. I am as responsible for them as if I were their true father."

"You're a better man than me," Hawk said with a grin as they carried the tools into the scullery.

Simon grinned back. "Don't I know it."

Hawk cleared a spot for the tools. While it was odd to think of adopting four and twenty orphaned schoolgirls, he supposed were he in Simon's boots, he might have been called to do the same.

"Put some pep into it," Simon scolded him, making a show of checking his pocket watch. "I've an investigation to get back to, old man, so quit dreaming and get back to work."

Hawk grinned and climbed up a wooden stool to position the brackets for the first shelves. "What are you investigating that is so important, big inspector? Has a gravy boat gone missing from Prinney's buffet?"

"It's an old case, actually." Simon dragged another stool to the wall to help hang the shelves. "Perhaps you could help. What can you tell me about Maxwell Gideon?"

Simon was investigating Gideon?

Hawk's skin went cold as pieces of the puzzle clicked into place.

He and his brother had met for the first time at the Cloven Hoof. They'd met *every* time at the Cloven Hoof, until Simon had been assigned across town. Had he been on a case from the very first? Was that the real reason the brothers had broken their silence after nearly thirty years?

"There's nothing to tell," Hawk said cautiously.

They both knew that wasn't true. Maxwell Gideon and his club were one of London's greatest mysteries. No one knew where he'd gotten the funding to start his gambling den, or how he gained the pieces of intelligence that allowed him to double and triple profits on an unprecedented scale.

No one *knew*, but of course Hawk had a few suspicions. He'd been an active participant in more than a handful of those backroom deals. In fact, funding for Hawk's port had been one of the key ventures.

Simon sent a long glance down the scarred shelf toward Hawk. "You are in there constantly and yet I've never seen you gamble. If your visits with

Gideon have nothing to do with the gaming tables, then why are you there?"

"Because he is my friend," Hawk replied flatly, irritated at the idea of being forced to choose loyalties. He would not be Simon's confidential source and he would not choose sides.

"I see." His brother raised a nail to the wall. "Well, if you think of anything, you know where to find me."

Hawk no longer felt like helping. He belatedly realized he already had made an unconscious choice by not mentioning to Gideon that the brother he kept meeting for drinks was actually a Bow Street Runner.

To Hawk's credit, the detail hadn't seemed relevant because Simon had never mentioned he was there at the Cloven Hoof as part of an investigation.

But now that Hawk knew the truth, he questioned how much of Simon's brotherhood was real and how much was the means to an investigatory end.

CHAPTER 14

*H*awk and his mother perched on the edge of their squabs as their coach inched along the enormous queue of carriages leading to the Grenville townhouse.

Due to their inability to reciprocate invitations by hosting fêtes or afternoon teas at their own home, he and his mother had long avoided society events. But the Grenville musicale was different. Not only was everyone who was anyone certain to be in attendance, even those in no danger of ever being granted an Almack's voucher were welcomed inside for the musicale of the Season.

Lord and Lady Grenville were as proper as any member of the aristocracy, and the reason why so many members of the *ton* had accepted that first invitation to something so trite as a musicale.

Their four Grenville siblings kept very different circles of friends. Dahlia the charity headmistress, Bryony the incorrigible hoyden, Camellia the scandalous opera singer, and Heath the mysterious secret-keeper. One never knew who might receive an invitation to take a seat amongst this crowd for an unforgettable night.

The one thing that was certain, was that anyone who had ever witnessed the musical Grenville siblings perform would do anything in their power to ensure they received a second invitation.

He turned to smile at his mother as the carriage wheels wobbled forward. "Are you looking forward to the performance?"

"I wish it weren't the only invitation you've allowed me to accept all Season," came her tart reply. Her bright eyes focused on the river of fashionable gentlemen and elegant ladies streaming up the walk to the Grenville front door.

Hawk did not reply. There was no point in mentioning that this had been the only invitation on the mantel. Or that it would likely be their only public outing all Season, before they returned to the country so he could stop paying expensive London rents.

Tonight he was not here to argue, but to be a good son and a respectable marquess. The latter was far more challenging than the former.

Every eye in the receiving salon would quickly note each minute, substandard detail about him and his mother. Although they wore their finest, there was no hiding the faded colors, the outdated fashions, the thin gloves.

Hawk had trimmed his hair just for this event and starched his best cravat within an inch of its life. Mother had spent so many hours curling and pinning her hair, he feared the intricate ringlets would be baked permanently to her head.

They could only hope to take their seats quickly,

lest the eyes of passersby have a greater opportunity to travel from the tops of their coiffures to their patched hems.

"Come," he said when it was finally their turn to alight from their carriage. "Let us enjoy the evening."

She smiled as she allowed him to hand her down from the coach, and the excitement in her eyes outshone the recent pallor in her cheeks.

For this, Hawk was grateful.

According to the most recent doctor, mother was unwell due to a depression of the mind that sapped her spirit. She was too thin because she was not eating, too pale because she never left her bedchamber. The cure was not medicine but a reason to enjoy life.

The diagnosis was a dagger to Hawk's heart. If he had the money, he'd escort her to every ball and fireworks display and theater performance London had to offer.

But he didn't have the money. Not yet.

Not for a long while.

His skin prickled with a cold sweat. Twenty-four hours was almost up. And with Simon investigating the Cloven Hoof…

As far as Hawk knew, Gideon's ethics might be questionable, but his business dealings were perfectly legal. But what if they weren't? What if there was some "i" not dotted, some "t" uncrossed, some law shamelessly thwarted, and the "guaranteed" exponential return disappeared in a puff of smoke?

Hawk could not take such a risk. The port was his future.

Rather than tie up his finances for another year, he would have to withdraw from Gideon's latest scheme and divert the vast majority of his earnings toward completing construction.

The sooner the port opened, the sooner the marquessate could be fully self-sufficient. Hawk would finally be free of debt. Free to court Faith. Free to truly *live*.

But until then... Hawk bit back a sigh. He would simply have to make do.

Even without investing funds with the Cloven Hoof, his friendship with Gideon was stronger than ever. In fact, as soon as the port opened, the Cloven Hoof would be one of Hawk's key connections to help spread word about the new opportunity to moneyed gentlemen with shipping interests.

He fervently hoped his brother's investigation was not trying to bring it down.

Hawk tilted his gaze toward his mother and nodded. He was making the right choice. Along with aiding in the port's launch, withdrawing the two thousand pounds would ensure he could provide for his mother's health. Perhaps even purchase her a few small luxuries. A new bonnet. A pot of chocolate.

Mother's wish was to live the life she had been, if not accustomed to, then at least promised. She could not bear to lose what little she had left. At the very least, she wished to die with the dignity due her station. Head held high until her dying breath.

Hawk was not ready to think of his mother dying, with dignity or otherwise.

Surely Mother had decades left to live. He would pay off the last of the debts, restore the marquessate's fortune, give her a line of credit on Bond Street to rival any duchess of the time, marry the girl he'd always wanted, and give his mother more grandchildren than she could count.

It was *not* too late. Plenty of time.

When they reached the door, the butler did not announce their names. This musicale was not the sort of soirée where the invited guests were the main attraction. The Grenville siblings could put on a performance to rival any stage.

When his mother stepped away to chat with a few friends, Hawk did not follow. His focus was not on the sea of famous peers mingling in the vestibule. The only face Hawk longed to see was that of Faith Digby.

He prowled the crowded room. Surely, she would be here. Dahlia was Faith's best friend. Even though Dahlia was the only non-musical sibling, her lifelong friendship with Faith meant the Grenvilles were practically family.

And yet he could not spy her anywhere.

When the footmen announced the doors would soon be opening, Hawk was forced to give up his search in frustration.

He found his mother amongst a circle of her old friends and proffered his arm. "Shall we take our seats, Madame?"

"Mrs. Merton's daughter is a diamond of the first water," Mother informed him in a pointed whisper. "It would be lovely if she could find a match in her very first Season. She and her mother are quite enamored with the idea of nabbing a title."

Whoever this chit was, she could not have appealed to Hawk less. "Title-hungry" was not a bedrock of a solid relationship, and "First Season" meant the girl in question could be little more than seventeen years of age.

Hawk still remembered how foolish he had been at that age. He had no wish to wait a dozen years for his wife to grow up.

"I suppose she's rich?" he asked his mother dryly.

"Only in the best way," Mother assured him. "Her second cousin is a duke and her grandmother is the daughter of an earl."

No repugnant connections to *trade* was the unspoken implication. This money came from the accident of being related to other individuals who had also been born to money. No embarrassing ties to factory or the textiles industry.

"Come." He placed his mother's hand at his elbow. "There's no time for introductions if we wish to be assured a seat for the musicale."

The horrible truth was that if their circumstances didn't turn about very soon, Hawk would be forced to consider making exactly the sort of match his mother had suggested.

But how could he think of such things when his head was still full of the earth-shattering kiss he and Faith had shared earlier that week?

Despite heading toward the audience chamber moments after the doors had opened, the huge salon was already packed with onlookers and the only pair of vacant seats Hawk could find were in the last row. He waited for his mother to take her chair, then settled himself beside her.

An excited hush rustled amongst the audience.

He tried not to notice how shabby his clothes felt against the richness of his cushioned chair, or how dull their best outfits were compared to the finery of the others.

No matter how out of place he felt amongst what should be a gathering of his peers, he was thrilled to see the liveliness return to his mother's face.

She was happy again. Perhaps she was finally in a good enough mood to consider his perspective about Faith.

"You must know, that 'diamond of the first water' is far too young for me," he told his mother quietly. "I much prefer a woman closer to my own age."

"Many girls wed husbands twice or thrice their own age," Mother pointed out. "Why should you be so particular?"

Hawk could have laughed. "You are the one who thinks the source of the dowry matters more the girl herself. Be honest. Would it truly be so horrific if the money had ties to trade?"

"Worse than horrific," Mother said with feeling. "When a dowry has ties to trade, then so does the girl. A Hawkridge would never devalue his title or his family in such a fashion. You would not shame me so."

"A history of trade does not preclude the possibility of being a good woman from a good family," he said firmly.

"This conversation is starting to remind me of the sort of balderdash you used to spout when you were a green buck. Do not tell me you've developed a *tendre* for another chit unworthy of your name."

"Not another one. The same woman," he said between clenched teeth. "Miss Digby is scarcely—"

"Do not speak her name to me," Mother interrupted with fire in her eyes. "That unfortunate child

149

did not interest me then and she does not interest me now. Your duty is to ensure your title's lineage, not sully it with commoners. You should wed Mrs. Merton's daughter and have done."

Hawk remained cold. "I don't even know Mrs. Merton's daughter. I want—"

"That is not what *ton* marriages are about." Mother's lip curled. "Your responsibility is to the Hawkridge estate, not to matters of the heart. Didn't you learn that lesson long ago?"

He clenched his jaw and faced forward, putting a temporary end to the subject.

It was a moot point anyway. Faith might have kissed him in a moment of weakness, but she was far from being open to entertaining the idea of a marriage proposal. Yet he hated the idea that his mother would never accept the woman he loved, even if Faith were willing to be courted.

"There is more to being a marchioness than mere bloodlines," he said stiffly. "Faith Digby has more intelligence and integrity than any debutante in this room. Being born to 'commoners' does not change that."

"Pish. I don't give a button if she—" A sudden wracking cough overtook his mother and she tumbled forward, gasping for air.

Alarmed, Hawk wrapped an arm about his mother in an attempt to calm her.

But the coughing did not cease. Heads swiveled as hundreds of rapt spectators craned their necks to find the cause of the noise.

Hawk ignored them. Mother's coughing spells never lasted this long. Or were so violent.

"Breathe," he whispered urgently. "Are you all right? Take a deep breath. Please try to breathe."

When it became clear that she could not stop, he lifted her into his arms and kicked a space between their chairs in order to carry her from the room.

What sort of the spectacle they made, the likelihood of this moment appearing in Betelgeuse's next caricature on the morning, were none of Hawk's concern.

Something was very wrong with his mother. Something far more insidious than a depression of the spirits.

When she finally stopped coughing, a fine mist of blood stained her once-white gloves.

He couldn't wait a year. He needed money now. A *pot* of money.

He needed Faith.

Hawk swore under his breath. He had wanted to do this right, but wooing Faith would take more time than he had. Yet what choice did he have? If she believed his motives remotely mercenary, Faith would refuse to give him the time of day, much less her hand in marriage.

And if he couldn't convince her his love had never waned…

Then he would absolutely have to marry any title-hungry debutante willing to have him.

CHAPTER 15

aith adored lazy evenings like these at home with her parents.

It was too early for the nightly bedtime ritual, so Faith was curled atop a pillow-laden chaise longue in her parents' Egyptian-themed front parlor while Christina played up in the nursery with her newest dolls.

Faith's attention was not on the orange flames crackling in the fireplace or the untouched glass of brandy on the table beside her. Rather, her mind was focused on the clear crisp handwriting of the sealed letter in her lap.

"When was this delivered?" she asked over the rapid beating of her heart.

Her parents exchanged a glance. Over thirty years after they had first met, the two lovebirds could still be found surreptitiously holding hands beneath the blanket on the settee.

Father took a sip of his own brandy before responding. "This afternoon, I believe."

Faith had been at the boarding school since early morning. It had been a long night for Dahlia, whose family had hosted a musicale the night before, so Faith had ordered her to sleep in and offered to cover morning duties herself.

Of course, morning duties led to noon duties which led to afternoon duties. Even though Dahlia had arrived at the school far earlier than Faith had anticipated, there was always more to do than time to do it, and the two women never secured a spare moment to chat.

Or possibly Faith had been avoiding her best friend, just like she'd been avoiding Hawkridge ever since they'd shared that devastating kiss. Faith did not want to confess her moment of weakness to Dahlia, or risk running into Hawkridge himself out of fear that she'd allow the transgression to happen all over again.

She forced her thoughts from the delicious memory and focused on the letter in her hand.

Receiving correspondence was such an unusual occurrence for Faith, that there could only be one source: the Fitz-Dwyer Academy she had applied to for Christina's admission. The school had been sent Faith's heartfelt letter listing every one of her daughter's best characteristics, as well as a letter of recommendation from Mrs. Turner who was the daughter of a lord.

Whether that was enough to give Christina a fighting chance was another question. But there was only one way to find out.

She retrieved the Pharaoh's-head letter opener from beside her glass of brandy and slipped the edge of its obsidian blade beneath the wax seal binding the letter. With trembling hands, she placed the letter opener aside and began to read.

Four short lines of text sent excited disbelief skittering through her veins.

"Mother! Father!" She could barely grip the parchment with the shaking of her hands. "Christina has an appointment at the Fitz-Dwyer Academy in a fortnight."

Her father stared at her. "Why?"

"There are many applicants but limited openings, so the interview with parent and child—or guardian and ward—are of utmost importance," Faith reminded him. "But don't you see what this means? She might actually be accepted!"

Her parents' eyes filled with instant dismay.

"I have a better idea," Mother said quickly. "Let's focus on *your* school instead. What if we sign over your dowry money? Do you still want that?"

"Absolutely. And I shall hold you to it," Faith agreed in excitement. "But that has nothing to do with Christina. Fitz-Dwyer is an exceptional school and an opportunity we must jump on at once."

Mother clearly did not share Faith's joy. "Would she have to live at the finishing school with the other students?"

"We've talked about this," Faith said patiently. "Chris deserves the best education we can give her. We are not shipping her to Egypt. She will be just outside of London. We can have her back on weekends and holidays and yuletide and—Mother, this is her chance. She'll have the very best resources."

Faith's heart swelled with relief and love. This invitation was everything she'd hoped for... But not a guarantee.

Her joy wobbled. This interview would likely be

as much about how Faith presented herself as Christina.

She would have to be more than respectable. Since she could not prove Christina's provenance, Faith could not allow bloodline to be a deciding factor. She must appear a model citizen, and Christina the perfect candidate.

A fortnight suddenly seemed like forever. They could not allow a hint of scandal to arise between today and the interview.

With luck, Christina would soon be on her way to an idyllic childhood full of experiences and educational resources beyond Faith's wildest dreams.

"Do not dare break your word," she warned her parents. "You agreed not only to allow, but also to finance, Christina's schooling. Fitz-Dwyer is the best way to make that happen."

"Of course we will pay for anything the child wants or needs," her father assured her. "It will just be lonely without her in the house."

Faith swallowed her fears. She had been trying not to think about that.

She could count the number of bedtime rituals she'd missed on a single hand. Once her daughter was installed at a finishing school, she would have new rituals. New people. New friends. New memories. It was bittersweet to say the least.

But Chris was growing up. Her mother and grandparents could not be the center of her world forever.

Faith wanted her daughter to be *happy*. To have every advantage she could give her.

This was Christina's opportunity to practice French and Latin with other girls, have lessons from a true dancing master, complain about sums or discuss literature, forge relationships that would last the rest of her life.

Faith would not keep that from her daughter, no matter how painfully she missed her.

"Perhaps while Chris is at finishing school, you'll finally have a chance to put yourself back out to market," Mother suggested slyly. "It's not too late for Christina to have an uncle, is it?"

Wasn't it?

Faith turned her gaze to the crackling fire. She was in no position to reenter the marriage mart. Not when her insides still tangled with butterflies at the merest thought of Christina's father.

She tried to consider him in that light and could not.

Hawkridge, for all his admittedly fine qualities, would be a terrible father. His failing estate would consume every penny of her dowry. Even if he were to someday actually offer marriage—and mean it—raising a child in poverty was the opposite of ensuring Chris the best advantages.

Faith's glance slid over to her parents.

And they would be impoverished. Her father would disown her for sheer stupidity if she even entertained the notion of going back to the man who had caused her such pain. Father would sooner light her dowry on fire than hand it to Hawkridge.

So of course she'd had to go and kiss the man. Like a complete hen-wit.

Although Faith had managed to avoid him ever since, she wouldn't be able to keep it up forever. Not with every one of her students clamoring for more dance lessons and the old abbey in constant need of repair.

From this point forward she would simply have to keep things between them civil. Professional. Distant.

A knock sounded at the front door.

Her parents exchanged puzzled glances. "Who would come to call at this hour?"

Faith lay the precious invitation from the finishing school atop one of the satin pillows and sprang to her feet just as Gostrell, their butler, appeared in the doorway. Perhaps it was Dahlia.

Gostrell cleared his throat. "A Lord Hawkridge to see Miss Digby?"

Faith resisted the urge to drop her face in her hands and melt through the parlor floor.

Her father was suddenly on his feet, his face purpling. "Throw him out at once."

"No," Faith hissed. "Please, pretend to tolerate his presence. You don't have to like him, but we cannot cause any drama. Christina's interview is in a fortnight."

Her father narrowed his eyes. "Did you know that self-important toad would be paying a call?"

"Of course not. I would never invite him here or anywhere. Especially not with..." She jabbed her finger toward the ceiling where Christina played above. The hairs on the back of her neck pricked with fear. "Now that he's here, we dare not cause a scene. We shall let him in and hope he leaves quickly."

After an interminable moment, Father nodded in acquiescence. Gostrell disappeared to fetch Hawkridge.

Faith retook her seat amongst the mountain of soft pillows. She did not wish to appear eager to see him by remaining on her feet.

She would probably seem obnoxiously indolent, reclining in a room filled with opulent antiquities whilst a brimming glass of expensive brandy dangled from her fingertips.

Good. She was not trying to make a positive impression. Hawkridge stomping off in disgust would be perfect. She needed him to go away.

Then all of a sudden, there he was. Filling up the doorframe like a Greek god dressed as a mortal man.

Despite the windy evening, not a hair was out of place. His greatcoat was not in the first stare of fashion, but it molded to his wide shoulders and defined the contours of his muscles so exquisitely, Faith could not imagine him in anything else.

Well, yes, she could imagine him in nothing at all… To her horror, heat spread up her neck and cheeks at the direction of her thoughts.

She rose to her feet but did not bob the requisite curtsy.

Her parents did not bother to rise.

"Mr. and Mrs. Digby. Miss Digby." Hawkridge's bow was fit for royalty. "Thank you for allowing me into your home unannounced."

Faith's parents still made no comment.

Hawkridge's wide, unblinking gaze darted from Faith to her parents to their butler in confusion.

One could cut the awkwardness within a knife.

Faith cleared her throat. "What brings you here this evening?"

"My townhouse is not two blocks away. I was out

for a walk and…" He glanced at her parents and then back to her.

Of course his townhouse must be little more than a five minute walk from theirs. Faith couldn't believe it hadn't occurred to her before.

Obviously she had noticed when her family fortunes had reached a level where the Digbys could afford to live in one of the nicest neighborhoods in all of London.

What she hadn't considered was who else must live in such a neighborhood. Their nearest neighbors were dandies and debutantes. Why wouldn't a marquess be counted among their numbers, too?

"I didn't realize," she said, hoping her horror was not evident in her voice.

"I doubt you would," he replied self-deprecatingly. "We only rent while Parliament is in session, and it's rarely the same townhouse twice. More to the point, we rarely leave our home. Had I realized our proximity sooner, I should not have waited until tonight to start taking evening walks."

"'We?'" Mother's eyes were as sharp as her tone. "Dare I hope you've married?"

Faith tried not to wince. Hopefully Hawkridge would believe her parents simply ill-mannered, and not viscerally opposed to his very existence.

"I have not," he answered with a smile, as if it had been a purely ordinary question. "In fact, I hoped to invite Miss Digby to take a carriage ride in Hyde Park tomorrow."

"She's busy," Father said flatly.

Hawkridge blinked. "From dawn to midnight?"

"For you, she will always be busy," Mother put in, leaving no further doubt as to their opinion of him.

Hawkridge's eyes met Faith's, but she could say nothing to help him.

A public carriage ride in Hyde Park was far more than he had offered her back when she'd given him everything. But she no longer wanted it. No longer wanted *him*.

At least, that was what she told herself.

"I fear we have begun on the wrong foot," Hawkridge said with understandable confusion.

He had no reason to believe Faith would have confessed her fallen state to her parents. Or that they knew he had taken their daughter's virginity before deciding she was not important enough for marriage.

"It's been some time since we've held a soirée at the Hawkridge estate," he tried again, smiling in the direction of Faith's parents. "But I will be sure to put your names on the guest list at our very next dinner party."

This time, Faith did wince.

One of the reason the others had mocked her was because her mother had been so flagrantly title-hungry. At the time, social-climbing had been her raison d'être. That had been a lifetime ago.

The idea that Hawkridge still believed he could buy her parents' benediction with nothing more than an invitation to sit at a marquess's table was an insult her mother would not bear.

"No, thank you." Mother trained flat eyes on Hawkridge. "We are busy that evening as well."

"It's late," Faith said quickly. "Let me show you to the door."

Since her parents had not bothered to rise to greet Hawkridge, they could not now scramble to their feet in a ham-fisted attempt to watch over them in the short distance between the parlor and the front door. There would be a few minutes in which they could speak privately.

"They hate me," Hawkridge said as soon as they were out of earshot.

She lifted a shoulder. "I wouldn't say that."

He stared at her in disbelief. "They did not bid me good afternoon or goodbye, much less invite me to sit or take tea."

"They do hate you," Faith admitted. "You shouldn't be here."

He blinked at her. "But why? What did I do wrong?"

"What did you do wrong?" she repeated with contempt. She counted his sins on her fingers. "Ruined their daughter. You stole my innocence and discarded me as if I were as forgettable as a penny whore. And you made no attempt to behave in a gentlemanly fashion thereafter, despite your lofty title." Her voice cracked with hurt and anger. "You'll have to excuse my parents if they do not wish to dine at your table. Perhaps you should count yourself lucky no blunt objects were hurled at your head."

"You *told* them?" Hawkridge's shocked expression would be comical if his actions hadn't completely changed the course of her life.

"I had to," she spat, furious he still believed he could act as if the past had never happened and he were completely blameless. "You ruined me and left me no choice."

"I...I did ruin you," he stammered, as if suddenly realizing he was not the victim of that particular turn of events. "And I did not behave honorably. But I didn't leave you no choice. You can't be ruined if no one *knows* you were ruined. It's not as though you were..." His face drained of color and he grabbed her wrists hard enough to bruise. "*Were* you?"

An eternity stretched between them. Faith's heart waged war in her chest, anger clashing with hurt, guilt clashing with vengeance.

This was the moment she had dreaded ever since the day she'd realized what her missing menses indicated. By then it had been too late to undo the past. To guard her innocence. To keep her virginity. To call back the overhasty letter assuring the lord who didn't want her in the first place that there had been no consequences to his actions.

He had made it easy to mind her silence by not bothering to be part of her life since the night he ruined her. There had been no opportunity to speak to him, which had quickly come to feel as though there was no reason to.

But here he was in her house. Face to face. With his gloved hand trapping her trembling wrists to his chest and Christina right upstairs. This was her chance to finally be honest with him.

It might also be her last chance to protect her daughter.

"No," she whispered. Her heart raced like the hooves of a thousand horses.

His eyes searched hers and narrowed with doubt at whatever they found.

She tried to wave the question away. "Hawkridge—"

"*Were you with child?*" he repeated, jerking her against his chest, his eyes wild.

She shook her head, her entire body trembling in terror.

He dropped her wrists as if they had burned him like coals.

"Liar," he seethed, his expression a mixture of shock and hurt. "You would hide a child from me?"

She shook her head again, not trusting herself to speak.

"If you gave my baby to some other couple, I will bring suit against all of you for child-stealing. And if you left my baby on the doorstep of some orphanage—"

"No," Faith said quickly. "I would never."

"Wouldn't you?" With a sneer, he gestured at her grand townhouse. "*Your* life seems fine. Your reputation unblemished in any way. What else am I to think?"

"It wasn't like that." She hesitated. "When you walked away—"

"You decided to keep a *secret?*" His eyes glittered with fury. "Ten years is an unforgivable length of time. I won't let you keep my child from me a moment longer. If I have to drag you in front of the courts and splash our names across every scandal column in London—"

"Don't," she whispered. "Please."

"Try to stop me." He jerked away from her to stalk toward the door.

Panic gripped her. "Hawkridge—"

He didn't slow. "By this time tomorrow, you will not have to answer to me, but to a judge who won't care how much textiles money you have."

She ran to catch up with him. "You have it all wrong."

"I have nothing wrong. You are a woman. I am a marquess." He glanced over his shoulder, his eyes cold. "You cannot keep a child from me."

Her stomach bottomed.

He would ruin her life. He would ruin *Christina's* life.

She had to stop him.

Even if it meant telling the truth.

"Let me explain," she whispered.

He folded his arms over his chest. "You can try."

Could she? A bubble of hysterical laughter tangled in her throat. She'd had ten years to practice a speech for this moment.

Nothing could have prepared her.

"Come back to the drawing room," she said. "Let's sit down and talk about this."

He drew himself to his full height. "Speak now, or I will see you in court."

She swallowed her fear.

Surely she could reason with him. Hawkridge was in no more position to be a father today than he had been back then. He would come to the same conclusion she had: Christina had been far better off right where she was.

There was no need for courts or scandal sheets or criminal charges.

Her parents were blameless. *Christina* was blameless. Lord Hawkridge could hardly say the same.

He had taken her virginity and walked away without a backward glance. Faith hadn't been important enough to merit gentlemanly behavior. To have rights. To have feelings. Her chin lifted.

She had made the best decision she could at the time. Christina had spent ten blissful years without the stigma of being a bastard. Of being unwanted. Of not being good enough for her own father. That was the sort of innocence that every child deserved.

Faith would not apologize to a man who had never intended to do the honorable thing by her in the first place.

But nor could she risk him making good on his threats.

"Yes. You impregnated me before you decided to walk away." She rolled back her shoulders and tried to breathe. "But I did not give the baby up."

Hawkridge's gaze flew to hers in shock. "Here? In this house?"

"This is not the best moment to visit the nursery," she said firmly. "Once you've calmed down and we've had a chance to talk, I can decide if it's truly in Chris's best interest to meet—"

"*Chris?*" Hawkridge repeated, his eyes flashing with unsuppressed rage. "If you hid an heir from me, woman, so help me God—"

"Stop it!" Her limbs shook with fear. "Leave Christina alone. You are not fit company to—"

"Nor will I be." Hawkridge curled his lip in disgust. "If you won't bring her to me, I shall find her myself."

Before Faith could stop him, he raced past the maid and charged out of the corridor toward the stairs.

She lifted up her hems and chased close behind.

CHAPTER 16

"*Nursery*," Hawk barked at the first maid he found after sprinting up the staircase. "Which way?"

The girl pointed a finger, more likely out of surprise than any desire to do a stranger's bidding.

Faith was right on his heels behind him. Hawk ignored her.

He took off down the corridor toward the chamber the maid had indicated. The door was ajar, and he managed to come to a skidding halt before sheer velocity tumbled him inside.

His blood pulsed so loud in his ears that he could not think over the din.

He had a child.

She was sitting in the center of a plush rug that cost more than his entailed estate had earned all year. Her back was to him, but he recognized her long golden-brown curls.

The girl from the school. The one whose fine clothing far outclassed the others. Now it made sense. She was not like the others. This was Faith's child. *His* child. And Faith had kept her from him.

Hawk whirled to face her. "How could you?"

She held up a finger to her lips and backed away from the open door.

He stalked forward, unable to believe Faith's treachery.

All this time he had believed that *he* was the one who needed to atone for the past. Now that he knew the truth, she would never be able to make the past up to him. She was a liar. A thief. She kept his sole child and hadn't seen fit to inform him.

His entire body shook with rage and hurt and powerlessness to change the past. Blast and damn. Now that he did know, what was he meant to do about it?

He spun away from Faith without granting her so much as a word, collected himself as best he could, and stepped into the nursery.

The girl glanced up at him suspiciously from the corner of her eye.

Christina.

His daughter.

"Who are you?" she asked, clutching her dolls to her chest.

A very good question. If only Hawk knew the right answer.

He was her father. He was Lord Hawkridge. He was the man who was going to throttle her mother the second he stepped outside this nursery.

None of which seems like the right response.

"An... acquaintance of your mother's," he hedged.

He did not want to begin their relationship with lies, but she clearly did not trust him and he had no wish to frighten her.

"You knew my mother?" Christina relaxed the stranglehold on her dolls. "What was she like?"

Hawk blinked. Was this a trick question? He would have absolutely nothing complimentary to say about Faith if he were forced to describe her right now.

"Don't you live together?" he stammered.

Christina shook her head. "I'm an orphan. I live with Aunt Faith and my grandparents."

Understanding washed over Hawk.

Faith hadn't just kept their daughter from him—she'd also kept her from herself. The only explanation for pretending her daughter was her niece was to shelter from the cruel realities of being a bastard.

That would be a noble gesture. Selfless, even. If it hadn't been so bloody unnecessary. No matter what his mother and advisors forbade, Hawk would have married Faith in a heartbeat if he'd had any inkling she was with child.

"I'm pleased to meet you," he said tightly and hurried out of the nursery before his anger could overtake him.

Faith was no longer alone in the corridor. Her parents flanked her like soldiers guarding a queen.

Hawk did not bother to hide his disgust. Faith was not his queen. She did not rule over him. And she would not rule over their child alone.

"You are unbelievable," he snarled. "Duplicitous and heartless."

Mrs. Digby stepped forward with fire in her eyes. "Duplicitous and heartless like the night she stole your virginity, ruined your chances at a good match, and never bothered to pay so much as a simple call, despite having promised you marriage?"

Hawk swallowed with guilt. Of course her parents hated him. They both knew exactly who and what he was. "I didn't know—"

"It shouldn't have mattered," Mr. Digby interrupted coldly.

"You think your title is your most redeeming quality," Mrs. Digby put in. "When in fact it is your *only* redeeming quality. Faith does not need you and neither does Christina. You are worthless even to your own estate. Don't think you deserve to come sniffing about her dowry now."

Faith's dowry. Hawk had completely forgotten. He dropped his chin to his chest.

When they had accidentally run into each other that first night at the school for girls, he had no reason to believe she was any better off than she had been when they were younger.

He'd learned otherwise, of course. Even if Simon hadn't accidentally let slip the precise amount of her dowry, the excessive opulence of every item in this townhouse would have more than sufficed as a clue.

Hawk had believed that before they could begin to hope for a future together, he would first have to win back her love. Eat crow. Atone for the unforgivable actions of that fateful night.

But she was the one who had to atone. Not for her actions that night, but for her failure to speak every day since.

And they thought he was here to what... place a ring on her finger and make her his bride? The thought was laughable. Any dream he'd once had of marrying her had vanished. Along with his dreams of a happy family.

A dowry like Faith's would enable him to open

his port on schedule, true. But it was also true that the thought of marrying her now filled his stomach with bile. He could no longer trust her.

It was more than a lie. She had hidden a child from him. Hadn't bothered to mention the slight detail even when all three of them had been under the same roof.

They might not have seen each other for ten years, but there had been more than ample opportunity to come clean over the past few months. His blood raced. This wasn't love in his heart. She had turned it into rage.

"You cannot put all the blame on Faith," Mrs. Digby said with a sneer.

"Can I not?" He gaped at her in disbelief. "The child doesn't even know her father."

"It's for the best," Faith said. Her tone was final, as if he had no say at all. "Even *you* must see that."

"I see plenty," he growled. "I see everything you've taken from me. I've lost the opportunity to know my child since her birth. I cannot give her lost time. I can't even give her my name."

"You didn't want to," she reminded him hotly. "At least, you didn't want to give it to me."

"I still don't," he said, his voice ice.

He had known Faith could no longer be the young girl he recalled from his youth, but he had never suspected it would come to this. That his relationship with her would become not his dream, but his greatest nightmare.

Through no knowledge of his own, he had abandoned a child.

When Christina had been born, he had been off visiting entailed properties. While she had been crying to be held, he had been at society balls hunting wealthy dance partners. He had missed her first laugh, her first steps, her first words. She had never called him *Papa*.

She never even knew she had one.

How could he fix this? He curled his shaking fingers into fists and pressed them against his sides. There was no way to undo the damage. No way to return what he had lost. No way to give Christina what she had been denied. A childhood knowing her father loved her, wanted her, cherished her.

Instead, all either of them had was emptiness where there should have been joy.

And Faith… She was the blade that twisted again and again. Instead of confessing the truth, she'd kept the secret. Decided his future *for* him. Denied their daughter a father, and him his child. She had played God, but delivered him to Hell.

Throat tight, Hawk stalked past her and marched down the stairs to the front door.

His temples pounded. He could not be in this house a second more. Its gaudy opulence mocked him. Its terrible secrets laid bare his heart. He could do nothing more tonight. He could not risk frightening Christina.

If he had known his daughter since birth, he wouldn't have to pray for the possibility that she might warm up to him someday.

But he had not been given the choice.

"Where are you going?" As before, Faith was right on his heels.

"Home to think." He shot her a warning glance. "You do not wish to have a conversation with me right now. You will not like anything I have to say."

She bit her lip. "It really is for the best."

Anger flared within him. Who was she to decide for him? Hawk would not be robbed of his child.

He enunciated each word so there could be no mistake.. "You cannot keep her."

"You cannot take her," she countered in alarm.

Like hell he couldn't. His head swam under the weight of all those lost years. Christina was his daughter.

He leaned forward and dropped his voice dangerously. "She is my child."

"And mine." Faith took a step backwards. "You can't have her."

His heart pounded in pain and fury. "If you dare to keep her from me a single moment more, I will haul you in front of the courts without a second thought."

"And prove what?" Her chin lifted. "That you're a destitute fortune-hunter who suddenly discovered me in possession of a fortune? It will be a brilliant scandal and you still won't get Christina."

"Of course I will." He stared down his nose at her as condescendingly as he could. "I don't need proof. I have a title. And soon, I will have custody of my child."

"A title." Her eyes flashed. "I have my dignity, which is more than you can claim."

He shook his head in disgust. "There is no dignity in lying to a child's father for her entire life."

"What lie?" Her hands curled into fists at her hips. "Other than a carelessly scribbled missive the same morning I was expecting a wedding proposal, I never heard your voice or saw your face for an entire decade until Simon invited you to supper. I never had a chance to *lie*. You were completely un-concerned with how or whether I was getting on with my life."

It had not been that simple.

His hands shook with anger. "You have no idea what I've been through."

"And you don't know me at all if you think I'll let you turn Chris's life upside-down. She's happy, Hawkridge." Faith shoved his chest as if to push him out the door. "Do you even understand that word? *Happy*. She likes herself and her life. How would it help to rip that away from her? What kind of man would do such a heartless thing? What kind of father?"

Of course he wanted Christina to be happy. But right now, he didn't give two figs about pleasing her mother. "You cannot keep her from me."

"You cannot swoop in and take her." Faith's eyes filled with tears.

He smiled icily. "We'll just have to see."

CHAPTER 17

a t noon the following morning Hawk found himself seated alone at an otherwise empty table, in an otherwise empty dining room, in a completely silent house.

This, in itself, was not new.

His mother would not wake for at least another hour. They were down to only two servants. A maid of all work and a footman who was also their butler and their driver.

Insipid tendrils of steam rose from the thin soup before him, but Hawk barely succeeded in choking down the first bite. Everything tasted like sawdust. The soup, the bread, the air.

What might his Parliamentary sessions in London have been like if there had been a child in the house?

He stared at the bowl of soup. He would never know what it would've been like. There was no sense trying to imagine the sound of little feet pounding too quickly down the stairs, a peal of laughter or the cry of *Papa, come play with me.*

It hadn't happened. And now it wouldn't.

Unless he did something about it.

Hawk couldn't get back the last ten years, but he could take control of the next ten. He just needed to come up with a plan capable of reuniting him with his daughter without causing her undue harm.

He idly stirred the stew before him then let go of his spoon with an anguished groan. Through no intention of his own, he was *exactly* like his father.

Making love to a woman he did not intend to marry, getting her with child, not raising his offspring as his own. The only point in Hawk's favor was that he hadn't known about the child's existence. But Faith was right. He had perpetrated the rest. He was no more righteous than his father had been.

Just because Hawk accepted his share of the guilt in the blame did not mean there was no fault to find Faith's actions. Or lack thereof.

She should have told him. Even if she believed he would not have married her, even if she was absolutely right, she still should have told him. But because she had not, he was a stranger to Christina and she to him.

Did that matter? Did not knowing until now make her any less his daughter? Any less his responsibility?

He pushed away his untouched bowl of soup and buried his face in his hands.

It didn't feel like there was enough room in his body for this much emotion. Anger. Hurt. Guilt. Would he help anything at all by telling her he was her father? But now that he knew he had a daughter, how could he possibly just walk away?

There were so few choices. If only there was

some way to legally make Christina his child! If there were a special license to purchase, a certificate to sign, a Justice of the Peace to bribe, anything at all that could make Christina his legal daughter, Hawk would do it in a heartbeat.

But there were no such paths. No way to add an child to one's family. No way to give Christina the protection of his name.

The only available options were guardianship and fostering. Hawk rubbed his face. Because he had failed to marry Faith back when he'd ruined her, Christina could never become his legal daughter. The best he could do was to make her his ward.

And then what? If he welcomed Christina into his home and never mentioned he was her father, would his guardianship be suspicious enough to do the same damage?

He slammed his fist onto the table with enough force to slosh broth from his bowl of stew.

The pregnancy had not been Faith's fault, but the current predicament absolutely was. There was suddenly a child he never knew about. The woman he loved, the woman he thought he knew, had lied to him. Hid the one aspect of his life he'd always believed he could do right.

It was unforgivable.

He no longer even wanted Faith in his life, and now he would be forced to do so to have a relationship with his daughter. He had been robbed of choice, then and now.

Nor was she the only one who had hid the truth.

Faith was not shuttered away in the country. Her reputation had not been ruined. How could an unconnected girl like Faith have managed to keep a secret as large as an unplanned pregnancy? Not without help. That much was certain.

Hawk pushed up from the table. He stalked out the door to head straight to his carriage.

He had a reasonably fair idea just who might've conspired to keep such a monumental secret. Faith's bosom friend Dahlia was the younger sister of London's premier secret-keeper and problem solver: Heath Grenville.

Who, until this moment, Hawk had counted as a friend.

When he reached the Grenville's front door, Hawk was ready to break it down by force necessary.

It was not.

The familiar butler showed him into the front parlor as if today were like any other day and Hawk's world wasn't falling apart at the seams.

The parlor contained three out of four Grenville siblings, hunched over a low table and playing some sort of rowdy card game involving flying playing cards and a shameless disregard of proper language.

Any other day, Hawk would've taken the empty spot between Dahlia and Bryony and launched himself into the fray as if he were part of the family. But it wasn't any other day. It was today, and if his suspicions were correct, Heath Grenville might not live to see tomorrow.

"You knew," Hawk accused him in a low, dangerous voice.

Grenville lay down his playing cards and turned to face him. To his credit, he neither denied the charge nor disingenuously inquired to what Hawk referred.

"You *knew*," he repeated in disbelief. "You knew and you didn't tell me."

"Somebody tell me," Bryony said with wide eyes. "I want to be indignant, too."

"Go away," Dahlia whispered under her breath. "This is about Faith."

Disgruntled, Bryony stalked from the room as slow as humanly possible, but not another word was spoken until the door clicked shut behind her.

"I always knew you were privy to secrets other people didn't even realize existed," Hawk told Grenville. "But I never thought you would keep the existence of my own flesh and blood secret even from me."

Dahlia paled. "You *do* know."

Hawk crossed his arms as he forced himself to contain his anger.

"I won't apologize," Grenville said evenly. "Faith asked if I could keep a secret and I said yes. If you know anything about me at all, it is that I do not go back on my word."

"*I* thought about it, though," Dahlia mentioned hesitantly.

Grenville slanted his sister a scathing glance and strode from the parlor, leaving Hawk and Dahlia alone to argue amongst themselves.

Very well.

Hawk turned back to Dahlia.

"Make no mistake. I had no sympathy for you at first," she said bluntly. "You were a blackguard unworthy even to be trod upon. But when I heard you mention Faith earlier this year and then you started coming around the school… I saw how much you were truly suffering. One couldn't help but suspect that you still loved her. And that if you loved her now, you have loved her all this time."

Hawk gave her a brittle smile. "Then why did you do nothing?"

"Too much time had gone by," she answered simply. "Think of it from Faith's perspective. Whether or not you agree with the choice she made, once she made it, every day, every week, every month, every year that you didn't know, made it all the more impossible to tell you. Not that you were anywhere to be found. If you had come by at any point while she was still panicking about being with child, I have no doubt she would have done everything differently. But you didn't. You didn't come then, and you didn't come after. So why should she have come to you?"

"I made a mistake. Several of them. I do not deny this." Hawk's fingers clenched. "But if I had known the truth sooner, I would've tried to fix my mistakes."

"Meaning what?" Dahlia asked. "You would have married Faith? No, you wouldn't have. You didn't marry her after taking her innocence. A child would have been just as easy to sweep under the rug."

"I *wanted* to marry her," Hawk ground out. "My mother, my guardian, and my advisors—"

"Would have 'advised' you to walk away. To send her to the countryside. To 'take care of the problem.' Perhaps send her a small sum to make up for any hard feelings."

Hawk snarled, "I would never have done such a thing."

"Wouldn't you?" Dahlia waved a hand dismissively. "If they could talk you out of marrying the woman you loved, you were in no position to insist upon being a father to a child you couldn't afford."

That was then. This was now.

"We'll never know," Hawk said bitterly. "Maybe you're right about me. Maybe I was too desperate for approval from my mother. Too terrified of causing even more harm to an estate I had just learned was built on nothing more than smoke and mirrors. Or maybe family meant more to me than you give me credit for."

"But would it have been better for Christina?" Dahlia asked, her eyes pleading.

Hawk's chest tightened. "You sound exactly like Faith."

"She's had ten years to think about it," Dahlia pointed out. "In the beginning there was nothing she wanted more than for you to come back on your own. Not because you had despoiled her, not because you had accidentally sired a child, but because you loved her and wanted to share your lives together. It never happened."

"She specifically requested me never to—"

"She was *angry*. Your presence in her life should never have been in question."

He had no response. Dahlia was right.

"Once she gave birth and held Christina in her arms," Dahlia continued, "Faith stopped caring about what *she* wanted. All that mattered was Christina. She hadn't been born into a title, but she had been born into a house of love. And month by month, as Christina's grandparents became wealthier, she quickly had far more advantages without you than she would have ever had with you."

Each word was a knife, a curved blade shaving away slices of his soul.

"Even if every word you say is true," he ground out in torment, "does my unsuitability back then mean that I shouldn't be allowed to do right by my daughter today? That it is too late for us to become the family we always should have been?"

Dahlia's eyes shone with empathy. "Only you and Faith can answer that."

Hawk stared at her for a long hopeless second before turning his back and exiting the parlor and their home.

Coming here had not been a waste of time, nor had it been the panacea he'd hoped for. The Grenvilles were not at fault for his current situation. That designation fell squarely on him and Faith.

Dahlia was right that they were the only ones who could reach some sort of conclusion. A compromise that complemented the needs of all parties, if such a feat could exist.

He was not yet ready to speak with Faith, but he was more than ready to get to know his daughter. Every minute without Christina in his life was another moment he could never get back. He gave his driver instructions and leaned back against the hard wall of his coach.

Hawk had not yet worked out all the details, but of one thing he was certain. There could be no future without his daughter in it. He could not live with himself otherwise. He would not abandon his own flesh and blood.

When the Season ended, if he couldn't afford to stay in London and was forced to return with his mother to their entailed monstrosity in the countryside, then by God he was bringing his daughter with him.

No matter what it took to do so.

CHAPTER 18

*U*nease prickled the back of Faith's neck. She pushed from her desk to go peek in on her daughter, just as she'd done every half hour all morning long. Ever since the disastrous revelations to Hawkridge two nights before, she hadn't been able to allow Christina out of her sight for more than a few moments.

Not that he would just *take* Christina from her, Faith told herself firmly. He might be a marquess, but he wasn't the *devil*.

Probably.

Faith stepped out into the school's corridor and let out a deep breath. The truth was, she was no angel either.

Christina would feel incredibly hurt to discover that her "aunt" was actually her mother. She might think Faith had been ashamed of her all this time. Unwilling to admit the connection publicly because Christina was in some way unworthy. Faith couldn't bear to put her daughter through such unnecessary self-doubt.

And that wasn't even the worst.

Christina would feel utterly betrayed to learn her father wasn't dead. That he had been living in the same town. Volunteering his time at the same school. She would never forgive Faith for keeping him from her all of these years.

Even if it truly had been out of love for her daughter.

She rubbed her temples. A secret this big would not get easier with time. But although Faith hadn't given up the idea of one day telling Christina the truth, this was not the moment to confess her sins. There was too much happening at once. Hawkridge had just come back in their lives. There was no way to know whether this time, he'd stay.

Or whether he'd do as his father had done and decide a lord's attentions belonged elsewhere.

Faith tiptoed down the hall toward the unfurnished dormitory Chris often used as a playroom. There was no reason to be so jumpy with fear. Everything would be fine. At least for another day.

Hawkridge could be impulsive, but he wasn't *rash*. Wasn't *destructive*.

But when she peeked through the crack in the doorway at the bare stone floor Christina shared with her toys, her daughter was not alone. Lord Hawkridge sat across from her on the dusty floor in his nankeen trousers, a doll in his hand.

Faith's heart skipped in alarm. When had he arrived? Who had allowed him in?

She swallowed her anger. Most likely, it would not have occurred to whichever student was on duty as butler at the time not to allow admittance to the school's dancing instructor. By now, Hawkridge was a familiar face. He had helped mend windows and hang shelves. Of course he would be welcomed in without question.

After all, it was not as though Faith could confess her reasons for wishing to keep him out.

Christina pointed at her toys. "And this one is Grandmother Doll and this one is Grandfather Doll and that one is Faith Doll."

Hawkridge held up his doll. "Which one is this one?"

"Me!" Chris laughed. "That's Christina Doll. This is my family. We love to play together."

Faith burst into the room. "What are you doing here?"

"Playing," came Christina's sunny reply as she bounced her grandmother and grandfather dolls from knee to knee.

Lord Hawkridge laid down the Christina Doll and jumped to his feet. "I came by to bring her a gift."

Faith glared at him. "She doesn't want a gift."

"I want it!" Christina clapped her hands and scrambled to her feet. "Is it a surprise?"

Hawkridge tore his gaze from Faith's and reached for a rectangular package on the windowsill. It had been wrapped with brown paper and tied with a blue ribbon, neither of which had been performed with a practiced hand.

He had wrapped the gift himself.

Faith scowled. She wasn't prepared to watch him do sweet things for her daughter.

Their daughter.

Christina tore open the paper with an abandon that would have shocked the other students at the school. In situations like theirs, paper was very dear.

A luxury to be treated carefully and reused as many times and in as many ways as possible.

Even in Lord Hawkridge's house, this was likely the case. What must he think of a daughter who took such things for granted?

"A book!" Christina squealed. She eagerly flipped through the pages and clasped it to her chest in delight. "There's a drawing on every page with every kind of animal in England!"

Before Faith could so much as take a step forward, Chris launched herself up and into Lord Hawkridge's arms for a spontaneous hug and then danced her new book about the empty dormitory as if she were twirling in the arms of a prince.

Hawkridge was frozen in place, his expression stunned, his eyes glassy.

Faith tried not to think about what it might mean to him that her affectionate child had hugged him. She tried not to think about what it meant to herself.

Seeing the two of them together was something she had always dreamed of, yet always dreaded. The specter had always followed over her shoulder like a dark cloud capable of portending either a thunderstorm or a rainbow.

It was far too soon to tell which.

"May I please speak with you in the corridor, Hawkridge?" she asked tightly.

He remained encased in stone for another moment, then nodded jerkily and made his way to join her out in the hall.

"She's wonderful," he said in awe.

"I know," Faith said. "That's why I want the best

for her. Not the best for you. Not the best for me. The best for Christina."

"I just want to be part of her life," he said, his voice tinged with regret.

"You should not have come today without informing me first," was all she said in reply.

She could not trust herself to say more.

"I'd like to make a schedule," he announced. "With Parliament in session, my time is limited but the hours are predictable. I should be able to spend a significant amount of time with Christina starting as early as today."

Faith shook her head. "Regardless of your schedule, once she begins finishing school, you cannot drop in unannounced to bother her. There will be specific days when she is free to spend time with her family."

"Finishing school?" Hawkridge took a step back. "You mean to send her away?"

"Not far," Faith admitted. "Just outside the city limits."

Frustration flashed in his eyes. "Now that she is finally part of my life, you're trying to keep her out of my reach?"

"I said just outside London," Faith repeated irritably. "Not the moon."

"It might as well be. I don't live in London." Hawkridge glared at her as if she were being purposefully dense. "I let an apartment while Parliament is in session, but as soon as it ends I must return to one of the entailed estates."

"And that is not my fault, but rather your decision." Faith tried to make him see reason. "Regardless of where *you* live, Christina needs an education."

"And so she will have one. But if I never see her, it will be as if nothing has changed. Yet *I* have." Hawkridge's gaze was wild, his face ashen. "Now that I know she exists, I cannot relegate her to sporadic visits once or twice a year when I happen to be in town for other reasons."

Faith winced. The situation he was describing was painfully familiar. His father had done exactly that. With Simon. Hawkridge was horrified at the idea of repeating the pattern.

"I won't stand for it," he said stubbornly. "It will not happen."

"You will not ruin this for her." Faith glared at him. "This is one of the best finishing schools in England. Garnering an interview with the administration was difficult enough. She does not need to count you as a liability."

He drew himself up taller. "I am not a liability. I am her new guardian."

Faith's heart dropped. "I won't allow it."

"I don't want to have to force you." His expression was as hard as stone.

She crossed her arms. "Without proof of parentage, you have little power over me. You cannot force me to do anything."

"A word from me can do a lot more damage than you realize," he said grimly. "Don't back me into a corner. The right to see my child is nonnegotiable."

Faith hesitated, her hands shaking.

While this threat was nonspecific, he did not require details to make his point. He was a man and a marquess. Those traits alone gave him plenty of power.

He could ruin Christina's chances at every finishing school in the country. He could ruin *this* school's chances at raising even another farthing for their students.

Now that she'd told Hawkridge the truth, there was no choice but to live with that decision.

Perhaps if they reached some sort of compromise...

If Lord Hawkridge were Christina's legal guardian on paper, he would not have "abandoned" her. Hawkridge could then allow her to attend school, and make friends, and live her life.

Decision made, Faith nodded and forced herself to meet his eyes. The courts might well side with him, regardless of pesky details like *proof*. She could not allow him to ruin their lives.

"Very well. You can foster Christina on one condition." She took a deep breath. "Where she goes, I go. You cannot take her anywhere without my knowledge or permission."

Hawkridge laughed, but it didn't reach his eyes. "No, Faith. I'm taking both of you. You will come as my wife."

CHAPTER 19

*H*awk waited in the receiving salon outside his mother's bedchamber in a cold sweat. The cough was back. It was worse than before. The doctor was inside.

He leaned the back of his head against the wall and listened as hard as he could to the murmuring voices on the other side. Not *voices*. Just one. If Mother was responding to the doctor's hushed queries, Hawk couldn't hear her.

Unsurprising, since she hadn't spoken or even exited her bedchamber in days.

There was sick, and then there was this.

Hawk slammed the back of his fists against the wall. Mother *couldn't* be dying. They couldn't afford it.

He could not wait another moment to marry Faith.

On the one hand, he should not waste his limited funds on something so ostentatious as a special license. On the other, he could not risk three weeks of banns and having Faith's friends and family protest their union in order to indefinitely impede their marriage with frivolous accusations.

But it was more than just her dowry. He didn't trust her to allow him in Christina's life of her own free will. Once Faith became his wife, they would both be Christina's guardians. Equals. As it should be.

His footman appeared in the doorway, red-cheeked and windblown. The young man had been given a stack of letters and instructed to wait at each residence for the recipient to pen a reply.

Hawk accepted the small pile of folded letters.

"Thank you." This would give him something to flip through while awaiting the doctor's verdict.

Most of his inquiries were dead ends. The investors had all signed very specific contracts, and were unwilling to part with another penny until the port finally opened.

One, however, had proven to be somewhat flexible. He would allow Hawk to take out a small personal loan against his own shares, in exchange for an exorbitant interest rate if the money was not repaid in full the moment the port became active.

The eye-watering percentages were less than ideal. Hawk had a sick mother, an unexpected daughter, and a reluctant wife to contend with. He would do as he must.

The door to his mother's bedchamber eased open.

Hawk snapped to attention. "May I see her now?"

"No." The doctor stepped out into the receiving salon and shut the door firmly behind. "Let her have her rest."

"Have you determined what's wrong?"

The doctor frowned. "It's unclear. The cause could be as temporary as the dreadful weather, as concerning as pneumonia, or as fatal as consumption. Until we know for certain, we must keep her comfortable and warm, and suppress the cough as much as we can."

Hawk's brain had stopped working after the word *fatal*. He blinked as fast as he could to hide the fear threatening to unseat him. Family had just meant the two of them for so many years. He could not bear to lose her so early.

The marquessate should be able to eke out another year until the next influx of coin. Mother, however, might not have that long. Hawk didn't want her to die believing he had let his legacy sink into destruction. But she was unlikely to appreciate his solution.

She was going to be furious when she found out about Faith. Even if he did not mention a word about Christina's parentage, Mother was perfectly capable of simple maths.

Especially when she had lived through this story before.

This time was different. Hawk steeled himself. It wasn't her life, but his. He wasn't seeing one woman and marrying another, but making a true family out of the one destiny had created for him. Or at least trying to.

Mother was still going to have an apoplexy.

It wouldn't matter that he was trying to do the right thing by being a true father to Christina. There was no right path for the marquessate that also happened to be the right path for everyone else. The best anyone could hope for in life sometimes was a compromise they could live with.

Hawk lowered his face into his hands. It was terrifying to admit it was not possible to be fully in control of one's life. He had believed he could do it. That he could defy twists of fate in the unexpected actions of others and forge a life of his own choosing.

But that wasn't what life was. It was making the best choices you could, one day after another.

There was absolutely no telling what the future was going to bring.

CHAPTER 20

*F*aith hunched forward uncomfortably on her favorite wingback chair in a sunny corner of her private receiving parlor.

She had spent countless hours curled against the soft pillows of this very chair, with a good book or a bit of embroidery or a cup of steaming chocolate or her daughter in her lap.

Today appeared to be a day like any other. Faith in this chair, her bosom friend Dahlia sprawled bonelessly on the chaise longue beneath the largest window.

How many other hours had been spent exactly like this? Might this actually be the last time she and Dahlia shared an afternoon in these familiar quarters?

The clock ticking on the mantel marched not toward the dinner hour, but toward the impending date in which she would cease to be Miss Faith Digby forevermore and become instead Lady Hawkridge, wife and property of the former paramour who now hated her.

"Well?" Dahlia's head swiveled on the pile of

satin cushions to face Faith. "Are you going to tell me what's bothering you or gaze pensively at your lovely Axminster carpet for the rest of the evening?"

Stare into oblivion was far more appealing to Faith than the current disaster of her own making, but there was no advantage to keeping Dahlia in suspense. "He asked me to marry him."

Dahlia sat upright. "Hawkridge?"

Faith nodded.

"I guess... Second time is the charm?" Dahlia suggested hopefully.

"Technically, he didn't 'ask' either time." Faith lifted a sardonic brow. So much for girlhood dreams. "The first time, he skillfully implied an official betrothal was forthcoming. And this time..."

Dahlia's eyes narrowed. "And this time?"

"This time he *informed* me of our impending nuptials." Faith hugged a pillow to her chest. "It was either agree or risk him upending Christina's life and ruining mine."

"Gallant of him," Dahlia muttered, then fixed a pointed gaze toward Faith. "Hawkridge would never purposefully ruin your life a second time."

"You didn't see his face when he found out about Christina," Faith said quietly.

Dahlia did not respond. Likely she was recalling the conversations she had shared with her husband, the unwanted bastard sired by Hawkridge's father. Her mouth twisted. "The difference is, Hawkridge is actually going to marry you."

Probably.

This wasn't the first time Faith had pulled Dahlia aside privately in order to confess that a wedding to Lord Hawkridge was imminent.

Faith rubbed her face. This was what she had always wanted. *He* was what she had always wanted. But not like this. Not as an afterthought, a punishment, his famous "responsibility" to yet another unwanted duty.

She had been so swept away by him in the old days.

The romantic walks, the unwavering intensity of his gaze, the way the world fell away every time they kissed.

That was what she had wanted with him for the rest of eternity. Not rancor and guilt and cold silences. She had never dreamed that one unguarded moment of love would lead them to ruin each other's lives and destroy all hope for future happiness together.

Dahlia's expression was sympathetic. "Don't throw yourself from a cliff just yet. The banns will take three weeks to be read, which gives us plenty of time to figure out how to make the best of this."

There would be no three-week reprieve for the calling of the banns. There would be no reprieve at all.

Bleakly, Faith lifted her head. "Special license."

Dahlia gasped audibly. "How did he—"

"I don't know." Faith hadn't thought he had the inclination or the spare coin, and yet he had procured the document faster than she believed possible.

Dahlia leaned forward. "Then when?"

"Sunday." Faith briefly closed her eyes. "You and Simon are hereby dutifully invited to be our witnesses and join us after for an intimate wedding breakfast hosted by my parents. As much as they hated what Hawkridge did when we were younger, they agree it's Chris's right to be raised by her birth parents."

Dahlia sighed. "They're right. It's not worth ruining Christina's childhood by dragging everyone into the courts."

Faith nodded and stared bleakly at the wall. After Sunday, this would not be her house anymore.

She would no longer have her private receiving parlor, her familiar bedchambers, quiet mornings in the family library. The bedtime ritual with Christina would be completely different, in some new and unfamiliar place where they were both strangers. They would be forced to live in someone else's home, where neither of them truly belonged.

"Of course we will be there," Dahlia said quickly. "And we are happy to sign the parish registry and return here for a…" Her voice faltered. "…party."

"There will be cake," Faith said sarcastically. "And possibly a tantrum."

Dahlia winced. "Chris doesn't want to go?"

"I meant from me," Faith confessed. "Christina doesn't know yet."

Avoiding the issue helped nothing, but she had no idea how to tell her daughter the news.

"I'm so sorry." Dahlia's face contorted. "There *must* be a silver lining."

"There is." If a bittersweet one. Faith gave a crooked smile. "A few days ago, I thought my greatest victory was finally convincing my parents to donate my dowry money to the school. Now they won't have to, and Mother can give it all to a lordling, just as she'd once dreamed."

Dahlia bit her lip. "You'll have to find a different

silver lining. Your parents already began the transfer. I received a notice from the bank this morning."

For a brief second, Faith was actually relieved.
He didn't deserve that money. Besides, her parents
would never let her or Christina want for anything,
dowry or not. The girls at the school were not so
lucky. Orphans had no one to turn to. No one except people like Faith. They needed her *and* the
dowry money. Her hands curled into fists.

She had worked so long and so hard to build up
the school. Had collapsed into bed many an ex-
hausted night after waking at dawn to perform ad-
ministrative duties, teach classes, mend hems, devise
fundraisers, give hugs, dry tears.

Without their school to give them shelter, every
one of their girls would return to a short and often
violent life in the streets. Faith shivered. The money
would keep the school afloat for at least another
year, which was plenty of time for her and Dahlia to
raise more funds and improve conditions even
more.

Except it wasn't, Faith realized suddenly.

Although her parents had sent the dowry money
to the school instead of to Lord Hawkridge, he
would control the purse strings. As soon as Faith
married, everything that was hers would immediately become his—including her half of the school.

Rather than spend her dowry on four-and-
twenty unwanted dependents, Hawkridge could
evict them all overnight and sell every teacup and
stick of furniture as profit for his estate.

It would be a heartless thing to do. But also, a
pragmatic one. He would be obliged to give the
Hawkridge finances priority in any and all decision-

making. His first duty was not to see to Faith's "pet project" but to his precious title.

A cold sweat sent chills across her skin. Having her own life in upheaval was one thing. She could not possibly risk jeopardizing the futures and the very lives of the students who counted on her.

"I need to arrange a meeting with Bryony's barrister," she blurted. "This evening."

"Done." Dahlia stood up. "I'll have her arrange it this very moment and send a note by with the time and location."

Faith threw her arms about the one person who had always given her unfailing support and unconditional love, no questions asked. There was little in this world more precious than a true friend. Faith could not have asked for a better one than Dahlia. "Thank you."

Dahlia's eyes softened. "Now promise me you won't spend the time between now and then seated in that chair, drowning in your own misery."

"I promise to spread the misery around," Faith replied with false earnestness. She rolled back her shoulders. "It is past time to inform Christina."

"Good luck." Dahlia squeezed her hand and disappeared from the room to find her sister.

Faith took a deep breath and forced herself to march directly to her daughter's play chamber.

Her heart twisted at the familiar sight of the sunny room Christina would no longer have, beside the nursery she would no longer have, inside the home she would no longer have. Faith's legs felt too stiff to walk upon, but she forced herself into the room. Postponing the conversation would not postpone the inevitable.

Christina was seated in the center of the plush carpet, her beloved collection of dolls encircling her on the floor as they all partook from a miniature porcelain tea set.

Faith took an empty place amongst the pillows. "Are any of your dolls married?"

"Of course." Christina laughed. She pointed at the two to her left. "Grandmother Doll and Grandfather Doll have been married their entire lives."

Faith took a deep breath. "And do you remember Lord Hawkridge?"

"Of course," Christina repeated, but this time she frowned rather than laughed. "What does he have to do with marriage?"

An excellent question. Faith forced a smile. "As it happens, he is going to marry me. He will become your guardian just like I am, and I will become his wife."

Christina's brow furrowed. "Will he live in the guest chamber?"

Faith swallowed a lump in her throat. "No, darling. We will live in his house. The wife must always move in with her husband."

"The wife." Relief crossed Christina's rosy cheeks. "But not the niece. I could stay with Grandmother and Grandfather if I wanted."

Christina was the *only* thing Lord Hawkridge wanted.

Faith hesitated. "I'm afraid it's not that easy."

"Because if I stay here, I couldn't be with you," Christina said slowly. Her bright gaze shone with determination as she reached forward to rub Faith's knee. "Don't worry, Aunt Faith. I won't leave you. When he marries you, we will go together."

Faith's eyes stung with heat and her whispered reply was barely audible. "That is very kindhearted, darling. Hawkridge will be pleased."

Christina stared down at her dolls' interrupted teatime. "Will my dolls have to play with a Hawkridge doll, too?"

Faith pulled her daughter into her arms and buried her face in Christina's sweet-smelling curls. "Let's see how things go with the real Hawkridge first."

CHAPTER 21

*L*ess than a week later, Hawk sent yet another sidelong glance at the woman seated next to him in his carriage, and still could not rid himself of the cloud of unreality that enveloped him.

Despite having spent the past two hours within arm's reach of each other, the only words he and Faith had exchanged were the rote phrases designated by the marriage ceremony.

The signing of the registry had been as silent an affair as the wedding itself. No one had clapped Hawk's shoulder in congratulations. Faith's parents and best friend had all given the new bride a restorative embrace in commiseration.

And yet they'd done it.

They were finally married, but his old coach felt like it was rattling them inexorably back toward the past rather than to their future. Would they ever trust each other enough to truly become a family?

He hadn't been back in Faith's life long enough to know whether the gown she wore was something old from the back of her wardrobe or a new confection commissioned specifically for the occasion.

In either case, she was stunning. She always had been. Regardless of the cost of the material that clothed her.

Sometimes, he thought her hair was her crowning glory. Thick glossy ringlets that had mussed so perfectly all those years ago when he had sunk his fingers into their brown silk. That memory could still warm him on even the coldest of London winter nights.

Other times, he thought it was her eyes that had so enraptured him. Sometimes a green so emerald they glittered as much as jewels, and other times as soft and mossy and warm as a bucolic forest surrounding a burbling summer spring.

Her eyes were expressive and ever-changing, windows not only to her soul but to his own. The thick brown lashes that framed them could melt him with a single flutter. He could still remember how it felt to see love reflecting back at him.

The memory ripped open a crater of longing almost too raw for him to bear.

He might never see affection return to her gaze. She trusted him as little as he trusted her. But while her sins were now in the open and in the past, he was still disappointing her.

Shortly after he'd informed her of his intent to marry her, he had learned from Simon that after a full year of pleading, Faith's parents had finally agreed to donate the money meant for her dowry to the school instead.

He had not spoken with the Digbys. Faith no longer required permission to wed, and with a ten-year-old daughter between them, Hawk had no need to beg for permission. But he suspected that part of the reason for the haunted look in Faith's eyes whenever someone had mentioned the school, was because the dowry money would no longer be going to the school.

Although she would never believe it, the ordinary act of accepting his bride's dowry wracked him with guilt.

He did not want to steal bread from the mouths of children. But he also had to provide for his own.

Accepting a dowry did not make him a monster. It made him the same as every other man who had accepted every other dowry in the history of brides and dowries. The very definition of a dowry was a gift of monetary value from the bride's parents to the groom upon the circumstance of their marriage.

Lord knew, his estate needed the money. Their *family* needed the money. So why did continuing an expected and long-standing tradition make him feel like such a scoundrel?

He would not think about that now. There was nothing he or Faith could do but make the best of their situation.

And as far as Hawk was concerned, the best of their situation—indeed, the crowning jewel—was Christina.

He would finally be able to get to know her. To be a good father, even if she believed herself nothing more than a ward. Excitement hummed along his skin.

"Starting tomorrow morning, I shall arrange scheduled visits with my daughter without you peering over our shoulders. She will never get to know me with you pecking between us like a mother hen."

Faith's eyes flashed in his direction. "I *am* her mother hen. You are the rooster that crowed once and flew away. Until I give permission for Christina to be unsupervised in your company, she will not—"

"Incorrect, Lady Hawkridge," he said softly. "As your husband, I do not require permission for anything at all."

Her eyes flashed. "Anything you still *own*."

A cold sweat prickled along his skin. His voice filled with danger. "What did you do?"

"I gave away the school," she whispered. "Before it could become yours. I signed my half back over to Dahlia the day before the wedding. It's legal and there's nothing you can do about it."

Relief washed over him. He hadn't even considered the school. He was glad it would not be his responsibility. Hawk had more than enough already just with taking care of his family.

"I don't want the school," he bit out through clenched teeth. "I want my daughter. You stole the first ten years of her life from me. It's finally my turn to have her, too."

There was light at the edge of the darkness. The dowry money would allow him to open his port ahead of schedule. Despite the guilt he felt at spending money meant for the boarding school, Hawk was in no position to turn it down. Once his port turned a profit, he would more than match the donation.

In the meantime, he would have to settle the worst of the overdue accounts, turn the guest chamber into a proper nursery for Christina, boost his mother's spirits with a new gown. He and Faith could start their marriage without worrying about money. Hawk's mood lightened at the prospect.

Her dowry was ample enough to allow them to live in relative comfort until his port opened. He had done the calculations dozens of times. Thanks to the unexpected influx, in less than six months he would finally be out from under his predecessors' debts and every shilling he earned could be used to spoil his family.

Whether this strained union would ever *feel* like a family was another question entirely.

He tried to look away from Faith but her despondent expression only reflected back at him from the carriage windows.

This was not her fault. She was far from perfect, but so was he. If he was miserable, he'd managed to ruin their relationship all by himself.

The news of Christina's existence still made him dizzy. But he had to stop allowing Faith's deception to make him angry. She had made the decision a decade ago, but she'd been living with the aftermath ever since.

A ruined spinster with a child that would never know her mother. He lowered his head. Punishing her further would be far beyond excessive.

It was time to move forward. To create a future far different from their past.

"We're here." Faith practically leapt from the coach moments after it turned onto the road leading to her parents' house.

Hawk was not nearly as excited to follow her inside. He had not made a positive impression the first time he had met the Digbys or any day since. His stomach was too knotted to be hungry.

When he followed his new wife inside her parents' home, Hawk was delighted to spy his brother standing just outside the archway to the dining room. The sole friendly face amidst a panoply that ranged from suspicious to devastated.

At least, he hoped his half-brother was still friendly toward him. If Christina's existence had been a shock to Hawk, to Simon it would have been tangible proof that Hawk was no better than their father.

His steps slowed. He would not blame Simon for being unable to forgive him for repeating the same history that had caused Simon such pain. Hawk could not even forgive himself.

"I'm trying to make this right," he said to his brother in lieu of a greeting. "I have yet to find a right answer, but I swear to you I am trying."

Simon's gaze went somewhere over Hawk's left shoulder. "Let us not discuss the choices you have made. But if I ever hear you refer to Christina as a 'mistake', then so help me God I will—"

"Never," Hawk said quickly. "I have made countless mistakes, but she is not one of them."

Simon nodded. "It will not be easy. I do not envy you."

"I envy you," Hawk muttered. "Your life seems so easy in comparison."

"Does it?" This time, Simon's smile reached his eyes. "Feeding four-and-twenty schoolgirls, chasing after my wife, drowning in case files…"

"Perhaps not 'easy,'" Hawk allowed with a laugh. "But you have a path. A plan. You know which direction you're going. That's what I'm trying to forge as well."

"If it makes you feel any better, I am often stumbling about in the dark."

"Unlikely," Hawk scoffed. "With what?"

Simon lifted a shoulder. "For example, I am no closer today to determining which, if any, of Maxwell Gideon's surreptitious dealings are legal and which are not. His reputation as a ruthless blackguard has made some believe he would not hesitate to manipulate and coerce others if it resulted in more profit for him."

Hawk's shoulders tightened. Once again, he was caught between loyalty to his brother and to a long-time friend.

No matter how ruthlessly Maxwell Gideon controlled his business, complete and informed consent was a primary requirement of every contract he signed. Hawk shook his head. Even though his own money was no longer at risk, he would not take part in casting doubt on another man's reputation.

Was Gideon a blackguard? Without question. But Gideon was also a pathologically *fair* one. His word was his bond, and absolutely unshakable.

"I'm sorry," he said to his brother. "I cannot help you. To the best of my knowledge, every deal Gideon has brokered is completely legal, even if the details aren't public."

Simon returned his gaze for a long moment before responding. "Then I am at a crossroads."

Hawk hesitated. "If anyone knows Maxwell Gideon secrets, it is your brother-in-law. Grenville knows everyone's secrets. But you will need far more than mere good fortune to wrest it out of him."

"I know." Simon sighed. "I've tried."

Hawk lifted a shoulder in sympathy. Heath Grenville was damnably good at his job. No matter how Hawk might have wished otherwise. He furrowed his brow.

Perhaps his brother's life was not nearly as straightforward as he had assumed. Not only was Simon's investigation not going as smoothly as he hoped, Hawk had swooped in and inadvertently redirected dowry money that had been earmarked for the school. He winced. Simon would be well within his rights to be more than disgruntled with him.

"About Faith's dowry," Hawk began.

"I'm sorry about that," Simon said quickly. "The transfer had already gone through before I learned it was underway, and they managed to spend every penny within a matter of hours. Contracting repairs for the school, new clothes for the girls, books for the library, staples for the pantry. All I can tell you is that every shilling was lovingly spent for a noble cause."

Hawk's brain barely processed his brother's words.

The dowry was gone.

Not only did it not come to him, it had already been spent. The guilt he had glimpsed in Faith's eyes was not because her marriage to him would deprive orphans of new shoes, but because he would not be receiving a farthing at all.

Hawk's pulse pounded in his ears. His port would not be opening early. There was no money for paying debts, for paying rents, for food and clothing. No money for doctors to treat his sick mother.

No money at all.

Fury surged through his veins. Faith *knew*, and hadn't seen fit to tell him. She'd done it on purpose.

"She gave it away?" he rasped in disbelief. "She told her parents not to give me the dowry?"

Simon winced. "They didn't rescind it from you personally, if it makes a difference. Faith convinced them to donate her dowry to the school before you had proposed marriage."

Hawk *hadn't* proposed. Hadn't courted Faith at all, then or now. What dibs did he have on a dowry that had been promised to orphans? None.

His eyes blurred at the irony. If Hawk would have paid a visit to her father back when he had first intended to, he and Mr. Digby would have signed a contract. The dowry money would not have been a mere cultural norm, but a legal obligation.

By securing a special license and using Faith's permission as a woman of majority in her own right, Hawk had completely bypassed the step of formally asking for her hand.

This was what his arrogance deserved. But that did not change their circumstances. Without Faith's dowry...

How would he afford to provide for his new family at all?

aith gripped her daughter's hand as Hawkridge's carriage pulled to a stop. Arriving at his temporary London townhouse didn't feel like a homecoming. It felt like stepping out of her own life and into someone else's.

She didn't feel like a marchioness. Her very presence seemed out of place, like she was a tired old gewgaw that ought to be swept back into the attic where such trinkets belonged. This wasn't her home or Christina's.

It wasn't even Lord Hawkridge's.

For her daughter's sake, she pasted on a delighted expression as if becoming mistress of someone else's rented townhouse was jolly sport.

Faith dreaded stepping inside not because she and Christina would be alone with Hawkridge, but because they would not.

His mother, they had been told, was too ill to attend the wedding. Regardless of the dowager marchioness's health, Faith suspected Hawkridge's mother would sooner lock herself in an ivory tower than witness him pledge himself to a nobody. Particularly not to the common bit of baggage she had warned her son against a decade ago.

Back then, Faith had still been hopeful enough and naïve enough to believe such differences didn't matter. That of course she could be a marchioness equal to any other. Someday win her mother-in-law's respect and love, as well as her husband's.

She was no longer the silly creature she once had been.

When the driver who had handed Christina and her out of the carriage dashed ahead of them up the walkway to open the door and welcome them into their home, it took Faith a moment to realize the young man had not lost his mind.

He was John the footman, the driver, the butler, and likely more.

No matter. Faith knew what it was like not to have servants at all. And although Christina had been raised in comfort, she had not been taught airs. Faith pressed her lips together and lifted her chin in determination. They would be fine. If anything, it should be a relief not to have to manage a large house.

Inside the entranceway to the townhouse, Hawkridge gazed at them in obvious discomfort. "Do you... Are you hungry? I can have the maid—"

Faith shook her head.

"We've just come from the wedding breakfast." This was true, although of the three of them, Christina was the only one who had enjoyed the repast. "Please don't have her go to any extra trouble on our behalf."

Hawkridge stared back at her for a long moment.

"Should you change your mind, this house is yours to command."

Except it was not. If his awkwardness was any indication, Hawkridge certainly meant well. But any house with so few servants and an obviously limited budget meant that Faith would be far wiser to ask which meals could be scared up from the larder than to attempt to impose her will upon a meager pantry.

"Christina, may I show you to your room?" Hawkridge asked their daughter.

Christina's hazel eyes gazed up over the Grandmother Doll and Grandfather Doll clasped to her chest. "Does it have a window?"

Hawkridge's obvious relief would have been amusing had their situation been different. "It does. Your chambers have the best windows in the entire townhouse."

Christina nodded. "Then I like it. Do the play chambers have windows too?"

Hawkridge's eyes met Faith's over the top of Christina's head.

She took pity. "This is a temporary townhouse, darling. Remember? There's no nursery or school-room here. But you do have a bedchamber with the very best windows."

"I want to see them." Christina held up her dolls. "Grandmother Doll and Grandfather Doll want to see them too."

"Then, this way, if you please." Hawkridge led them up a simple stairway leading to the next floor. "Your valises will be right up. I shall be honored to give you the grand tour in the meantime."

Faith followed her daughter and her husband up

the stairs to the sleeping quarters, where her mother-in-law presumably also resided.

How did it feel to have one's childhood fantasy finally realized?

She was a marchioness. *His* marchioness. And it made her want to cry. This was not what she had wanted, for herself, for him. She wanted the fairy story. Had expected it. But fate had held other plans.

She hung back to give Hawkridge a chance to bond with his daughter.

Christina was suitably impressed with her bedroom windows. The huge square in front of the Digby house was just visible in the far corner.

Before they had left for the wedding that morning, her parents had offered to decorate the townhouse with anything Faith lacked. Chandeliers, books, Egyptian artifacts, anything at all.

But it was already April, and this was a rented apartment Hawkridge didn't even intend to keep. In a few months, the Season would be over. Where would she and Christina be then?

"So you did it despite my warning," came a disgusted voice from the corridor. "You always were too selfish and self-important to consider how your actions reflect on others."

Faith whirled to face Hawkridge's mother. "Don't speak to him like that."

"I wasn't," the dowager answered coldly. Pointedly.

Faith's cheeks flushed. She laid a protective hand on Christina's shoulder.

Hawkridge stepped forward, his voice a low growl. "Mother."

The pale-cheeked dowager coughed into a

stained handkerchief. "What can I do? My feelings have never been important in this family, so why should hers be any different?"

"That is enough," Hawkridge said firmly. "You should be resting."

"I agree." She swayed and gripped the doorframe as if the floor had begun to pitch with the tide. "This is nothing to get out of bed for."

Faith quickly revised her plans. There is no point in insincerely attempting to win her mother-in-law over. All she and Christina could do was to be compassionate, be themselves, and hope for the best.

The sudden wedding had been a shock to all of them. And Faith had dreaded it just as much as her mother-in-law.

"Christina, I would like to introduce you to my mother, the dowager marchioness, Lady Hawkridge." He lowered his voice to a whisper. "She's very sorry she was too ill to attend the ceremony."

Christina frowned. "I thought Aunt Faith was Lady Hawkridge now. Is she the same as your mother?"

"That chit is nothing like me," the dowager spat in fury, pointing a trembling pale finger at Faith. "I would have refused to attend that wedding even if I weren't sick. I regret living to see a commoner rule over the respectable estate I once managed."

CHAPTER 23

*H*awk rolled his head, trying to work out a kink in his neck.

A sleepless night tossing restlessly on the settee in his study was not how he dreamed he'd begin his marriage. But things between him and Faith were already complicated enough. They would need to figure out how to share each other's lives before either of them was ready to share the marriage bed.

He made his way to the dining room and brightened considerably to discover Christina seated at the head of the table with a towering pile of toasted bread.

Rather than rush into the room and disturb her, he took a moment to observe her from the shadowed corridor. His heart flipped.

Hawk had broken his fast alone for as long as he could remember. Neither of his parents could be roused before noon, and there had been no other siblings living in the house.

In all his imaginings of one day sharing ordinary moments like these with the woman who would become his wife, it had not occurred to him that it would perhaps bring even greater delight to share rashers and eggs with a child.

Just as he was about to cross into the dining room and present himself, a hand brushed against his elbow.

He jumped.

It was Faith. Of course it was Faith. The servants would never touch him. He had just been so focused on dining with his daughter that he hadn't heard footsteps approach from behind.

He turned to face her. "Lady Hawkridge. I trust you slept well."

"I woke up alone." The voice was hesitant, her eyes confused.

"I didn't wish to wake you."

"I was awake half the night waiting for you." She tilted her head to regard him, keeping her voice low so their words would not carry to the breakfast room. "Either I fell asleep before you arrived, or you never came to consummate the marriage."

"We consummated a decade ago," he said dryly. He met her eyes to allow her to see the sincerity of his next words. "I have spent every night since dreaming of making love to you again, Faith. I shan't come to your bed until that's exactly what we are doing."

She swallowed visibly but did not lower her eyes. "It is breakfast time. Have you eaten?"

The question was far from an invitation to her bedchamber, but at least she had not scoffed at the idea of one day truly making love. A small victory, but there had been so few of them recently that Hawk was quite willing to take it.

"I was just about to go in," he said. "Care to join us?"

He started to proffer his arm then hesitated. The sight of his daughter had put him in too good a mood to have it spoiled by his wife refusing to take his elbow or recoiling from his touch. A rush of emotion made him dizzy with hope. Just this once, it would be lovely to dine as a family.

"I cannot stay." Faith backed away from him. "I am needed at the school unless..." Her eyes filled with dismay. "You wouldn't forbid me from volunteering my time, would you?"

Hawk spirits dipped. He tried again. "I hope to never forbid you from anything. If you would like to continue volunteering, you are more than free to do so for as long as we remain in London."

Her eyes dimmed at the reminder of their time limit. "Perhaps I'll wait until Christina is done with breakfast so that I can drop her at her grandparents' house on my way to the school. Unless you require the coach? I am happy to take a hack instead."

He raised his brows. "I'll take you to the school myself. Christina will not be going to her grandparents."

"Of course she will. Chris stays with them whenever she's not with me." Faith frowned at him. "They enjoy their days together."

His smile was bleak. "I am certain they do. They shall continue to have such days, but today is not one of them. I, too, expect to spend time with my daughter."

"*Ward*," Faith hissed, casting a speaking glance in the direction of the dining table.

"With my ward," Hawk amended. He would take

more care in the distinction. "Today while you are at the school, Christina will be with me."

Faith shook her head. "I am not certain that is a good idea. She is not used to you."

"How can she ever be, if we do not begin getting used to each other?" he asked reasonably. "I do not wish to argue with you. But I also do not require your permission."

"I could stay home," Faith said quickly. "I could take her to see her grandparents myself."

"You could," he agreed, "if you wish to cease volunteering at the school and thus prevent your parents from their special time alone with Christina. Is that what you intend?"

She glared at him in disgust. "You know it is not."

"Then we are in agreement." He strode into the dining room and paused to look over his shoulder. "Christina and I will be happy to take you to the school after breakfast, unless you prefer to take a hack."

Christina glanced up from her tower of toast to smile angelically. "I didn't take too much, Aunt Faith. I will eat every bite. I promise."

Faith gave a tight nod. "There has been a change in plans. You will spend the day with Lord Hawkridge. No sour faces, please. I will hurry home as fast as I am able."

Christina shook her head. "Today I go to my grandparents. We are going to make paper boats and float them on the lake."

"Next time." Faith's smile was overbright. "Be good, darling. I'll be back in a trice."

When Faith stalked away down the corridor— presumably preferring a hackney cab over Hawk's company—Christina pushed her plate of toast away and crossed her arms in a huff.

She glared at Hawk. "I don't want you. I want my grandparents."

His stomach tightened. "We can go to the lake together. I love to float paper boats, too."

"I don't want to float them with you. I want to float them with Grandfather."

"We can go out for ices," Hawk continued cajolingly. "What flavor of frozen ice do you like best?"

He ignored the recriminations in the back of his mind. They did not have the money to make such extravagances a habit, but surely just this once...

"I don't want ices," his daughter said flatly. "If I can't go to my grandparents' house then I want to go to school with Aunt Faith."

"Tomorrow," he promised. "Today you will have adventures with Uncle Hawkridge."

Christina was singularly unimpressed. "You are not my uncle."

"I could be *like* an uncle," he offered hopefully.

She shook her head even more disparagingly. "You could not. You are not my family. You took my family away from me."

Hawk wondered if it was too late to halt Faith before she managed to catch a hackney. He'd been parenting for all of five minutes and could clearly use some direction.

"What if we *visit* your grandparents," he began slowly, "and then sail paper boats in the lake?"

Christina frowned as she considered his proposal.

In the ensuing silence, Hawk's skin pricked with pins and needles. This was worse than the first time he'd ever asked a girl to dance. There would be other girls, other dances. But there would not be another opportunity to have a good "first outing" with his daughter.

"We visit them first?" she asked.

Hawk nodded. "Right after you finish your toast."

Christina slid a guilty glance toward the empty doorway where Faith had stood. "I took too much. Can you help me?"

"I would love to." Truce established, Hawk sat next to her so that they could both reach the same plate.

When they arrived at the Digby residence, to say Faith's parents were surprised to discover Christina in Hawk's company would be a vast understatement.

Mrs. Digby looked over his shoulder in alarm. "Where is Faith?"

"At school," he said quickly. "Christina and I are out on adventure today. Our first adventure was dropping by to say good morning to you."

"It was my idea," Christina put in. "Lord Hawkridge wanted to sail paper boats at the lake first."

"Hawkridge wanted to sail paper boats at the lake?" Mr. Digby's tone was skeptical.

"That might've been my idea, too," Christina said. "Are there any biscuits?"

"I shall have Cook make some." Mrs. Digby cast a raised brow toward Hawk. "That is, if you've an hour to spare before your next adventure?"

He affected an offended mien. "Only a very foolish man would be in too great a hurry for biscuits."

She did not smile in return, but nor did she

wound him with biting comments about the many ways he had been foolish in the past.

"Did you receive the gift we sent?" Mr. Digby asked Christina when his wife stepped away to ring the maid.

Christina pulled a face. "Yes. Thank you, Grandfather. I'll try to love it."

Gift? Hawk frowned. He had no idea what the Digbys might have sent. Hopefully it wasn't a pony.

Mrs. Digby returned. "Shall we remove to the library whilst we await fresh biscuits?"

"Yes!" Christina exclaimed and raced from the room before anyone else could answer.

"Get used to that," Mr. Digby muttered under his breath as he set out in pursuit of his granddaughter.

Hawk felt out of place following Faith's parents through their magnificent home. When he entered the library, his jaw dropped. He had never seen such a collection shoehorned into a townhouse before, even in a residence as large as this. No wonder Christina couldn't wait to disappear inside.

"This one!" Christina flew out from between two rows of bookshelves with a colorful tome held aloft. "Grandmother, can you read it to me?"

Mr. and Mrs. Digby exchanged a glance.

"You can read that on your own," Mrs. Digby said to Christina. "But why don't you read it to Lord Hawkridge?"

Christina pouted, clearly about to argue.

"I hazard he's never seen such a fine book on butterflies before," Mr. Digby said to his granddaughter. "Just imagine Lord Hawkridge's face when you describe the cocoon."

Christina brightened and flung herself to the thick carpet at Hawk's feet. "Sit."

"We've talked about chairs, Christina," Mrs. Digby reminded her. "Lord Hawkridge is a marquess and cannot possibly—"

Hawk dropped to the carpet next to his daughter. "I don't mind at all. What's this about a cocoon?"

The next hour disappeared in a flash as Christina read to him about the life-cycle of caterpillars, the flowers of England, the birds of London.

Although she stumbled over a few words, her reading level was far higher than Hawk would have guessed for a girl her age. Hell, he guessed half the pinks of the *ton* would've twisted their tongues over words like *bulbous buttercup* and *metamorphosis*.

Mr. and Mrs. Digby sat side-by-side not ten feet away. Hawk expected to feel spied upon, as if he were not good enough to play nanny, much less be a father.

He quickly surmised, however, that watching Christina play on the floor from their vantage point on the richly decorated chaise longue was one of the Digbys' favorite pastimes. The amused glances they exchanged, the way they mouthed words from the book even before Christina spoke them, the brief caresses of one hand on the other's when they thought Hawk wasn't looking.

That was perhaps the most mind-bending of all. Hawk could not recall a time in which his parents had shared the same settee, much less a furtive caress. Faith's parents were still in love. She'd grown up knowing love like that, commitment like that, *happiness* like that.

So had Christina. She would have no reason to

doubt that her future husband would treat her just as tenderly.

Hawk's shoulders sagged when he realized Faith had been right. When he'd rescinded his impending proposal because he couldn't afford to keep her, much less start a family, she had been faced with a difficult decision.

Regardless of whether the right thing to do would have been informing him of her pregnancy, had Christina really been any worse off growing up in a loving environment where money was never a worry?

She would forevermore be Miss Digby, rather than Lady Christina. That part pained Hawkridge because it was the one thing he could have given her.

But the rest of it: a magical library, a charmed life, a loving mother and two loving grandparents... There was no price he could put on her happiness.

He set his jaw. From this day forward, he, Faith and Christina would determine their joint future together.

When the last of the biscuits had been consumed, it was finally time to bid farewell to the Digbys. Hawk expected tears, or at least repeated accusations that he was stealing Christina's family from her.

Instead, she shocked him to the core by taking his elbow and skipping toward the coach without complaint.

"Thank you for taking me to see my grandparents," she said happily as she wiggled onto the squab.

"Any time," he replied in wonder.

Perhaps he was not doing so badly after all. They

had started on the wrong foot because she had believed he didn't care about what she might want or need. But after a dozen biscuits and at least as many illustrated scientific primers, he had proven himself not to be completely heartless.

Her grandparents had been instrumental. Had they spoken ill of him, he had no doubt Christina's original negative impression would have cemented rather than softened. But because Mr. and Mrs. Digby had put the needs of a child above their personal dislike of their son-in-law, Hawk had a chance.

He flinched at the memory of how his own mother had treated Faith and Christina upon their arrival.

The dressing-down he had given Mother once they were back in her private chambers had been well deserved. But from now on, he would not wait until his wife and child were out of earshot before he defended them. He could never again let them doubt the place they held in his heart.

Hawk's coach was already halfway to the park when he realized that he had no paper with which to make folded boats to float on the water.

"I am very sorry," he said, once he had explained the situation. Their first father-daughter outing and already he had cocked things up.

She patted his shoulder. "That's all right. I should have reminded you."

He tried not to laugh at what was clearly an echo of something her mother must often have said to her. "Next time?"

"Next time," Christine agreed with a smile.

"Very well." Hawk thought for a second. "You have two choices, Miss Digby."

Her eyes lit up. "Do I?"

He nodded solemnly. "Would you like to return home and play with your toys? Or would you like to walk about the park with me anyway, and perhaps come with me while I complete a few errands after?"

Christina thought it over. "I can choose whichever I want?"

"Absolutely." Hawk gazed back at her. "You're almost a young lady. I am certain you know your own mind."

Pleasure flooded Christina's face at the compliment and she lifted her chin arrogantly. "I do indeed. And I have decided to spend the day with you."

Hawk had not thought she would choose him. He grinned, despite the sudden tightness in his throat. "Shall we start with the lake?"

The next few hours with his daughter were full of more fun than he'd had in years. They walked every inch of the park, picked a bouquet of flowers, spied a trio of red squirrels, shared hot cross buns, and fed the crumbs to baby ducklings.

When at last it was almost time to return home, the last thing he wanted was to leave the magic of the park for errands on Bond Street. But he was not just a father. He was also a marquess. And men like the tailor had been waiting long enough for their accounts to be settled.

Even if all Hawk could do was to pay pennies on every pound owed.

But when he and Christina stepped inside the tailor's shop to place another paltry twenty pounds toward the total, the tailor shook his head in confusion. "There's nothing to pay. Surely you haven't forgotten?"

Hawk blinked.

The tailor smiled expectantly.

"Forgotten what?" Hawk shook his head in confusion. When he had come by the month before, there had been five hundred pounds outstanding on the account. "I haven't been by all month."

"No, of course not." The tailor laughed, as if this were all a silly misunderstanding. "But Mr. Spaulding was quite clear the sum was to be paid off in your name."

Hawk froze. His *brother* had paid off the sartorial debt? For the father too self-righteous to give Simon a legitimate birth? That act of selfishness had cost Simon his rightful place as the heir. He was the first-born and should have inherited the title, but instead he had received nothing.

Which meant these were not his debts. Even if Simon were using Faith's dowry to close out the accounts, Simon needn't feel responsible in the slightest for a single penny of their father's obligations.

"Thank you," Hawk said tightly. He turned to march toward the door.

Christina's hand tightened on his elbow. "Where are we going now?"

To have a reckoning with Hawk's presumptuous brother.

He glanced down at his daughter. "Do you mind if we stop by the school?"

Christina's hazel eyes lit with happiness. "It'll be nuncheon. I can visit with my friends."

Perfect. Hawk did not need his daughter to witness the conversation he was about to have with Simon.

The man had claimed that the ladies had spent every penny of Faith's dowry before Simon even knew about it. If instead he was using it to pay off debts in Hawk's name, it should be up to Hawk not Simon to determine how the marquessate's accounts were settled.

When they arrived at the school, Simon was just leaving for Bow Street. Hawk sent Christina inside to chat with her friends.

"I've just come from the tailor," he said by way of greeting.

"Ah," Simon nodded. "Then you know."

Hawk shook with anger. "You said the dowry money was gone."

"It is," Simon said. "But my promotion came early. A matter I resolved for Lady Pettibone impressed the right people. The Justice of the Peace felt I deserved compensation."

This thunderbolt only turned Hawk's guilt into shame. The money wasn't from the dowry that had been meant for Faith's future. It was a hard-earned bonus that had been meant for *Simon*.

"What has that to do with me?" Hawk demanded. "You have a family of your own. The school needs your money. I did not ask for your charity."

"All the ladies in the school are part of my extended family," Simon agreed. He placed a hand on Hawk's shoulder and looked him in the eye. "But so are you, little brother. You may be a marquess now, but I'll be your big brother until the end of time."

Hawk's throat was suddenly too tight for him to speak.

Simon glanced at his pocket watch. "Be back by seven if you want to join us for the Headmistress Dinner. And don't think about skipping out on your duties as dancing master this week. 'Newlywed' does not mean a gentleman leaves twenty-four eager girls without a dance partner."

Before Hawk could respond, his brother leaped onto his horse and rode away.

He swallowed his guilt. Simon did not have ulterior motives after all. He was not trying to use Hawk's inside knowledge of the Cloven Hoof to make an even bigger name for himself amongst the Bow Street runners. Simon had got his promotion completely on his own. He had not wanted the bonus for himself but for his family.

Hawk had never known having family could feel like this. Someone spending an unexpected windfall to help you, rather than himself. Someone choosing to spend time with you rather than her dolls. Fresh baked biscuits even when one did not deserve them.

His heart warmed. He had become a far richer man than he had ever dreamed possible.

CHAPTER 24

*A*fter the fourth day in a row of grueling parliamentary sessions, Hawk was ready to hang himself with his cravat.

Sitting through the sessions was his duty to his title and to the Crown, but surely there was a limit to how much any man could be expected to withstand arguments on gossip-column caricatures and Princess Cariboo sightings.

There were so many more important topics to discuss. Construction of the Waterloo bridge. The reintroduction of the gold sovereign. Hawk finally escaping the Palace of Westminster to spend time with his family.

He had been married less than a week and already one of the best parts of Hawk's day was returning home from Parliament, knowing Faith and Christina would be in the house waiting for him.

When his carriage pulled up at the front walk to their townhome, an entire day's exhaustion vanished into the air. Hawk all but sprinted up to the doorstep, letting himself in and beating his driver to the task.

But when he opened the door, nobody was there to greet him. Not even the maid.

He frowned and tilted his head. The townhouse was silent. Perhaps the honeymoon, such as it was, was over. Faith and Christina likely had any number of better things to do than sit about waiting for Parliament to wind down, while their stomachs growled in displeasure.

The house was almost eerily quiet.

Before his mother had fallen ill, she had been the one to greet him. Often with recriminations about this, or complaints about that, but at least he had known she was well.

Since becoming bedridden, she had ceased to greet him by the door, but her wracking cough was violent enough to make the house tremble. Yet there were no such rumbles.

Alarm coursed through his muscles. For a woman who was not willing to leave her bedchamber, complete silence might mean something horrible had befallen her. Something too dreadful to consider.

Hawk sprinted up the stairs to the sleeping quarters and skidded to a stop just outside his mother's receiving parlor.

She was not in bed, but nor had she succumbed to an untimely demise while Hawk was at Parliament.

His mother's quarters had been rearranged such that she was now bundled not into her four-poster canopy, but rather upon a chaise longue beneath an uncurtained window.

He could hardly see her beneath the multiple

layers of old woolen blankets and suspiciously bright-colored satin pillows piled up on the chaise.

The tea table had been dragged from the unused corner of the room in which it had stood for the past several years, and now stood between his mother's chaise longue and a footstool, upon which perched Hawk's wife.

Before his disbelieving eyes, his mother cast a handful of cards toward Faith's face.

Just as he stepped forward to intervene, Faith tossed two playing cards of her own in his mother's direction with a gleeful, "...and I'll raise you three!"

Hawk's mind blanked. What the devil? This was the throwing card game the Grenvilles had been playing. Faith had taught it to his mother.

His mother was out of her sickroom tossing playing cards about with a low-born *commoner*.

He backed away from the open door and collapsed against the wall in awe and relief. Mother looked better than she had in a month. She was going to pull through.

More importantly, so was his family. Somehow Faith had managed to soften the one woman Hawk could've sworn could not be melted.

He had no idea how she had done the impossible, but her methods were likely the exact talents that enabled her to be a beloved teacher to students who had never heard a kind word prior to becoming wards of the St. Giles School for Girls.

Compared to some of those challenges, he supposed gentling his mother had been child's play.

The corner of Hawk's mouth lifted. *Literal* child's play. He would not soon forget the sight of his mother tossing playing cards with abandon.

He peeked around the corner one last time. He could not rightly claim that he was looking at his wife with new eyes. Not when he had always loved her.

But for a short while, he had allowed the anger in his heart to blind him from the treasure he already had.

If Faith could work such magic with Mother, surely all of them working together could turn a household of virtual strangers into a true family. Create a true home.

He turned away from the laughing women and made his way to the end of the short corridor where Christina's bedchamber stood.

She sat in the center of her small room, on a rug Hawk had never seen before but strongly suspected had come from her old bedchamber. Or at least from her grandparents. A ring of even more brightly colored pillows encircled her, several of which were adorned with one or more dolls.

Hawk stepped into the room and inclined his head at the maid folding freshly laundered pinafores into Christina's armoire.

"May I join you?" he asked his daughter.

She pointed toward one of the pillows. "Your spot is there."

"I have a spot?" he asked in surprise.

"Your spot is by your doll," she said impatiently, as if he were being purposefully dimwitted.

"I have a doll?" Hawk echoed in bewilderment.

Christina leaned forward with a huff and yanked up the doll that had been lying on the pillow she indicated. Short, light brown hair, a wide smile, evening dress far more elegant than anything remaining in Hawk's wardrobe.

He sat down on the pillow and accepted the doll. "This is me?"

"That's Hawkridge Doll," Christina said, as if explaining the obvious to a baby. She pointed at each of the figures sitting on the pillows. "That's Aunt Faith Doll, Grandmother Doll, Grandfather Doll, and Christina Doll. Plus their animals. Hawkridge Doll is the newest."

He blinked at her. "When did you get it?"

"Grandmother and Grandfather sent it to me." Christina marched a wooden pony from one pillow to another. "I promised to try and love it."

Hawk glanced down at the doll in his hands then back to his daughter. "Why would you promise to try to love Hawkridge Doll?"

"Well... He hasn't been with us for as long as the rest of the dolls, but he's still family." Christina's hazel eyes hesitantly met his. "Aren't we?"

Hawk nodded and walked his doll across the carpet to press a kiss to the top of Christina Doll's curly head. "Forever and ever."

CHAPTER 25

*O*n Saturday afternoon, Faith hung back with her husband as they watched their daughter scamper through the flower-lined paths and towering statues of the Bagnigge Wells tea-garden.

After all these years, she had finally married the man who had haunted her dreams for a decade, yet this moment was the first time that actually felt like courtship.

He wasn't behaving like a rakish buck afraid that someone should espy him flirting with the wrong element. Nor was he acting like an autocratic husband, laying out mandates without regard for her feelings or opinion.

Indeed, in the weeks since they had been wed, Hawkridge had been treating her like a... beau.

It was an exhilarating sensation. More so than the wedding had been, which was nothing more than a ceremony required by law.

Escorting her and Christina to a public tea-garden was something he had chosen to do. Gazing down at her time and again to ensure her comfort or her happiness, something he could not help but do.

Such attention was more than heady. He made her feel like she mattered. Like he didn't care who knew he had married her, because he had chosen her and she was wanted. She and Christine both.

She curled her fingers tighter about his arm. If their future together were half as peaceful and sweet as this moment, perhaps they *could* make it.

"I've been meaning to ask you." He slanted her an amused glance. "I had no idea you were a miracle-worker."

"A what?" She looked up at him in bafflement.

"My mother," he said, as if the word alone was more than explanation enough. "She can be…difficult. And she has not been fair to you. Yet I saw her immersed in a card game with you as if you'd been bosom friends for decades."

"Oh, that." Faith widened her eyes innocently. "Easy. I promised she could throw the cards at my face."

"What?" Hawkridge choked in horror.

"I'm *teasing*." Faith squeezed his arm. "I understand your mother. When I became your marchioness, I realized that the one thing the dowager hated more than me was feeling useless. She was bored and frustrated and lonely. From her perspective, the only thing worse than having Chris and me around would be *not* having us around. We were better than staring at the wall."

Hawkridge blinked. "You *and* Christina?"

"Chris has been asking to play the throwing-card game for years. When she was younger, I worried the maths would be too complicated. But I figured, if I happened to teach Christina in your mother's sitting room, where your mother couldn't help but overhear the rules of the game…"

"Clever." Hawkridge grinned. "But how did you convince her to play?"

"I didn't," Faith answered. "Christina did. She simply asked the dowager if she'd like to join us."

"And won her over just like that?"

"Being cold to an upstart commoner one fears will ruin the life of one's son is one thing. Being rude to an innocent child is another. Your mother has better breeding than that."

"You used *good breeding* against her," he breathed in awe. "Diabolical."

Faith laughed. "The game did the rest. It's addictive. Who *doesn't* enjoy tossing playing cards in the air and gloating at one's opponent?"

"No wonder my mother loves it," Hawkridge said wryly. He gestured to a fully bedecked table in the path just ahead. "More tea?"

She shook her head.

Now that the subject of familial relations had been broached, perhaps this was as good a time as any to have a long overdue conversation. She and Hawkridge were within eyesight of Christina but out of earshot of the other passersby. Faith swallowed her nerves. In an environment as peaceful as this, perhaps they would not argue.

"Christina seems to have taken to you," she began quietly.

Hawkridge's entire face lit up. "I adore her. You have raised her brilliantly. She is smart and thoughtful and kind."

Faith blushed with pleasure. "Thank you. Right now, she is also the center of my world."

He frowned. "*Our* world."

"For now," she allowed. "I presume you will soon want heirs."

His brow furrowed. "It is my duty to ensure the continuation of the line."

She nodded. "That is not in question."

"Then what is the question?" He gazed at her down at her. "Please speak plainly."

She took a deep breath. "I do not want Christina to feel that your legitimate children are more important to you than she is. Even if by Society's standard, that's exactly what they are."

His eyes shuttered. "*Our* legitimate children."

She nodded miserably. "Exactly. Chris should not suffer just because she was first."

He turned to grasp her urgently by the shoulders, his gaze intense and his voice adamant. "Christina will never hold a lesser place in my heart than any other child."

Faith glanced away to blink the sudden stinging from her eyes.

He did not let her go. "Are you listening? Birth does not matter. You have never meant less to me because you were not born to the aristocracy. I am *jealous* of your relationship with your parents, and their love for each other. You are richer than me even without counting money."

She forced herself to meet his eyes.

"That is what I want for Christina," he continued, his gaze fierce. "She will never doubt her place in our hearts because we will not give her reason to do so. She has been raised in love, and I hope that never changes. She will be Aunt Christina to our heirs, and I will give her reign to spoil them or chastise them as she sees fit. They in turn will have no choice but to love her, probably more than they will love their strict and domineering father. Christina will not be lesser. She will be the favorite. Of her own siblings."

Faith bit her lip. That sounded lovely, but these were dreams and not certainties. "Will she have the same advantages? Will her peers not view her as intrinsically inferior?"

"You cannot know how much it pains me that it is too late to give her the protection of my name." His voice was hoarse. "But that is the only thing she will ever lack. Her gowns will be as lovely, her education as complete, her dowry not a shilling smaller, her place in the family as secure as yours or mine."

"What kind of education?" she pressed. "Chris was going to attend the Fitz-Dwyer Academy, which is the finest finishing school in the area. Now what shall we do? Will we employ the cheapest governess we can find, after we remove to one of your entailed estates in the countryside?"

Hawkridge took her hands. "All decisions about our children will be made by the two of us together. I may have the legal right to rule my house as I please, but that kind of house is not a home. We are a family. So tell me, is it your opinion that we must send Christina to the illustrious Fitz-Dwyer Academy?"

"I don't know," Faith said miserably. "Of course we should. For Christina. But I cannot bear to be without her for six months or more at a time, when I have never been away from her for a single night. The wait between visits would be torture. I don't know if I am strong enough to say yes, even though my parents have already promised to fund her tuition."

He ground his teeth. "I do not intend to ask your parents—"

"Then you shall be glad to know you shouldn't have to. They made this decision before they knew you were back in my life. This decision has nothing to do with you or your finances, but rather with what is best for Christina."

"Then you do think the academy is the wisest choice we could make for our daughter?" He held her hands to his chest. "Would it affect your decision to know that we may no longer need to remove ourselves to the country estate?"

Her breath caught. "I thought we could not afford—"

"We could not. But family can do unexpected things." The corner of his mouth lifted as if recalling a pleasant but mystifying memory. "We can afford the townhouse a few more months, at least."

Her shoulders drooped. He didn't mean they could stay in London forever.

His expression was pensive. "If we find someone to rent the last unoccupied cottage, we could perhaps remain in London for the rest of the year."

Slim hope. Renting the entailed cottage had thus far proved difficult, because the property required more repairs than the Hawkridge estate was currently in a position to offer.

Which meant it was likely to become their new home.

He met her gaze. "Please don't be glum. By next season when my port has opened, we could find ourselves in much nicer circumstances than I can currently offer. More importantly..." His face blossomed into a hopeful grin. "Much closer to Christina."

Faith's heart melted as she realized Hawkridge wasn't just courting her. He was trying to court her and Christina both. He had not only married the two of them in a package deal, but had also welcomed them into both his home and his heart.

How could she fail to do any less? Making this marriage succeed required both of them working together. Even if opening herself back up to him terrified as much as thrilled her.

CHAPTER 26

*B*etween the sunny afternoon at the tea-garden and the candlelit dinner about the supper table with his family, Hawk had not experienced a more perfect day. He did not wish for it to end, although of course it must. Christina was already abed. The house was silent.

He and Faith were alone in an empty sitting room. Two strangers with far too much history to know how to begin a new chapter.

"Thank you," Faith said softly. "For today. The tea garden was lovely."

"My pleasure," Hawk said, and meant it. "Was it Christina's first time at a—"

Faith shook her head.

Heat pricked the back of his neck. Of course it was not Christina's first time anywhere. Just because *he* could not recall the last time he'd splurged on a visit to a tea garden did not mean Christina and Faith had been similarly restricted. His happy glow began to fade.

Just because his first outing with his wife and

daughter had been an earth-shattering glimpse into the life they could have had, the sort of life he still intended to give them, did not mean the day was special in any way for them at all.

It was just tea. With a man who might as well be a stranger.

No. Hawk did not accept that future. From this moment on, he and Faith would *talk*. He wouldn't settle for husband and wife on paper. Not when they had once been friends. Not when they could still become so much more.

If they could just break free of the past.

If a man with his sins even deserved the luxury.

"Even if it wasn't Christina's first tea garden—" he began.

"Seeing you with Christina today—" Faith blurted at the same time. Her cheeks pinkened.

"What were you going to say?" he asked.

She shook her head, her eyes pained. "You first."

He gazed back at his wife for a long moment and tried to think how best to begin. At last, he took her hands.

"I loved it," he said simply. "Being with you and Christina… It's better than I dreamed."

"I never imagined she would one day be raised by both her parents." Faith's smile wobbled. "Like a family."

"Not *like* a family." He slid a knuckle beneath her chin to force her to face him. "We *are* a family."

"*Christina* doesn't know that." Faith's anguish swirled about them like a winter breeze.

"She *does*," he countered. "She *will*. I'll tell her so every day if need be. Just because there's no legal way to give her my name does not mean Christina shall lack for anything else. I will ensure she does not."

"How?" Faith whispered. "We cannot undo the past."

"But we can surpass it," he said fiercely. "If Christina and the entire world need to know the truth about her parentage, I shall proclaim it from every rooftop. She is my daughter. I am her father. Now and always."

Faith slumped. "I should have told you I was with child."

Yes. And she *would* have told him, if he had not left her. If he had kept his promise.

His heart twisted. He had judged her harshly for raising their daughter in secret, but he could not claim she had done a poor job of it.

Regardless of the past, she had not hesitated to tell him the truth when he reentered her life and they finally spoke. She was trying. Not just to make up for the past but to make something of their future. Just like he was.

"I should have been there," he answered roughly, hating himself for the coward he'd once been. "There would have been no secrets if I had stood by your side."

"We'll never know. I didn't give you the chance." She shuddered. "I can't fault you for never forgiving me. I cannot forgive myself."

She could not forgive herself for having no faith in a rogue who had promised her forever only to abruptly walk away and never look back? *He* was the one who deserved no forgiveness.

Hawk's resolve hardened.

It was time to face all their old hurts. To vanquish the past once and for all. To let Faith know how much she meant and the lengths he was willing to go to ensure her happiness.

She was a good person, an exemplary mother, a truly miraculous daughter-in-law even to someone as irascible as his mother. She was a good *wife*. But far more than all that, she was important because she was Faith. His life-mate. His soul's other half. His lover and best friend.

The only way to move forward was to rid themselves of the past.

To finally speak the words aloud.

"I understand your decision not to immediately inform me about your pregnancy," he said slowly and clearly so she could not fail to hear him. "And I understand how quickly you found yourself in a position where you could no longer publicly admit it at all."

She froze in place, her eyes wide and glassy with guilt.

He lifted her hands to his chest so she could feel the sincerity in each beat of his heart. "I *forgive* you, Faith. I forgive you for keeping Christina's existence from me. I forgive you for every hard decision you had to make that continues to haunt you with guilt."

She blinked rapidly without meeting his gaze.

His heart clenched. "There's nothing to feel guilty about anymore. We're together. All three of us, at last. Your lie of omission was made with our daughter's best interests at heart. I could not possibly seek vengeance for so noble a motive as that."

He looked straight into her eyes. "It is past time for you to forgive yourself."

Faith's eyes shimmered and her hands trembled in his.

Hawk slid from the chaise to kneel before her, keeping her hands pressed against his heart. "The wisest part of me forgave you the moment I met Christina. It just took the most feather-witted part of me this long to admit it out loud. I forgive you, Faith. Wholly and completely."

The corner of her lips wobbled into a hopeful smile.

He swallowed. This next confession would be so much harder. He gripped her hands tight. "The one thing I cannot do is forgive myself for putting you in a situation where you felt you had no options. I *gave* you no options, when instead I should have been right beside you all along. Not just as the father of your child. As your husband."

"You didn't know," she whispered, her eyes vacant.

"I love you," he said above the pounding of his heart. "I can be an impulsive, arrogant fool, but my love for you is stronger than any trials that could come our way. You are not just part of me. You are *all* of me." His voice cracked. "You gave me hope when I had none. You gave me *love* when I had none."

She stared up at him, speechless.

He lowered his eyes in pain. "You taught me I could be a better man. I knew that much then just as I know it now. And because of that, because of all the hurt I caused, I will understand if you can never feel the same."

Silence stretched out between them. Terrible, crystal, razor-sharp silence.

She would not forgive him. He could not forgive himself. There was no hope at all.

Just the ticking of a clock on a distant mantel. Counting out the hours in the rest of their lives. The days they would spend together. The hearts that would remain locked apart.

Unless something changed. Unless one of them was strong enough to wreak a miracle.

Nothing else could save them.

Stunned, Faith pulled Hawkridge's strong hands from his runaway heart to hers.

After seeing him with Christina, she was plagued with guilt over the lost years father and daughter would never recover. Even if the resulting quality of life had been the right choice for Christina, forgiving herself for making the decision was proving harder than ever.

He might not have been the right man for her back when things had been moving far too quickly for either of them to think rationally about their action, but he was the perfect man for her now... and a wonderful father to Christina. It was time to let him know. All of it.

"I do forgive you," she said softly, pressing his hands to her chest.

His body jerked, but he remained locked in silence.

She opened her mouth and poured out her heart to him. "I forgive you for taking the virginity I so freely offered. I forgive you for failing to offer for me because I was neither rich enough nor noble enough to save you from the mess your father and the estate's temporary guardian had made. I forgive you for not coming to see me when each year that went by made the gap between us more and more impossible to close."

He shuddered beneath her fingers, his face stoic.

"I forgive you, Hawk." She lifted his hands to her cheek.

He was trembling just as she was. As if he heard her, but could not quite believe.

She pressed a soft kiss to his palm. "Do you hear me? *I forgive you.*"

He stared back at her in anguish.

She brushed a tendril of hair from his brow. "I forgave you the first time I saw you cross-legged on the carpet with Christina. I forgave you when you helped Simon repair windows at the girls' school, without any expectation of accolades for your efforts."

He blinked as if her words barely penetrated his darkness.

"I forgave you when you defended my honor," she continued gently. "When you danced the minuet with an orphan and the child of a street sweeper, when you made friends with your bastard half-brother, when my father who had sworn to drive a dagger into your heart on sight called you his son-in-law, and teased my mother for not ordering enough biscuits from the kitchen."

He remained perfectly still, the unsteady tremor in his muscles the only clue to his inner turmoil.

She placed her hands on his cheeks and forced him to meet her eyes. "I love you. I forgave you every single time you made our daughter laugh. You bring joy into our lives, Hawk. It is past time you forgive yourself."

With a violent shudder, he pulled her into his arms and hugged her like he would never let her go.

CHAPTER 27

Faith gripped her daughter's hand as they followed Hawkridge and her parents into Vauxhall Gardens for a balloon launch.

Christina's eyes were full of anticipation and excitement. Faith wondered what shone in her own: pleasure or trepidation?

Not only was this the first outing they would share with both Hawkridge and her parents, this was by far the most public place Faith, Christina and Hawkridge could possibly be seen together.

The Bagnigge Wells tea-garden had been a lovely afternoon, but also a very quiet one. The venue had been falling out of favor as much with the smart set as the common folk for the better part of the past decade.

The Vauxhall pleasure gardens, on the other hand, were overflowing with life. By the look of this afternoon, not a single soul in London dared miss a daredevil pilot fly away in a hot air balloon.

Hawkridge grinned over his shoulder, pausing to link arms for reinforcement before forging ahead through the dense crowd in search of the best vantage point. He appeared just as excited as Christina.

Faith and her daughter had visited the pleasure gardens many times, but never on a day as crowded as this. They were but tiny droplets in a vast sea of shouting children, shrieking pie vendors, fine ladies with bonnets taller than Christina. Many heads boasted Lunardi hats made of wicker with fabric atop like a slightly deflated hot air balloon.

Christina had begged for one, but Faith had thought the hats ridiculous. Now she felt as though she and her daughter were the only ones gauche enough to sport plain, ordinary bonnets that could have sprung whole cloth from Ackerman's.

Faith clenched her jaw at the irony. No matter how hard she tried to ape the aristocracy, to commission gowns and accessories that matched every stitch and color from the latest fashion plates, she could not uphold the mirage. One did not *study* to be a member of the *beau monde*. One was born to it or one was not.

And Faith and Christina were not.

At least they had worn sensible shoes. Despite the crush of people with their clashing odors and perfumes, the area still smelled of fresh rain and the ground was soft and muddy in spots.

Christina did not mind the mud or the jabbing elbows or the deafening ruckus of voices clamoring to be heard over the noise of a band practicing in the orchestra pit and a flock of goldfinches squawking overhead.

Chris was having the time of her life. Thrilled to be in such a lively venue on such an exciting day. She had her grandparents, her Aunt Faith, her Uncle

Hawkridge. The balloon launch was no more than a dollop of cream atop an already rich puff pastry.

Faith was silly to fear such an idyllic day. Nothing could happen to them here. Nothing could happen to her and Christina at all.

This was her chance to prove to herself she could absolutely share a normal life with Hawkridge. That she and her daughter could enjoy any public place or activity as someone of his class might, with their heads held high.

Of course she could. Faith was a marchioness now and therefore untouchable. She was a "better." No one would dare make her or her daughter feel as worthless as they had done when Faith was a child. There was no longer any need to be timid or fearful amongst Society. She could finally just live her life.

She hoped.

So many people had flocked to the pleasure gardens in the hopes of witnessing the balloon launch that it was impossible for Faith to feel like she and her family were the center of anyone's attention. The relative anonymity of a sprawling crowd was pure bliss. Instead of darting nervous glances over her shoulders, she could feast her eyes on the view right in front of her.

Here, amongst all walks of life from every corner of London, Hawkridge was by far the most handsome. He did not need to drape himself in the first stare of fashion to be head and shoulders above every other young buck or lordling or rake who considered himself the catch of the *ton*.

Faith stood with her mother and daughter, and frowned as her father drew Hawkridge a few feet away. What on earth could Father want with her husband?

There was not quite enough space amongst the jostling crowd for them to truly move out of earshot. Faith hoped her shameless eavesdropping was not easily betrayed in her face.

"By now you've realized the extent to which my family's fortunes have blossomed in the years since you first met my daughter," Father was saying to Hawkridge.

Hawkridge's brow furrowed. "I am pleased by your good fortune, although your finances are no business of mine."

"Nonsense," Father said briskly. "You are my son-in-law now, and I cannot treat you more shabbily than I would treat my own daughter. Let us be frank. Tell me how much you need. I may have the bank draft some portion to your account."

Hawkridge's neck flushed scarlet above the ivory of his cravat. "I do not want your charity."

"It is not charity," Father insisted. "Surely you are not so churlish as to deny an old man the opportunity to bestow a simple gift?"

Hawkridge clenched his jaw. "Apparently, I am just that churlish, when the 'gift' means my father-in-law does not trust my ability to support my family."

"For once," Father said dryly, "I am in no doubt of your intentions. Be practical. Does 'accepting charity' make one a lesser man, if one does so to support his family?"

Hawkridge's chin lifted. "I am not too proud to recognize when aid would be a boon, but I *am* too proud to passively allow a third-party to solve my problems for me. This is my family, and I am my own man."

Father assumed an identically stubborn stance. "And *I* am not willing to take no for an answer. Not where my daughter and granddaughter are concerned. So how do we resolve this?"

A muscle flexed at Hawkridge's temple as he considered his reply. "The most I would be willing to concede is a short-term loan in the precise amount of money I know my port will earn in its first three months of operation."

Father frowned. "If what you need is within my power to give, there is no limit to what I am willing to negotiate—"

"There is a limit to mine," Hawkridge interrupted quietly. "If such terms are not agreeable to you, then I'm afraid we cannot resolve this matter in your favor."

Father beamed at Hawkridge and relaxed his stance. "My wife was right about you. I'm pleased to say your character is much stronger than I gave you credit for. You have acquitted yourself surprisingly well. It is only because of your loyalty, sincerity, and commitment to your family, that I arranged this morning for both dowries to be deposited into your accounts forthwith."

Hawkridge blinked in obvious bafflement. "What dowries?"

"Mrs. Digby and I settled on terms after the wedding breakfast," Father explained, as if nothing about this extraordinary conversation was out of the ordinary. "Through no fault of your own, we had given the sum designated for Faith's original dowry as a donation to her school. It is only fair for that same amount to be matched in a dowry to you."

Hawkridge's jaw worked soundlessly for a moment before he said, "You put me in a position where I am unable to say no. We have signed no contract requiring such a concession, but if you are determined to make it, I will not need to break the lease on my townhouse. Faith and I will be able to live in London close to Christina even after the Season ends."

Joy flooded through Faith's body with enough force to make her feel weightless. They would stay in London. Near Christina. Near her parents. Faith need not fear a miserable existence in a country cottage far from everything she knew and everyone she loved. Christina would have both her parents within half a day's journey anytime she might need them.

"Since you have graciously agreed that it would be ungentlemanly to refuse a lady's dowry," Father continued with a crafty smile, "I now inform you that Christina's is equal to the size of Faith's."

Hawkridge frowned. "It is my duty to provide an appropriate dowry for Christina's future husband."

"And you shall," Father said heartily. "You are accepting not one, but two women into your home. Therefore both 'dowries' belong to you. Christina's *ward* gift is not for her future husband, but rather her new guardian. It should be spent on items relating to her personal growth and comfort. When that dreaded day comes in which Christina must throw herself onto the mercies of the Marriage Mart, I trust the dowry you will have amassed for her by that time will be her equal in every way."

"More than her equal." Hawkridge drew himself

even taller. "She will not need the trappings of an attractive dowry to attract the man of her dreams, but I will ensure that hers is the envy of the *ton* all the same."

"Then we are in agreement." Father shook Hawkridge's hand. "Take good care of my girls."

"I will protect them with my life," Hawkridge said simply. He watched in bemusement as his father-in-law turned away to rejoin their family.

Faith's own head was swimming as Hawkridge shook his head in wonder before making his way back to her side. "You will never believe the conversation I just had with your father. His surprise doesn't solve all my problems, but pushes my timeline forward enough for me to secure our financial future myself. The port will open earlier than hoped. I am at sixes and sevens."

Christina spun around to face him, eyes wide. "Why sixes and sevens?"

"It means my mind is spinning." Hawkridge dropped to one knee and took her hands in his. "But my heart is not confused at all. You are not some 'duty' or 'responsibility' to me."

Christina nodded. "I'm your ward."

"More than that," he said, his gaze intense. "So much more. The difference in our surnames is nothing more than a legal distinction. My heart knows the truth and I want you to know, too. Never doubt your place."

Faith's breath caught. She had never thought... Never dared to hope—

"Where is my place?" Christina asked with wide eyes.

"With me," he answered simply. He pressed a kiss

to her forehead and smiled. "For all intents and purposes, you are my child. My daughter." His gaze met with Faith's and he reached for her to join them. "*Our* child."

Faith's heart swelled as she wrapped her arms about them both. She had always told Christina she thought of her like a daughter. She had never expected Hawkridge to one day feel the same.

"I love you, darling." She pressed her cheek to her daughter's hair. "You can think of me like a mother if you like."

"I always have," Christina admitted with a dimpled grin. She lifted her eyes to Hawkridge. "Does this mean I can think of you like a father?"

"I insist upon it," he said gruffly. "I shall be mortally offended if you do not."

"Then I will," Christina promised him and patted his knee. "I am quite pleased that you married us."

A choking laugh rumbled from his throat in surprise. He cast a twinkling eyed gaze up at Faith. "As am I."

All she could do was nod in response, her throat suddenly too tight to release the emotion in her heart.

"Christina." Hawkridge cleared his throat. "If our family were to someday have more children..."

"Could I be their sister?" Christina whispered in excitement, bouncing in place. "Even if I'm not a Hawkridge?"

"You *are* a Hawkridge," he corrected fiercely. "No matter what your surname is. Now and forever."

"That's a 'yes', darling." Faith finally found her voice as she stroked her daughter's cheek. "You would absolutely be their sister. They will be quite lucky to have you."

"Then I cannot wait." Christina clasped her hands together and wiggled in place. "I will be the best big sister England has ever seen. I can read their bedtime books!"

The sides of Hawkridge's mouth twitched. "May we join you from time to time?"

"From time to time," Christina agreed, then suddenly squealed and pointed between the crowd. "Look! Is that the balloon?"

"This way," Hawkridge shouted to Faith's parents. He linked arms with her and Christina in order to lead them to a slender clearing just up ahead.

Faith gasped aloud with her daughter when they reached the little hill and could finally see the cordoned-off area where the great balloon was preparing for launch.

The balloon's endless yards of fabric bore the bright colors of the Union flag. Brilliant red, deep blue, blinding white. It appeared to have been made in long, triangular patchwork pieces. The cage beneath the balloon was bedecked with ribbons and feathers, and a smart pair of steering oars.

The music from the orchestra suddenly swelled as the band ceased practicing and launched into a rousing number designed to heighten the emotions of the crowd. Faith highly doubted the delirious crowd required any aid in this regard. The palpable excitement was already a hair's breadth from complete hysteria.

When the pilot ducked under the cordon and strode toward his enormous bobbing balloon, the crowd's deafening roar shook the very ground beneath them. The pilot locked himself inside the balloon's thick carrying basket and turned to adjust the flames that would take him airborne.

"I can't see," cried Christina. "Why is there smoke? Is the balloon on fire?"

Hawkridge swung her up and onto his shoulders as if she were weightless.

"It's hydrogen," he explained, pointing between the straining balloon and its cage. "Look, it's already lifting him, despite his extra weight in the basket."

Even as Hawkridge spoke, a quartet of impeccably dressed footmen ducked under the cordon to run forward and yank free the ropes anchoring the balloon to the ground.

Before their very eyes, the huge colorful balloon rose higher and higher. Every soul in Vauxhall craned their necks so as not to miss a single moment.

Faith presumed the orchestra was still playing, but the music was far too difficult to detect over the delighted screams of the crowd.

They watched and watched until they could no longer discern the wave of the pilot's flag from inside the cage, and the balloon was nothing more than a red and blue dot disappearing toward the horizon.

"What did you think?" Faith's mother asked her granddaughter.

"It was *wonderful*." Christina gaped down at them from Hawkridge's shoulders in openmouthed delight. "When can we see another one?"

Hawkridge laughed and lifted her back down to the ground. "We can return for as many as you like."

"Hawkridge, is that you?" A grating laugh accompanied the disbelieving voice. "What the deuce are you about?"

Faith spun around in horror. Her heart sank.

If she had spent the past ten years dreaming of being reunited with Hawkridge, she had spent an equal amount of time praying never again to have the misfortune of running into Phineas Mapleton.

He had been the worst of the bullies when she was younger, capable of turning even the few friendly faces against her.

Her hopes that Mapleton had moved elsewhere had clearly proved fruitless. All she could hope now was that enough time had passed that he no longer recognized her.

"Spending an afternoon with my family," Hawkridge replied evenly. "Don't you have more important people to rub shoulders with?"

"Don't you?" Mapleton's laugh was ugly. "Not one, but *two* dukes are eagerly awaiting my company, and here you are with…" His eyes widened and he chortled with glee. "Dear Lord, never say you're still dallying with that Digby chit, after all this time."

Faith's hand tightened around her daughter.

"We were wed this past fortnight," Hawkridge said coldly. He took a menacing step forward. "And I shall thank you not to speak ill of my marchioness and her family, because you will not like my reaction."

"I would never speak *ill*," Mapleton protested, then frowned in Christina's direction. "Whose moppet is this?" His jaw dropped open. "Never say the Digby chit allowed you to sire a bastard back when we were children!"

The blood drained from Faith's countenance and she swayed, light-headed with fear. Hawkridge's horror-struck, wide-eyed countenance could only mirror her own.

Their first true public outing, and already their greatest secret had been exposed within minutes.

"Oh, posh," Mapleton slapped Hawkridge on the shoulder and let out another braying laugh. "I am only bamming you. Back then, you weren't desperate enough to risk being forced to wed the daughter of a textile monger. Come to think of it, I heard about some charity school she and Dahlia Grenville had put together." Mapleton turned his sardonic gaze toward Faith. "Is this creature one of the unfortunates you girls rescued from the streets?"

"That's my Aunt Faith," Christina shouted hotly. "She's not a girl. She's a lady!"

"And that's quite enough from you, Mapleton," Hawkridge said icily, stepping forward with his hands clenched into tight fists. "Leave while you still can. I am perilously close to meeting you at dawn."

"Over a pipsqueak of a poor relation?" Mapleton spluttered in disbelief. "I never thought you'd be so sensitive in your old age. Very well then, esteemed Hawkridge family and dubious distant relations. I bid you farewell."

Hawkridge's cold gaze did not waver. "May our paths never cross again. Your life now depends upon it."

CHAPTER 28

*H*awk gazed across the candlelit supper table at Faith and Christina. Despite Phineas Mapleton's best attempts to ruin everyone's day, the family outing to the pleasure gardens had been a huge success. Hawk looked forward to countless more days with his wife and daughter at his side.

This one, however, appeared to have come to a close. Hawk gave a wistful smile. It was now half eight in the evening, and he had just caught his ten-year-old trying valiantly to stifle a yawn.

He turned to Faith and lowered his voice to a murmur. "I'm afraid I have kept Christina up later than is her wont."

"No, Uncle Hawkridge," Christina said from the other side of the table. "I'm not tired at all."

His heart flipped.

Faith grinned at Hawk. "I'll take her."

Hawk hesitated. "Would it be all right if we did it together? Like a family ritual?"

Her gaze softened and she gave his hand a squeeze beneath the table.

"Let's ask her." Faith turned to their daughter. "Chris, would you like to pick out two books tonight so Lord Hawkridge and I can both read to you?"

Christina squealed and launched herself from her chair. She was halfway to the open doorway before she returned to the table and climbed back up in her seat with a dutiful sigh. "May I be excused from the table?"

"You may." Faith rose to her feet. "We'll be right behind you."

Hawk leapt up and offered Faith his arm. They took the stairs together, well in the wake of Christina's scampering footfalls.

"I swear she'll have a proper library the very instant I am able," he said to Faith.

She gave him a half smile. "In the meantime, she has borrowed more than her body weight in books from her grandparents' library. And besides, it makes going to visit them even more special. Instead of having everything at our fingertips, Chris must choose only as much as she can carry to bring back home."

Home. As much as it warmed him to hear Faith refer to his townhouse with such a term, he very much wished he were in a position to provide both of them everything they wanted.

If he spoiled them, so be it. Hawk would far rather his women take his largesse for granted than to lie awake despondent over advantages they no longer had.

Soon, he promised himself. One year.

Once the port was finally open, the marquessate would finally be out of debt.

From that moment on, every penny he raised

would be for his family, his tenants, his estate. Not the overdue accounts created long before he had ever inherited the title. If all went according to plan, Christina would have every advantage available to her long before the time came for her come-out.

A shiver went down his spine. He was not at all prepared to think of his daughter as a debutante.

She was ten years old, and part of him hoped she would remain so indefinitely. He loved watching her run up and down the winding walks of the tea-garden. The way her bonnet flopped backwards when she tilted her face up at the many statues decorating the paths.

He loved her round little cheeks and her big hazel eyes. Her delight when a butterfly had landed on her shoulder, and that her immediate reaction had been to look at him and whisper, *remember our book?*

Hawk did remember. He wanted a thousand more such memories, a million more shared moments. He wanted days like today to be special not because they were so few and far between, but because his *family* was special, and their lives were always this full of happiness.

"Which books have you chosen?" Faith asked as they entered Christina's bedchamber.

Chris held two aloft and pointed at her pillow-strewn bed.

"Sit," she demanded. "I wish to snuggle against you as we read."

"It's a trick," Faith stage-whispered to Hawk. "We cannot leave her at bedtime if we are trapped beneath her."

It sounded perfectly lovely to Hawk, who immediately positioned himself in the center of the bed with both arms outstretched. "Well?"

Christina launched herself on top of him and rolled to the other side. She nuzzled her head against his chest and curled against him.

With an exaggerated, long-suffering sigh, Faith made a production out of daintily mincing toward the bed, gathering her skirts, wiggling her hips up onto the mattress, and ethereally floating backward until she curled into the other side of Hawk's embrace.

Christina giggled uncontrollably. "Do it again."

"Minx," Faith said with a laugh. "Now where are these books?"

Chris propped the first one on Hawk's waistcoat. "Help me hold it."

Faith obediently steadied the other side.

Hawk could not have helped with the book if he wanted to. Both of his arms were busy holding his women close.

"Chapter One," Faith began in a calm, smooth reading voice. "Nelson and his puppy set forth one afternoon for a brisk walk to his grandmother's house."

"'It's too sunny,' said Nelson when the clouds parted above in the sky." Hawk interrupted, giving a whiny falsetto to the character's dialogue. "'Grandmother will never recognize me, should I become brown as a nut.'"

Christina hiccupped with laughter and joined in the fun. "'Woof-woof,' said the puppy, which is dog language for *human boys are very stupid*."

"That's not what it says it all!" Faith gasped in mock outrage. "A puppy would never speak ill of its master."

"A smart puppy would," Hawk protested innocently. "Especially if his master was a very stupid human boy."

Christina giggled and read the next line, changing the words to make the boy even more insipid and his puppy the beleaguered voice of reason.

It took twice as long as it should have to read both bedtime books aloud, but Hawk couldn't remember the last time he'd had so much fun or laughed for so long.

Today they had felt like a family, but tonight Hawk truly felt like a father.

Moments like these were not mundane, but even more precious than he had imagined. The soft warmth of his girls snuggled against him, Christina's peals of laughter as he and Faith tried to outdo each other with ridiculous dialogue and outlandish accents.

Hawk was not at all certain whether it was he or Christina who was more disappointed when story time ended, and it was time for her to go to sleep.

Out in the corridor, he paused with Faith outside the master bedchamber. This was where he and his wife always parted for the night. Where reality sliced through his lingering euphoria and reminded him just how far they had left to go.

She relinquished his arm but did not immediately remove herself to the sanctity of her bedchamber.

Hawk was glad. He did not want her to go. Not after a day like today.

"Today was wonderful," she said softly. "And tonight was truly special. Thank you for being so kind to Christina."

Hawk's heart twisted. He answered gruffly, "I am not being kind to her. I am treating her as she deserves to be treated. She will never lack for love and respect under my roof or anywhere her feet should take her."

"Thank you," Faith repeated, her whisper even softer than before.

He was not certain he deserved it.

Despite the magic of tucking his daughter into bed, he was still simmering with anger just below the surface.

The lion's share of his ire was rightfully directed at Phineas Mapleton, a self-important pompous arse who lacked the good breeding to realize when his efforts to make himself seem bigger than others resulted in the exact opposite.

But as intolerable as the loudmouth gossip had been for as long as Hawk had known him, Mapleton was a small part of a bigger picture. Nor. was Phineas Mapleton the only villain.

Hawk's original hurt and anger at the discovery Faith had kept his daughter from him had been perfectly understandable. He had not been in the right, however, to judge her so harshly for maintaining the secrecy once it had begun.

The only reason disaster had been narrowly avoided today when Mapleton had quite correctly determined that Christina's approximate age would correspond with the time of Hawk and Faith's ill-advised dalliance, was because Mapleton's prejudice against the lower classes blinded him to the idea that such an unlikely union was even possible.

Had Hawk *not* been present, had he not been in the picture at all or anywhere near it, and Faith had been but an unwed mother daring to show her face as a fallen woman with her unwanted bastard in tow, a run-in with Mapleton would not have ended nearly as well.

Hawk had vastly underestimated the risk involved for the lies Faith had told Christina. The sacrifice of denying her parentage and pretending to be an aunt instead. The agony every time Christina inquired about a mother or father she could never know the truth about. The fear of the daily possibility that despite Faith's best efforts, the ruse would be discovered anyway.

He had thought earning Faith's forgiveness would be the end of it.

He had been wrong.

Now that they were out of earshot of Christina's bedchamber, out of earshot from his mother's sick quarters, out of earshot from the footman out at the rented mews with the horses or the maid banging pots somewhere inside the scullery, Hawk took Faith's hand and dropped to one knee.

"How could you forgive me?" The words clawed their way out of his swollen throat. "I judged you for your part in a situation that was far outside your control. I see that now. No matter how hard you tried, Christina's future must never have seemed secure. Perhaps to you it still does not, even now."

"Is this about Mapleton?" Faith's shoulders caved, her tone lifeless. "He made my life miserable when we were younger, and many others have stepped forward to fill his void in the years since. I am used to people disregarding me because I was not born to a title or a legacy. I am used to them belittling my parents, criticizing the hard choices they made that created a better world for Christina and me." Her voice broke. "But no matter how hard I tried to steel myself against the barbed words of their mockery, I can never get used to hearing them spew filth about my daughter."

"Nor should you ever have to," Hawk growled. He rose to his feet and pulled her into his embrace. "Neither you nor Christina nor your parents will hear vitriol like that ever again. I will ensure it."

Faith laughed humorlessly into his cravat. "What can you possibly do to stop it?"

"Tomorrow, I pay Mapleton a visit he will not soon forget," Hawk said between clenched teeth.

"And then what?" Faith asked. "If I have learned anything in my seven-and-twenty years, it is that there is always another Mapleton. Always someone else to gleefully step in to make someone else feel small."

"You do not deserve such treatment," Hawk said firmly. He led her across the parlor and seated her next on a chaise longue. "I have not had much reason to throw my title and influence about these past several years, but I have never had greater motivation to do so than now. It will be nothing for me to make it unfashionable for an unwise word to be spoken about my wife or my ward." His muscles shook with anger. "Indeed, I shall relish the opportunity to teach arrogant pups like Mapleton how deeply words can cut."

Faith lifted glazed, hopeless eyes toward his face.

"Do you truly have the power to ensure terrifying moments like today never happen again?"

"I do." He took her hand into his with determination. "And I will. You need never again fear being humiliated or disparaged. Not by any of them, and certainly never again by me."

Faith's breath hitched as hope returned to her eyes.

"You don't have to be afraid anymore," Hawk said gruffly. "We're together now. In every way that matters."

The sole sconce down the hallway was not bright enough to fully distinguish her features, but the faint glitter of candlelight reflected in her eyes as she turned to gaze up at him.

"*Almost* every way," she whispered.

Hawk lifted his hand to her face and rubbed the pad of his thumb against her cheek. They were at a precipice, he realized. Teetering on the brink of two possible futures. One option in which they remained strangers who treated each other with politesse for the sake of a child.

The other possibility was infinitely better and commensurately more terrifying a risk. Truly becoming husband and wife. Treating each other not with polite manners, but with trust and honesty. Sharing an intimacy far deeper than the physical.

It would take both of them working together to create a marriage in more than mere name.

He stroked her cheek. She had accepted all the duties and responsibilities of being a marchioness without question. A new home with strange surroundings, a prickly new husband mired in the past, a mother-in-law who had been determined not to like her at all costs.

His wife had handled it all with grace and brisk efficiency, despite continuing to maintain a staggering quantity of outside responsibilities, such as two dozen dependents counting on her at the St. Giles School for Girls.

With Faith, nothing got in the way of anything else. There was time for everything. Everyone was important.

Even a rash fool like Hawk.

"If you need something," he said, his voice urgent. "If you want anything at all and it is within my power to give, you need only say so and it shall be yours at once."

"In that case…" She covered his hand with hers and pulled it away from her cheek.

Hawk's heart sank. Of course she wouldn't want him. She had learned that lesson long before.

But rather than let go of his hand, she laced her fingers with his. "Would you like to sleep in here tonight?"

Surprise surged through Hawk's veins, then hope, then desire. There was nothing he wanted more.

Blood rushed through him so quickly that he had no memory of crossing the threshold and stumbling to the bed. Somehow, the door was latched behind them and they were rolling across the mattress, limbs tangled, mouths barely parting long enough to gasp for air.

This was nothing at all how he dreamed it would be, nothing at all like the old bittersweet memories, but immeasurably better. Sweeter. Hotter.

Hers were not the tentative kisses of a girl afraid to seem too forward, but those of a grown woman who knew full well what she desired and was not ashamed to take it. Faith wanted *him*. His body grew even harder with desire. She was everything he had been waiting for.

Her skin was as soft as he remembered, but now boasted the most tantalizing curves. Her breasts were larger than before, her hips shapelier, the curve of her derrière tantalizing enough to steal his breath. His heart beat so quickly he was afraid she could feel each pulse.

After ten excruciating years without her, he was about to be intimate with the first woman he had ever made love to, and it felt like the first time all over again.

He had yearned for her since the moment they had met, and his longing had only increased since their marriage, knowing she slept just on the other side of a thin wall.

But he did not wish to push her before she was ready, take more than she wanted to give. This time, he had to be certain it was truly what she wanted. He did not wish for her to wake up tomorrow morning with more regrets. Hawk would have none at all.

As much as his desire to make love to her raged within him like a tempest, the only way he could live with himself for doing so was if they made love together.

He broke the kiss so she would be forced to meet his eyes. "If I stay here tonight, I will do so every night. I do not wish to share your bed for only a moment, but for the rest of our lives. It is your decision."

Her gaze flickered uncertainly.

Hawk's heart stopped. He had ruined the moment. But she needed to understand that her consent was equally as important as his own.

He held his breath to await her response.

CHAPTER 29

Faith did not untangle the fingers she had laced about her husband's neck as she considered his question. More importantly, what it meant to her that Hawkridge had felt strongly enough about gaining her consent to risk the possibility of her pushing him away.

His question was more than fair. As was his position. If she invited him into her bed, it would have to be as his wife. Not as a singular occurrence or some hurried rendezvous to be quickly forgotten or ignored.

Of course she wanted him. The wanting had never lessened. Him handing her the reins to control the speed of the relationship did not make her wish to flee away from them, but rather leap heedlessly into his arms.

He had afforded her more control in the past few moments than that foolishly hurried night they'd shared ten years ago.

Back then, there was no discussion. She had assumed a marriage offer was imminent, and as a gentleman it certainly should have been forthcoming.

But as a lady, Faith should not have put herself in an uncertain position. Things might have moved too quickly for a conversation any deeper than a few exchanged moans of pleasure, but she had not been too naïve to understand what they were doing.

He was asking her not to be naïve now. To welcome him into her arms and her bed because she wished to for herself, not because she was obliged to as his wife.

Hawkridge was more than a husband. She could not have asked for a better father figure for Christina. Seeing her little girl breathless with hiccupy laughter as she cuddled against him with a bedtime story had long since dissolved the last of Faith's doubts.

All this time, she had been worried he would not feel the same about *her*. The green country girl. The daughter of a factory merchant. The outsider.

She might not have been born good enough for a lord of his class, but he'd chosen her anyway, was still choosing her right now, giving her the respect and the freedom to decide whether or not to choose him back.

The decision had been made as soon as he'd asked the question.

Faith laced her fingers higher into his hair and pulled his mouth down to hers.

"Yes," she whispered between kisses. "You may share my bed tonight, and the next night, and the next. Now show me how well we belong together."

Without breaking their kiss, he pulled her shoulders up off the blanket to unlace the back of her gown.

Heart thundering, she slid her fingers from his

hair long enough to tug his cravat from his neck, to free the many stubborn buttons of his jacket, his waistcoat. She pushed fabric from the wide expanse of his shoulders and hurled each item forgotten to the floor.

Her dress slid from her body, her whalebone stays joining the other garments on the carpet below. He somehow managed to shuck his boots as quickly as she could kick off her slippers, and rejoined her on the bed.

With trembling fingers, she tugged the lawn shirt from the waistband of his trousers and pushed the soft material up over the hard planes of his stomach, up over the muscular warmth of his chest, over the full width of his shoulders, until it too slipped from her fingertips over the side of the bed.

Now there was nothing between them but his trousers and her thin cotton shift.

He was bigger than she remembered. Stronger. More solid. Yet as hard and firm as his muscles felt beneath her eager hands, his touch was tender, as if he wished not to ravish her but to savor every moment.

Tonight would be better than the last time, in every way. Not only because she could finally be the wife she'd always dreamed of being, with the husband she'd always dreamed of having. This time, she came to him not as a passive waif or some lesser hopeful, but as his equal. As Lord and Lady Hawkridge. Joined both in marriage and with their bodies.

She could not wait a moment longer.

As their kisses increased in hunger, their hands

crashed and tangled in their urgency to divest each other of their last remnants of clothing.

She managed to fumble open the fall to his breeches, pushing them down over his narrow hips with one hand as she curved the other about his manhood.

He gasped into her mouth, shivering with plea-sure even as he ripped her shift from her body. When his fingers slid inside, it was her turn to cry out in pleasure. The many lonely nights she had touched herself in remembrance of their coupling did not compare to the exquisite reality of once again having his hand between her legs.

She pushed him, not away from her, but onto his back so she could straddle him. She lowered herself onto him as slowly as she could. But much as she tried to make the splendid anticipation last, her body was too slick and ready, her need for him too great.

He was hers now. Wholly and completely. Not for one night, but forever. In victory, she sank down until she fully sheathed him, locking their bodies to-gether. Ripping asunder the shields that guarded her heart.

"This is better than my best fantasy," he panted, his gaze hot and locked with hers. "And all of my fantasies have been about you."

Her muscles tightened and spasmed against him in response.

He leaned up to capture one of her bouncing breasts in his mouth, gripping her hips as he drove deeper and deeper within her. She arched her back, grinding helplessly against him as waves of pleasure took her. With him, it was not a surrender. Their bodies took what they wanted. What they *needed*.

As she reached her peak, his body tensed and bucked beneath her, joining her thrust for thrust and pleasure for pleasure in mutual satisfaction.

She fell forward against his chest. He cradled her to him, pressing a kiss to her hair.

"Don't fall asleep," he whispered. "We have ten years to make up. It's going to be a long night."

She laughed and punched him lightly on the chest. "Just one night? You had better cancel your engagements for the rest of the Season. I am not certain I shall even allow you to attend Parliament now that I know your talents are better served between these walls."

His arms locked about her without further comment, but the skip of his heartbeat against her ear told her everything she needed to know.

At last, they belonged fully and completely to each other.

CHAPTER 30

"*L*ondon is such a dreadful bore once the Season has ended," said one debutante to another somewhere behind Hawk's left shoulder.

He could not have disagreed more. The end of Parliamentary sessions meant his time had been significantly freed to share more moments like this one. His entire family crowded about a small table in the middle of Gunter's tea shop to celebrate the grand opening of the new port.

Faith sat to his left, Christina to his right, Hawk's brother immediately opposite him, and Dahlia just to Simon's right.

While his daughter might disagree, this was Hawk's favorite part of their new weekend ritual.

Her grandparents would fetch her from school and gad her all about town on Saturdays. Her parents had her all to themselves Saturday evenings and Sunday mornings. Then Sunday afternoons, before it was time to return Christina to finishing school, the entire troupe would meet at Gunter's tea shop with one noble goal above all others:

To order a heaping scoop of every single flavor on the menu, then attack the resulting mountain with their spoons before the rest of the family gobbled all the ices up first.

Hawk hung back, allowing his boisterous family to elbow each other in pursuit of flavored ices amidst infectious peals of laughter.

He was so grateful for all the blessings in his life. His marriage to Faith grew stronger every day. Christina was an absolute delight. Dahlia had even taught Hawk a secret Grenville strategy to the throwing-card game. It gave him his only hope of beating Faith and his mother whenever those two vixens teamed up against him. Not that his mother had much time for card games these days. From the moment she began to regain her health, she'd left her sickbed far behind.

Life was absolutely beautiful, and Hawk's wife was the most beautiful of all.

Since that day in Vauxhall several months ago, Faith had not been forced to endure any more uncomfortable public outings.

The odd looks his family garnered nowadays were due to their lively games or loud laughter, and a tendency to invite others to join in on their fun.

Faith had grown into her role as marchioness with aplomb. She was no less "important" societally than Hawk himself, and no more scandalous than her best friend Dahlia, who continued to run their charitable boarding school in the St. Giles rookery with Faith's help.

Simon's bastardy had affected him deeply during his youth, but today he was highly respected as a man and as a high-ranking inspector.

Hawk often teased him that they could not enjoy a private conversation anywhere without a deluge of citizens interrupting to thank Simon for the various and sundry matters he had resolved for them.

As soon as the last of his mother's doctors had proclaimed her back to her full health, she had wasted no time in rejoining Society. She was the queen of Bond Street. In honor of her return, she had even purchased a bonnet piled high with yards of intricate lace, fourteen colorful flowers, and a fake bird. She and her fashionable cohorts were promenading Hyde Park at this very moment. Hawk grinned. He was thrilled at the return of his mother's health *and* happiness.

When the last of the ices disappeared, Christina set down her spoon and leaned her head on Hawk's shoulder. "Next holiday, I want to spend a few extra hours at the school."

He frowned. "At the finishing school? You'd like your grandparents to pick you up later in the day?"

Christina shook her head. "Earlier. They always take me to visit my friends at my other school in St. Giles, but I never have enough time to get everything done."

Faith leaned forward with curiosity. "What are you trying to get done?"

Christina's eyes shone. "I teach them everything I learn at the finishing school. It's ever so much fun. It's like we're all there together!"

He exchanged grins with his wife. The daughter they had once worried so much about, now had more friends in both schools than she could even count. Every one of them vying for her endlessly divided attention. Christina was in no danger of becoming a wallflower.

"When can I have a party?" she asked. "It would be so much easier to see all of my friends if they were in the same place at once."

"A party?" Faith's eyes widened in amusement. "I'm not certain that's the best idea."

"I don't know," Hawk mused as he glanced about their motley table. "For the right people, there's always a way."

Sometimes when one least expected.

Just that week, his port had secured an important contract with the East India Company.

He was not only treating his entire family to Gunter's delicious ices, Hawk had also repaid his debt to his father-in-law... and secretly paid off his brother's recent commission for new desks and writing sets for the boarding school, just as Simon had done with the old account at the tailor's.

Hawk grinned. He couldn't wait for his brother to realize how neatly the tables had turned.

"Speaking of parties..." He made a show of pulling out his pocket watch and affecting great shock at the lateness of the hour. "We had better hurry if we're to catch the fireworks at Vauxhall."

In no time, his family was on their feet, linking arms to file out the door two by two.

He pressed a kiss to Faith's temple. As they stepped outside beneath an endless starry sky, a shooting star streaked overhead.

Faith squeezed his hand and grinned up at him. "Let's make a wish."

"Why bother?" Hawk bent down to steal a sweet kiss. "All of mine have already come true."

EPILOGUE

One year later

Faith stood just outside the arched doorway to the Hawkridge family library and leaned back into her husband's embrace.

Safely ensconced in the shadows, he wrapped his arms about her and pressed a kiss to the top of her head. From this vantage point, they could watch in amusement as over thirty schoolgirls scampered up and down the library's many ladders and shelves and aisles like a houseful of rambunctious puppies.

"This is their third meeting," Faith whispered in wonder. "I am never certain if their joy comes from reading the books or running around trying to find them."

Hawk grinned and rested his cheek atop his wife's soft hair. He was pleased and proud to have been able to provide this library for his family. But he was even more proud of their daughter, whose monthly Children's Book Club was nothing short of a resounding success.

Someday, Miss Christina Digby would make her

curtsey as a debutante, her dowry the rival of any other, the young lady herself not only sponsored by Lord and Lady Hawkridge but also a sharp-tongued dowager marchioness who had quickly become Chris's greatest champion.

But today she was an eleven-year-old girl enjoying the simple pleasure of sharing her love of books with other, equally high-spirited little girls.

Despite the wide range of ages and backgrounds, Christina's sunny personality and boundless energy made it impossible for any of the children to obsess over class differences when there were so many books to explore.

Outside these walls, the rookery-born schoolgirls might never find themselves crossing paths with finishing school debutantes. But during the monthly book club meetings, these were not heiresses and orphans, but a giggling, playing tornado of happy little girls.

"Someday they'll fall out of love with the idea of a book club," he said morosely. "We'll be forced to read them ourselves."

Faith's tone was wry. "That won't happen until the day the girls start noticing how handsome lads their own age are, with their curled hair and crooked cravats."

Hawk groaned. "Please tell me our little girl will *never* be grown enough to fall in love."

"Why not?" Faith turned around to face him and wrapped her arms about his neck. "It worked out well enough for us, did it not?"

Hawk answered his wife with a kiss so full of wicked promise as to leave them both breathless.

"When the girls go back to school, we're not leaving our bedchamber for a week."

"Make that a fortnight," Faith corrected him, tilting her mouth up for another kiss.

Temptation had never tasted so sweet.

THE END

~

THANK YOU FOR READING

Love talking books with fellow readers?

Join the *Historical Romance Book Club* for prizes, books, and live chats with your favorite romance authors:

Facebook.com/groups/HistRomBookClub

Join the *Rogues to Riches* facebook group for insider info and first looks at future books in the series:

Facebook.com/groups/RoguesToRiches

Check out the *12 Dukes of Christmas* facebook group for giveaways and exclusive content:

Facebook.com/groups/DukesOfChristmas

Check out the *Dukes of War* facebook group for giveaways and exclusive content:

Facebook.com/groups/DukesOfWar

And check out the official website for sneak peeks and more:

www.EricaRidley.com/books

In order, the 12 Dukes of Christmas:
Once Upon a Duke
Kiss of a Duke
Wish Upon a Duke
Never Say Duke
Dukes, Actually
The Duke's Bride
The Duke's Embrace
The Duke's Desire
Dawn With a Duke
One Night With a Duke
Ten Days With a Duke
Forever Your Duke

In order, the Rogues to Riches books are:
Lord of Chance
Lord of Pleasure
Lord of Night
Lord of Temptation
Lord of Secrets
Lord of Vice

In order, the Dukes of War books are:
The Viscount's Tempting Minx (FREE!)
The Earl's Defiant Wallflower
The Captain's Bluestocking Mistress
The Major's Faux Fiancée
The Brigadier's Runaway Bride
The Pirate's Tempting Stowaway
The Duke's Accidental Wife

Want to be the first to know about new releases?

Sign up at http://ridley.vip for members-only exclusives, including advance notice of pre-orders, as well as contests, giveaways, freebies, and 99¢ deals!

ACKNOWLEDGMENTS

As always, I could not have written this book without the invaluable support of my critique partners. Huge thanks go out to Emma Locke and Erica Monroe for their advice and encouragement. You are the best!

Lastly, I want to thank the *Rogues to Riches* facebook group, my *Historical Romance Book Club,* and my fabulous street team. Your enthusiasm makes the romance happen.

Thank you so much!

ABOUT THE AUTHOR

Erica Ridley is a *New York Times* and *USA Today* best-selling author of historical romance novels.

In the new *12 Dukes of Christmas* series, enjoy witty, heartwarming Regency romps nestled in a picturesque snow-covered village. After all, nothing heats up a winter night quite like finding oneself in the arms of a duke!

Her two most popular series, the *Dukes of War* and *Rogues to Riches*, feature roguish peers and dashing war heroes who find love amongst the splendor and madness of Regency England.

When not reading or writing romances, Erica can be found riding camels in Africa, zip-lining through rainforests in Central America, or getting hopelessly lost in the middle of Budapest.

~

Let's be friends! Find Erica on:
www.EricaRidley.com

Made in the USA
Middletown, DE
15 January 2022

58746917R00179